MW00903242

PRAISE FOR LEON ROOKE'S FICTION

About OH!
"Rooke breaks the rules, makes up new rules, fractures and twists the story form with breath-taking aplomb, while communicating a generosity of spirit and joie de vivre *that is endlessly attractive. I've never read a writer I felt had so much fun doing what he does."*
DOUGLAS GLOVER — THE GLOBE AND MAIL

About SHAKESPEARE'S DOG
"It is witty and full of panache . . . A real sleeper, a veritable find, a novel to thoroughly delight and amuse the most jaded of readers. Rooke won the $25,000 1981 Canada/Australia Literary Prize for it."
PUBLISHERS WEEKLY

"The most idiosyncratic and diverting of biographies of a man whose life stays shrouded in a lost quotidian . . . Leon Rooke's capacity for unusual kinds of empathy was already amply demonstrated in his last novel, 'Fat Woman.' In 'Shakespeare's Dog' he's put his talent to the test and passed triumphantly . . . a robust delight."
HARPER'S

About A GOOD BABY:
"A haunted and haunting novel . . . in which past and present, and even heaven and hell are fatally intermixed. A quest fable, a murder mystery and a morality tale all rolled up into one . . . deliciously inventive."
THE WASHINGTON POST

"Story-telling at its most compelling, a narrative to rivet a reader's attention, told in a bardic idiom that gives the novel the authentic tilt of a hillbilly yarn . . . irresistible."
CHICAGO TRIBUNE

Who Goes There

Leon Rooke

TORONTO

Exile Editions
1998

This edition is published by Exile Editions Limited,
20 Dale Avenue, Toronto, Ontario, Canada   M4W 1K4

Sales Distribution:
McArthur & Company
c/o Harper Collins
1995 Markham Road
Toronto, ON
M1B 5M8

Layout and Design by MICHAEL P. CALLAGHAN
Composed and Typeset at MOONS OF JUPITER, Toronto
Printed and Bound by AMPERSAND PRINTING, Guelph
Author's Photograph by John Reeves
Cover by Tomi Ungerer

The publisher wishes to acknowledge
the assistance toward publication of the Canada Council
and the Ontario Arts Council.

The Canada Council
Conseil des Arts du Canada

ISBN 1-55096-254-X

A portion of this novel, entitled "There Are Bodies Out There,"
appeared in *98: Best Canadian Stories*, edited by Douglas Glover.

For my old pals
Bruce and Maria
and John and Rosie

CHAPTER ONE

UGG

"Bud?"

"Yes."

"Where was I?"

"Jack Dreck."

"Jack?"

"Yes."

Okay. Jack Dreck, his tight slick hair, his white bony hairless ankles, is reading the fine newsprint through splayed knees, going uh-oh, there's mayhem in Angola, uh-oh, them bikers over in Enfield are on the war path.

Ugg, I goes.

Like if he don't tell us the latest then we are never to know civilization's carrying on.

Outside the EatRite, this is, on the loading ramp: me and these gooneybirds grabbing the break.

Mental don't want any, he goes. He's off carrots. He's into unwashed spinach, so's he can tongue the grit.

Ugg, I goes, pulling a face.

"Grit's good on yous, girl," Mental goes. "Yous a kid, yous dint eat dirt?"

No, I dint, I goes.

"I dint either," goes Jack Dreck from Meats.

Dint is how them two speak. Juice them till doomsday, they don't never catch on. They's I.Q. below sea-level, see?

"Bud?"

"Yes?"

"See?"

"Yes. I see. Go on."

"Where was I?"

"Sea-level."

"Oh. Okay."

Okay. Then I'm going Ow! again. I'm scratching like fury at what is crawling up my leg. A bug invisible to the naked eye is creepy-crawling under my stretch tights, me with my whole hand under there zitching away. Bed-bugs, could be, from the girl's scummy habitat.

The bug moving on, taking more snips. Me going Ow, Ow, Ow! digging the nails.

There's blood under the full five, though no bug.

I'm looking back at Jack Dreck gawking at me zitch.

"Need help?" he goes.

Flicking his tongue as he scans the works.

"Pubescent flesh," he goes. "Ain't it rich?"

Me and him and Mental all shaking into hysterics. Cackle, cackle, we goes.

My mini, good softest leather costing a pearl, is hiked up over my hips.

Jack Dreck, or Dread we call him to his rear-end, is rearranging his keg seat. He only sits his fat bum on a thing with newspaper rolled in a back pocket to keep dreaded diseases at bay. He won't sit in movie house or cafe without his newsprint. Trains, buses, forget it.

"Yous remind me the time I had the crabs," he's going now. "Yous scratching like that. Man, did them buggers itch me. Yous put them louse under me pap's jeweller piece yous could see theirs eyes. See these, like, cauliflower ears them crabs had. Their feet, their big teeth."

Double ugg, I goes. Don't say 'yous'.

Mental, he's swinging his head to and fro, like as how it's magic, lips to part and form words.

"I pass them crabs on to sixteen bedmates," Jack Dreck goes. "I couldn't accept the firm knowledge I had them crabs. See what I'm saying?"

Me and Mental going Uh-huh.

"Or I'd of went to a doctor."

"Un-huh," goes Mental. "Would of had."

Un-huh, un-hum, him going.

"My pistol leaky too. Yellow dribble night and day. My women-folk thought it was I couldn't refrain from dwelling on them."

Ugg, I goes. That's horrific, Jack.

"I was young," he goes. "Crabs won't going to kill me."

"It won't going to kill him," goes Mental.

There's birds up in the sky, breaking fast as can shoot. The climate is turning goose-bumpy.

"But after a year," goes Jack Dreck — "after a year, year or two. After a duration, them crabs expire of old age. Jack is his noble pure self again."

That'll be the day, I goes, to Jack Dreck's grin.

Then he's got to show me and Mental how it was he went through them years, zitching night and day his beleaguered scrotum.

"Scrotum?" goes Mental.

Me and Jack Dreck dissolving into fits when Mental goes,

"Yous family jewels," goes Jack Dreck. "Man, I was covered like plaster."

La, la, I goes, watching them birds.

Up in the brainless sky the clouds in a minute have turned cyclone gray. The cloudies are twisting theirselves inside out.

The wind going whoosh-whoosh.

The air is sprinkly.

It's so ugly up there. It's cyclone and hurricane both up there.

I am thinking I'll wash and curl my hair when I get to my corpse home. I'll stay in till midnight admiring myself behind bolted door, the same as would any girl of like pluckish mind. Then I'm off over the rooftop. I'm the Night Prowler from Hades in this burg.

"Don't do that," Mental is going in a low, womanish squeal. Me looking around to eye-catch what he is talking about, for the sound is somebody else up inside his mouth. He isn't though, not going "Don't do that" about anything out there in the wide world's greater realm. He's got both hands deep in his pockets. He's doing it to himself, his eyes glazing some.

I decide to myself I'm not studying Mental. Mental is an embarrassment to the upright species.

He's a lefty, I note.

La, la, I goes, primping my hair.

That bug thing is crawling up my leg again, under the purple spandex tights where it's found home behind a girl's tender kneecap.

It's killing me, I goes.

Jack Dreck is reading.

"There's drought in the sub-continent," he's going. "There's bloodshed in . . . in I can't say it."

"Why won't you let me?" goes Mental in my face.

This anguish in his.

"What's the big deal?" Mental goes.

The same as he does on other days when Mental's got me pushed up against the cold storage or out by the Dumpster where we are made to stash all the off-color perishables so's the Food Bank people can't get at that produce to give it to the deadbeats so's the deadbeats can go and have more babies, at gigantic cost to us serious tax-payers.

So claims my foster pop, the dictator, Fast Eddie.

Mental sometimes out there saying while he rubs me, I'll pay yous ten pennies a minute. I'll give yous my white apron. I'll give yous my shoes. But sometimes not saying anything, condensation on his brow, those hips going rub-a-dub-dub, him squinting, his tongue lolling.

Jack Dreck on the loading ramp these times, revving his behind, going, "Don't let her tell you different. She wants it."

Which I did and dint, the way it goes. On my own time, I mean, or with my dream party, I'm for it. Otherwise, though my mind is hinged to the sex shelf and my spirit body is willing, the rest stands pat. Kiss it, the boys going, all this past year since I shot up. But hold off for your true love till yous — you — are fourteen, my pal Dotty back in the Neck goes, is how she views that issue. Her fifteen and already married once, though it annulled and not mentioned in the family chronicle except during punch-the-nose drag-outs.

"Give it to me good," goes Mental.

Me polishing my gold anklet.

Well, stand up, I goes to myself.

This ought to keep you, I goes to him. I wipe my finger across the chassis, then under his nose, then move on off the ramp, because our ten minutes have dibbled and dabbled and now it's back to business with EatRite's fruits, veggies, meats. All the glorious nourishment for the smart shopper.

The wind going *whoosh-whoosh*, ripping and roaring. It suddenly nighttime out there in what a minute ago was precious sunshine.

"Oh, dog," goes Jack Dread. "There's Crisp."

He is dead right. There by the tomatie load in the back room is my foster pops, Edward S. Crisp, Sr., EatRite HQ central on account of his being manager.

The tomaties bin is all rotted tomatie, juices seeping through the lattice-work. Hydroponic, $1.69 the pound. Foster Pop is sniffing and stalking and smelling the puddle. He is tearing at what remains of his turkey-crop hair.

Him going, "Now what? Now what?" — all grossed out.

"Fuck you all, you are dumbos or what?" he's, like, going.

"Yous are all fired," he's going.

Which is how he goes anytime a minute turns sour, like his little thing is caught in the zipper.

Jack Dreck is whispering this in my ear. Then using his tongue.

Jack Dreck is slowed down since his stroke. He's keeled over one day, I'm told, at the fish counter, his face buried up to the ears in tuna fillets.

I've circled wary of eye around behind Foster Pop's backside since I was crawling and the earth sunk into jelly. I'm easing out the Employees Only door. Eying Foster Pop's flaring buttocks which are like two mattresses stitched side by side.

"Yous!' he's going to me.

"Just a minute, yous bony, long-legged bitch," he's going. The floor is covered with wilted lettuce, close to like being scenic autumn leaves, plus loose taters, onions, carrots, squished melons.

"Hold on yous," Foster Pop goes. He's crossing to the proximity, breathing hard. "Girl, yous signed for this load," comes the bellow. "Why dint yous check it first?

"Why dint you?" he goes. "Yous been in my temporary employ one week, already yous ruining EatRite.

"Yous have signed your death warrant," he goes.

"You zonked out pussy," he's, like, going.

Like although I'm his flesh and blood, so to speak, I'm the last one he'll let get away with even the minutest rupture in the EatRite universe.

I've got my hands up, anticipating the belt.

"Dock her pay," goes Mental, right up in Foster Pop's red face.

Me thinking, Traitor, all the times yous have rubbed me.

When Foster Pop hits me I know I'm going to bounce and I've got my hands, my eyes, spinning around to find where. His fist gets me on the side of the head. I don't even see it coming. Next, he's kicking. I hit the metal door and go oomph. I bounce off binned grapefruit, careen into taters on a trolley. "I told Sen-Sen she ought never of had yous," he's going.

My fabled mother, he means. His one and only sister, dead these thirteen years in a drag race, her carrying me.

He's still stalking the prey, my head ringing. So I just scream out without thinking, Yous smarmy shits!

Yous smarmy shits!

Yous smarmy shits!

Three times. Like what goes for one goes for all, a la the Three Musketeers. Which is not what I mean, though I am not correcting myself. I am getting out of there.

"Yous get yous butt back here," he's going.

Him laying down his laws, for the close-knit fabric of the universe.

I give him the up yours freestyle digit.

Where to now? my inside head is going.

I'm only in this burg for the school holiday, see? Seeing old friends, earning the dollar.

I should of stayed in the Neck, my head's inside is going.

"What's the matter with yous," goes Pokey at checkout as I'm flying.

I've got angst, I goes.

Out on the street rain is falling like it's meant to be a secret plague. It's so fine a mist it's like moisturizer on the face. Like the rain has come in disguise to mildew the human race. My fine bootgear is a surface of pin-head bubbles. I'm soaked through to skin. Wind is swirling debris inside smallish pools in the alley corners where the no-home people are in congregation around sizzling fire-barrels. Them, like, oohing and aahing and going Oh shit. Throwing up a merry hand for the groovy toasting and shaking their hips in the monsoon weather, going Marry me, Sex Pot.

Me going, Just say when. Spanking the air. Those old alkies such a hoot.

The streets are like Black Death. It's like meanest night.

I drift over to the homeless congregation, holding tight to my tie-dye scarf from Home Ec. Wind is rocking me to and fro. I ankle up to my best-known no-home mate, Prince. My half-brother, him being of the EatRite chain: a freaky disowned boy now going by the name Prince Charlie Smack. The Smack part being obvious to one and all, from one look at his wasted self; the Prince part coming from how he greets society with hands slung in the dirty suit coat pockets, them thumbs ever hooked outside, a ratty ascot rimming the chicken neck.

"Hi, Butter," he goes.

He's looking at me through red-rimmed eyes, making room as his mates one and all goes, "Hi there, Starkie-Larkie, Hi-yo, Butter, gimmie five!" Smack's grimy hand on high, waiting for mine. "Hey, Broomstick, show us yous tits," goes the rabble. Then laughing like demented.

In no mood, I goes to Prince. Your precious Daddy hit and fired my can.

"He dint!" goes Prince, balling his fists and squinching his eyes.

"May he burn in hell," goes Prince, though I know he puts no treasure in that idea.

Tomaties, I goes.

"Fucking tomaties," he RSVPs.

An old alkie is lifting me up, hands cupping my rump, this whole time.

Him swinging me up and down. You can smell the pee on him. His whiskers are something; my face will be ruint.

"She don't weigh a feather," the alkie goes. "Eighty-five pounds max," he goes, letting me slide down his frontside to earth.

Yous is one to talk, I goes.

"Don't say yous," goes Prince. "You ain't that stupid."

"I'm stupid and proud of it," goes a handful of the dregs.

A whole week on holiday among the EatRite veggies and I've not added an ounce.

Peaches, six each day, that's all I'm letting in my mouth.

Three, four times a day these alkies are weighing me.

"It was spring we'd picket EatRite," goes Prince.

"Yeah!" goes a handful. "Picket that mother."

Yeah, yeah, yeah, they goes.

Prince's breath is raspy. His eyes is watery. His nose is beet-red and runny. His little goatee is scraggly. All around his lips is scabbed, some festering. Prince is as stringbean bony as me; he's done the plastic surgeon razor cuts to his own self's face to no avail; yous — *you!* — can still see Foster Pop's gross features slammed on him nosewise, earwise.

But Prince's heart is a heart of gold.

Wind is bristling cold. I feel cold through to my bones, though no bug, thank god.

I'm off, it clears, I goes.

We regard a minute the inclement foul weather.

"Back to the Neck?" goes Prince. "Back to Cutt country?"

Un-huh, I goes.

"Fuck Cutt!" yammers the dregs.

"You still at Etta's?" Prince goes.

Un-huh.

The Neck is a burg forty miles east; Etta is my dead mother's oldest auntie, burnt-out and sliding fast.

"What grade you in now?" Prince goes.

Prince is cosy sometimes. You can talk to him like a deep sister.

Seventh, I goes. I'm in seventh. Going on eighth, I'm thinking inside my head. Ever I make it.

"Well," goes Prince after a minute. "A sound education is a wise investment."

Ugg, I goes.

I'm feeling right weepy. My cheeks are cold. I'm clapping my hands, doing the foot hops.

"You can't put your money in bonds, then put it in a solid education. Education will leap you right past life's rigors," he goes.

Him a drop-out.

I leave here this time, I goes, I'm never coming back to this burg. I swear it.

Yous is my only true family, I goes. I won't never see yous no more.

"Un-huh," Prince goes. "Don't say yous."

He looks at me admiringly. He takes both my hands up to his heart.

"It's been right terrific knowing you, Little Butter. Look after yourself now."

Dead Mama was the one party on earth called me Little Butter. In her womb I was then. Prince is the one party remembers.

"Bud?"

"Yes?"

"Where we going, Bud?"

"I'm taking you to Ginger's place. You liked Ginger, dint you? You'll be safe with Ginger."

"Who's Ginger?"

"A friend."

"Whose friend?"

"My friend."

"What does this Ginger do?"

"She waitresses."

"Where?"

"Back there. The restaurant. The Watergate. Remember? She served you a bowl of pasta Bolognese."

"I bet she's your girlfriend. Do you love her, Bud?"

"She's not a girlfriend."

"Don't you have a girlfriend, Bud?"

"Idena. She's my girlfriend."

"Dump her, Bud. Let me be your girlfriend. Let me stay with you."

"No. Too dangerous."

"Oh. Okay. But I don't know no Ginger. I don't know nothing about that pasta you said. Where was I?"

"In your tale? Your dead mama. Prince."

"Oh, yeah. Right on! Okay."

Okay, so Prince unleashes upon my bodyworks a big embrace. I'm totally spaced. It's the first I've known Prince to touch a member of the immediate family. A finger touches Prince, he screams. Touchy, see, touchy isn't his bag.

Then he's fingering his scabs.

Whoosh, whoosh, goes wind.

I've been picked, I goes.

"Picked?"

Un-huh. I'm a School Three-Day Intern in the nation's cap. I've been honored.

He goes, "Yeah?"

Yeah, I goes.

"You don't say," goes Prince. "What's that mean, 'intern'? Three days, you said? Honored?"

Yeah, I goes.

"Well, hot dog!" he goes.

Miss Chudd is taking our whole class, I goes. We're going on chartered bus. Miss Chudd says I'm to be that old Senator, Senator Cutt's right-hand girl.

"Woo!" goes Prince. "I've always knowed you would make it." He's beaming.

I'm looking at him, thinking Foster Pop had hit him every day Prince was living home. Foster Pop would chase him through the house in their underpants, cracking his belt. No dope-dealing homo under my roof, Foster Pop went.

Prince is sliding secret dollars in my paw. "Take the bus," he's going. "I don't want you thumbing no rides with no evil shits."

He's remembering the family man in the Escort has come at me on the thumb-ride down to this burg. The Escort man has, like, gone, "That's the nicest nothing skirt I ever did see." He's gone, "My guess is thirteen." He's gone, "I've done drugs, yessir, I been around." He's gone, "Why don't you sit in my lap like you was driving, little lady? See if I got anything you like." Then that man is driving up a lane deep into piney woods, going, "You do good by me and I'll do good by you. I even let you hold my wallet."

This little Pooh bear on his back seat.

Prince and me stand bunched together breathing the cindery air. We can't hardly hang in place. Wind is whipping like almighty god. Icy rain is slamming down. The air has dropped 50 degrees in zero minutes. Everywhere you look something is flying. It is flying from the roof-tops, going clankety-clank, going ka-boom. That rain kitchen-knife sharp. Each minute or two the screen lifts, letting you see the whole realm clear. You see people screaming, their arms wrapped around lamp post and bush and fire hydrant. The motorized citizenry creeping like cat burglars, and yous — *you!* — can't hear yourself speaking, so's what's the point in uttering a word?

Holding on to my tie-dye scarf so's it won't be snatched into next week, along with my eyeballs.

But I must of squandered a minute in reverie, because when I open my eyes I goes, Where did everybody went?

Prince is gone, and the alkies too. They have been swept away. Even the fire-barrel is gone. A heap of barrels and muck are slung up over each other at the alley dead-end, burning and flaring cinders, the building beside there going up in flames. The fire impregnable against heaven's relentless wind.

I'm seeing hurricane, my mind goes.

The wall crumbles and volleys fire anew in the same breath; behind the wall, behind the flames, you can see dense smoke and faces emerging from time to time, then them bodies retreating again. It's ghosts I'm sure. It is a car-park in there. Car engines are revving, some poking along, others hitting the gas hard. Cars are criss-crossing each other in the bedlam, banging first one fender then the next; they are all turned around with none able to see the big blinking EXIT which is clear as pie to my sensors. I move a snitch, running low, and there in front of me is a whole bank of cars lined up and honking. The humble city servant planted in his booth behind the red-tiger crossbar not letting the wise shopper depart until they forks it over.

Over yonder whole buildings have toppled. Street poles have bent. Wires are singing. There's a Grayhound bus on its backside, the wheels spinning.

"Bud?"
"Yes."
"How you doing?"
"Fine. You?"
"Great!"
"Good."
"Yeah. Like fuckin' great."
"Don't use that word."
"Okay, Bud. Let me stay with you."
"No."
"Them Watergate people scare me, Bud."
"You can't stay with me."
"Okay, Bud."

Okay, my stomach is clutching. My inside's got hands clawing to get out.

"It's our afterlife," someone goes. An unseen woman's voice addressing the realm.

Ugg, I goes.

"There's safety in numbers," she goes.

This tall dressed-up woman steps out of the smoke, on her face a smile like from a billboard.

"I'm cool," she goes. "Are you cool?"

I'm in love.

"In Gunga Din did Kubla Khan," she goes.

We have the hysterics a minute, this party and me, crumpling down to our knee-caps. Us laughing till hiccups set in.

"Don't shoot till yous see the whites of their eyes," she goes.

Us whooping it up, my sides splitting.

Whoosh, whoosh, goes wind. *Splat, splat*, goes rain.

She's waving folding cash in the tight fist.

"I tell you, this here raw nature cuts into a working girl's time."

I fix her at can't be past 30.

Fanning smoke from our faces as we hug the walls, holding on to them and each other as we scurry-foot along.

Ka-boom, ker-bam, the realm goes.

"I know where there's refreshment to be had," she goes. Her chattering away, going Oomph in the blindness when we ram each other.

The sidewalk is rippling. There's swooshing mud. There goes another tree.

We turn down steep steps out of the wind, clear of rain for the second, lamps lighting up the run-off which is gushing down the steps, running up over our treasured footgear. She's packed herself off today in red lipstick, red gigantic purse, a red belt, red stiletto heels. Straps over those biggish feet thin as her gold watch band.

It is dark night in the city and we are the Prowlers from Hades.

Clickity-clack and splish-splash, we goes.

Roof tops goes ker-bam. There's broken tree-tops up and down. There's glass knee-deep. People are screaming and running.

I'm whipping after her through a slam-black cistern type thing, and suddenly perceive where I am. I've played with my jacks here when I was knee-high, going, What are yous going to be when yous grow up? Going, Which party is it most whips yous? Going, My mama was killed carrying me, now I'm here orphaned to Foster Pop and Foster Mom, who do yous stay with? Pansy-caking and cooking in mud and playing man and wife, playing Drag Race, when we are not scratching out each other's eyes. Going, This is how yous touch yous self. Going, This is how, and if yous do it right sludge will pour over yous finger and down yous legs and yous face will go chigger-bite red and yous wont breathe 'til the cows come home.

"Well, you're a moody one," my woman friend goes.

Producing the giggles again.

Yonder at the cistern's end is a baby carriage flying. Yonder is dead things. Yonder is a streaking cat. Muck is flowing. A hunch-backed man in a light suit has it whipped right off him. There goes umbrella and benches and flying dogs.

There's snakes hissing along. Even on good days you see snakes on the walkways in this tidal burg. They are so smart they wait for the right traffic light.

Up by a pole is a brown bag. We dread to see what is inside that bag.

"Go on," she goes, poking me.

You go, I goes, poking her.

Won't neither one of us touch that bag. Then the wind's got that bag flying, unleashing in us both the joyous hilarity.

"Home again," she goes.

Down by the dock this is. Planks and huts and boats bobbing in the dark sea.

The next minute we are pulling out chairs in this wide-floored place built over the whooshing waves.

"Darling One," she's going. "Yoo-hoo!"

It's right pleasant, I find, and well-lit, kerosene lanterns ablaze in the rafters. It's warm. There's a fishy smell, calming to the nose, and below the boards where we sit drawing human breath you can hear the waves slamming.

There's sea-kelp and the odd crawdad washed up in rows along the plank seams. There's lobster bones and dreck.

When waves hit the whole structure wobbles and rattles.

"It's been here a hundred years," she goes. "Ain't going nowheres now."

She's stripping off wet goods. She's making herself naked.

She's got bosoms to die for.

"Honey," she goes. "The men I've heard say that as they are choking me!"

You can hear whistling wind and waves chopping away the sea-walk. But it's pleasant, I reckon, after our duress.

"I can't serve no underage," goes a man's loud call.

But she and me are taking no notice of lowly men.

She's going, "You never seen a dress-up black woman before?"

I'm admiring her shoes. The label in her dress says Hoodwinked.

My party is looking at her hands palm-down on the wobbly table, going, "Can you believe it? Would you probe this?" Mile-long cherry nails have come unstuck. A lone one clings to her pinky. Then she's stooping her head between them slender legs. She lets go with this amazing screech, me going, *What! What!* She up-ends the both legs across the wobbly table corner, jiggling her toes. Appraising the damage.

"No underages allowed on these premises," the third party is going.

"That's Willard, my love-in," she goes. "Willard thinks gloom is a thing so thick he can ladle it on my plate."

Willard don't sound the least gloomy to me, I'm thinking.

Then she goes to him back there, "Just kidding, honey."

I can see the top of his honey head moving back there.

A popsicle wrapper has glued itself to my friend's ankle bone. Sea-weed and smelly muck and black smudges are on there.

"The enemy has struck," she goes.

A slither of glass inches long is embedded neatly in the one calf.

How gross, I goes.

She's picking at it.

Blood is scragglety. Like it's peeping out to see what's going on.

"Mercurochrome will fix that," she goes. "On my side of the tracks it was cold biscuit by day, mercurochrome by night."

The glass has a black one side, a mirror you can see your face in, on the other. She's twisting around to get a good look at herself.

"Look at that hair!" she goes. "Why dint you tell me?"

She's got a headful, rinsed deep red, dear as a Setter dog.

My name is Pure Envy, I goes.

"Yours is all right," she goes. "Yous just need taken in hand."

Me and her clang our heads together so's we are side by side in the mirror. She winks the one eye and together we slam off into gales.

The big toe on her foot has falsy nails shooting out like elephant tusks; the poor other nails are all rough dollops chewed down to the quick. Like in the privacy of her own den she'll sling that foot into her lap to gnaw at them toes till the chickens roost.

Then she sets to work slowly wiggling out that glass. She unscrews the salt shaker top, pours salt over the gash.

We are making gagging faces. The floor is rocking and sloshing. I'd faint, I wasn't pinching myself.

"I be my healthy self in Paradise," she goes.

Blood seeps up through the salt pile, us watching.

"That's enough of me," she suddenly goes, swinging her legs down. "Let's study on you, girl."

My boots have weathered the furor though there's tears and rents, holes and zig-zags, in the stretch hose. I'm ruint. That's eight dollars at Wal-Mart, misspent unless you possess the quick hand.

The itch is something horrible, I goes, lifting my rump and sliding down the stretch tights.

"No juvenile undressing on these premises," goes the deep voice.

A bug in there has been snitching my skin all day long, I goes. It's killing me.

My peeled skin is shocking white; it's purled, puckerish, tattooed. Wormy to behold. It's past disgustment.

"Honey," she goes, "at least you have lost your baby fat."

This induces a new round of delirious mirth.

I shake the tights and something skitters out.

Water sloshes in my boots so's I begin the big unlacing job.

My friend is under the table, scooting about, bumping her head, going, "Ooo," going, "Ah," going, "Yous stupid bugger, I'm going to git yous." At last going, "I've got yous now, son of a bitch!"

I'm dipping my head up and down, but she's a mystery to behold.

I goes, don't say 'yous'.

"Well who ever heard such a thing?" she goes under there. "'Yous' is a stupid word. Yous wont find that ignorance occupying my mouth."

Now she's back in her chair, opening a palm.

"Dint you say so?" she goes. "Isn't that critter the ugliest thing?"

She's got my bug in the beautiful hand.

She pokes the thing.

That bug is dead, I goes.

She pokes and pries, going, "Show some zip, yous."

That insect is reddish and black. It's got four bent hind legs; it's got two tripod-type jobs mounted to the front. It's got a helmeted head.

"Are yous catching yous Zs?" she goes to the bug.

We have us a round of hilarity at that.

Then I'm going, That's the son of bitch has been plaguing me?

Knee to thigh I'm a splotch of red holes and furrows, of wells and welts that bug has made in me. Skin is itching to hop off.

You can't tell the other legs that bug has. It's got my skin in its mouth.

"I think it's a he," she goes.

We cackle a while at that.

The bug is the size of a green pea, but flatter. It's packing my flesh into a hard ball with its front tripods then firing the glob into his mouth.

You can see his eyes are on us. Circling orbs are catching the light.

Suddenly a wing lifts; we screech, clattering back. We are both flinging and screeching the wild screeches. We are slapping at our arms, legs, and full bodyworks. *It on me!* we both goes. *Get it off me!* we are, like, going.

We are dancing and slapping, feeling it crawling. The bug is zitching first this one place then the other.

We are dancing and hopping and having the best time.

"No dancing!" goes a fog-horn voice.

Willard is settling a tall ice bucket by our table. A bottle sits snug in the ice.

She grabs an ice chunk, sucks it between her teeth. Water drips down.

"There goes love, life, and the pursuit of happiness," she goes.

We uproars ourselves anew.

"Pop!" goes Willard with a finger in his mouth. Then the cork flies.

"Willard was with Do-Wah-Ditty if you remember them," she goes. "Willard, do her your 'Do-Wah-Ditty.'"

But Willard is gone.

"Here's to precious drink," she goes.

She guzzles it down.

Next she's rooting inside her purse, pulling out linty pills. On the table they goes rolling.

"Honey, I've got to have these," she goes, "for what I must tell you.

"That there is an usher," she goes, poking one. "This here is more your size, an usherette."

I've seen these, I goes. Prince Charlie Smack moves these.

We down usher and usherette, chased by precious drink.

I see I'm barefoot, boots slung to the wall. We are underwater in that corner, my boots sloshing. My stretch purple tights I see slung over a chair-back above a puddle.

Everywhere you look you see discarded garb. Round and round I'm going.

Willard is sitting on my friend's lap, humming do-wah-ditty in her ear.

"Don't be selfish," she goes to him.

He gropes out a blind hand my way. I'm leaning in to help.

Her and me are looking deep into each other's eyes.

"I can't feel nothing," he goes.

"Butter is underage and white," he goes. "One is enough to get me killed."

"You been killed before," she goes. "One more time can't hurt us."

"Try your mouth on the haystack," she goes.

The minute she's said mouth mine have sprung up. I can't believe it's my own self there.

"Soft-talking's good, too," she goes.

Do-wah-ditty, he starts up.

I'm in a swoon, making space for his whole arrival. I'm squinting, wanting to witness the first mouth on me but fearful of jinxing the minute.

I hold his hat. I hold it above his head while he . . . then I realize his mouth isn't there. He's off to the backroom, going, "That's sufficient encouragement for the underage. Let me see what I've got back here I can fry up."

There's a great noise out on the docks. The sea-wall, the dock-walk, all crumbles. Shipping docks, warehouses, the whole sea-side is tumbling out to sea.

"Bud?"

"Yes?"

"You're the first grown man I've ever liked. I can talk to you."

"Good."

"Where are we going?"

"To Ginger's."

"What's her place like?"

"You'll like it."

"He dint really put his mouth on me, you know. That was wishful thinking. The Senator did, though."

"Un-huh. I know."

"He made me hold it. He hurt me, Bud. Bud, can't I stay with you?"

"No."

Okay. Then she goes, "Do you know who was in that other car killed your mama?"

Wind has slammed our door open and flung hinges, door and what-all out into the heaving realm.

There's bodies out there.

"Bud?"

"Yes?"

"There were bodies out there."

She goes, "Every summer you been coming here I been watching you grow."

She goes, "Anyway, you lived. Mine dint."

She goes, "We was hitting eighty-eight, going side by side, when the tire blew. Then ka-boom."

She goes, "There won't no EatRite in this burg in them days."

She goes, "Them was dark times."

She goes, "I lost two brothers to the peril."

She goes, "Honey, you are skin and bones. We got to fatten you up."

She goes, "The bet on that drag-race was $5. Five would buy yous a carton of Camels in them hard times."

Don't say 'yous', I go.

"Yous are right, honey," she goes. "'Yous' is ignorance speaking."

She goes, "The one thing I learnt from my mama was to rinse out my knickers each and every night."

She upends her purse on the table, she goes, "Here's loot, honey. It's all yours."

Out flows the bills.

"The tricks I've pulled for you," she goes.

Then she speaks a strange thing. She goes, "Dint you ever grow wildflowers? Me and mine, we just toss handfuls into every field."

Mama ought not to been drag-racing, I goes. Her carrying me.

"Honey," she goes. "You are telling me."

On the floor my bug has been busy. It is down there doing something along a twig; now it is crawling up over the twig.

"I can hear its grunts," she goes.

We both can.

It's like the bug must grunt if it's to clear the twig. It keeps on grunting, getting so far then tumbling back. But it's on top and over the twig now and seems to be stretching itself. It's doubling in size, then I see, no, it's something else, because the thing is leaving one part of itself behind. It's crawling out of the one part, the husk or shell part, and moving on away with this new slimy part. Though not fast, with a lot of foot-grappling and grunting, because a long sticky mucous-type string connects the old and new halves.

Her and me are down on our knees over the thing. Our faces mere inches above what's going on, the both of us silent, clenching each other's hand, when the mucous part snaps. Plops of sticky stuff hit our faces but what brings shivers of glee is how when the stringy part snaps the bug is caught by surprise. It shoots head over heels. Ping, there it went, popping up against the wall, then tumbling back on its backside.

La, la, I goes.

Grasping for air, wriggling these teensy thousand legs. Us crawling on our knees to get over it again, then both of us puckering up and blowing at that bug. The bug arights itself. It starts, it stops, it thinks to hobble off. Then it halts again. It's busy doing something, no guessing what. But pretty soon it's heaved a mound of seaweed up over itself. All to be seen of that bug is the odd leg, the occasional quiver of weed.

Quién esta, I goes.

"Bud?"

"Yes?"

"Do you know what that means?"

"What what means?"

"Quién esta."

"It means Who goes there. You were saying it to the bug: who goes there."

"Okay. Just checking. Bud?"

"Yes?"

"That Senator and those Watergate people? They'll be looking for me, won't they? They'll be trying to rub me out, won't they?"

"It's likely."

Okay. Just checking. Then she goes, "It's saying goodbye. That bug has done ate of human flesh, now it's saying so long."

She goes, "That there's a hurricane bug."

The pile stops quivering. It's out of sight now.

She fluffs a bit away from the pile with her false nail. She fluffs away more. She keeps fluffing and next there isn't any pile left, only a mere hole going down straight down into wood.

We blow into the hole.

"Wonder is it going in there to raise a family," she goes.

Ugg, I goes inside my brain, though already I'm thinking up names.

"It's heart-breaking," she goes, "what a bug has to put up with."

Then water is seeping up through that hole, and here comes the bug.

It's a drowned rat.

We get up, brushing our wet knees. Floodwater is in past the door and over in the corner is inches deep. It's clammy-cold to the naked feet. Her and me cackle, joining in the delirious embrace.

There's fish scales and fish heads and fins and every which thing in that water.

"Try these," she goes, slipping two nuggets inside my mouth.

We shoot the realm the high V.

I've been honored, I goes.

"I know it, honey," she goes back, giving me back-pats. "Glory is thy name."

She goes, "You are your mama's very own self. You are her to a T, down to them freckles over yous nose."

Down crashes the tears.

"Me and her were two hellcats," she goes.

We laugh 'til we cry, at that.

"The day yous mama was killed in that drag race was Cutt Day here in this burg. I bet you dint know that."

No, I dint know that.

"You watch out for that Senator, honey. He preys on young flesh."

The water goes slosh-slosh. It is over our ankle bones, rising by the minute.

"Bud?"

"Yes?"

"Here's how it ends."

"Okay."

Beyond the door there's naught but rubble within heaving waves. But there's light to be seen far out at sea.

Is it the sun? I goes.

"No," RSVPs my friend. "They are burning virgins out there."

Ugg, I goes.

In the meantime there's hours to live.

"That's it, Bud."

"Hours to live. Okay."

"You could see them, Bud. Far out at sea. On these little rafts. All the burning virgins."

"Well here we are," says Bud.

"I'm scared, Bud. That Senator Cutt is going to git me. Those people are mean."

"I'm meaner."

"Oh. Oh. Okay, Bud."

CHAPTER TWO

THE SENATOR

The Senator, that Thursday night of the Watergate meeting, was in an ugly mood. Koppel on previous occasions had been short with him. Tonight he had been downright disrespectful. Insulting, argumentative, rude. In the New America the Senator envisions there will be no Koppels, no disrespect shown those occupying such august positions as his own.

Entering 3303, he tells the amazingly thin, amazingly young girl who comes in behind him to go clean herself. "You stink," he says. "Scrub the soles of your feet. Wash under your arms. Clean your ears."

The girl, Cutt's newest intern, known as Little Butter, makes sniffling sounds. Her red nose runs. She has been weeping the full three days she has been under the Senator's tutelage.

A man is asleep in his clothes on the sheetless bed. The Senator leans on his walking stick, perusing the sleeper's form. The face is not one he recognizes, although the features are so familiar he can name the very town, the very street, the very house where the man was born. He prods the sleeper with his walking stick.

"Get up. You stink. Go and wash your face. Then get out."

"I'm not your dog, Senator," the man says, blinking his eyes. But the man goes. The Senator hears running water in the bathroom, the man gargling his throat, spitting.

He hears a yelp from the girl, her sudden cry. The slam of a door.

No one respects another man's property any more, the Senator thinks. All is dog-shit by the lamp post. The bush-beaters are ever clawing to pull you down. It matters not what exalted post you occupy. Perhaps George Washington, perhaps the Pope, Mother Teresa before she died, got respect. But not so. There are all those Mother Teresa jokes, for instance, which he has himself delighted in telling. Mother Teresa, the Pope and President Clinton up a plane soon to crash. One parachute.

When the Senator's own mother, Agnetta, a young woman although she looked old, was dying, her eyes shot as spinning discs from the sockets. The Senator himself was there to see it. He can still vividly recall the room's smoky lamps, the sour smell. The discs whirled four times around the bed of his mother's death room, buzzing like bees, before finding an open window; then they darted as pulsing orbs through the sky, following a brief parallel trail before splitting off. Only one eye returned, a lump of dead coal. It whirled through the open window, thumped back into the waiting socket.

"Who is making all that racket?" Agnetta said. "Did you feed the cats? Why are the lights off?" Then a hand grasped at the lump of coal, her buttocks and feet quivered, the throat rattled, and she died.

The funeral parlor director was perplexed. "What happened to your mother's other eye?" he asked. "Why, my God, man, that's coal! Oh, never mind. I'll put a marble in the socket. Look as nice as the day she was born."

But the Senator wanted that lump for himself and when no one was looking, before the final sealing of the casket, he snatched it.

A boy he was, then. Carrying that lump in a pocket. Over the years, rubbing that coal smooth.

The Senator wonders what has happened to that eye. Which son of a bitch stole it from his pocket when he wasn't looking.

The Senator, Roy Otis Cutt, is 88, recently elected to his 24th uninterrupted term. Tonight on Ted Koppel's *Nightline* he bemoaned the demise of democratic principle through five decades of unbridled liberalism; the runaway public purse, the dog-eat-dog. Koppel said, "Thirty seconds, Senator." Koppel plagued him with an embarrassment of questions about the government's policies on disappeared Vietnam veterans. "Thirty seconds, Senator. Make it brisk." In the New America these thirty-second big shots will hang in the wind. "You're getting along, Senator Cutt. Does retirement loom? Thirty seconds, please."

The son of a bitch.

The Senator is reposed on the vacated bed; the girl has loosened his tie, loosened his belt, removed his shoes, his socks. The Senator is famous for his black silk socks. A trademark. For fifteen minutes he has napped. He wakes to near darkness, feeling momentarily detached from his body. Then, slowly, here it comes back. His fucking old man's body. His joints ache. The mattress carries the faint smell of vomit. Of stale beer, urine. The fabric feels gritty, lumpy, against his backside. His pecker tells him it wants to urinate, but he's been down that road. He isn't yet ready to endure the sting. Although he will regret this decision, should he wet the bed. He rubs the heels of each hand into his eyes. The joints of his hands are stiff with arthritis, the fingers numb; some minutes go by before he can induce the swollen fingers to bend. His knee caps hurt. He has abdominal pains, nausea; his shoulders are sore, the neck stiff, his eyes sticky, his breathing ratchety. Wagon wheels over coarse ground, over gravel, he thinks — that's the sound of his breathing.

It is hell getting old, and the worst hell is how you're not tottering anywhere near the grave in one breath but in the next you are. He wonders which breath it was betrayed him.

Son of a bitch, he thinks. I'm a son of a bitch, but I been here before.

Often these days, when he naps, the Senator is again back home. His dead mother lifts herself up on her elbows, fixing him with one dark, baleful eye. She is saying: "I never cared for life. Why do you make such a fuss about something so inconsequential?" Then her body crumbles into ash, her remains wash into oblivion.

He remembers the time at home when there was a run of cats so numerous that they took over every cushion in every chair and every inch of floor and ate from every bowl. You opened a cabinet door and there was a cat hissing at you. You pulled open a drawer and there another cat was. Pick up your coat from the closet floor, thinking to run out into the snow, and there was another cat licking its slimy kittens; if you looked through the dark window outside there they were like monkeys high up in the trees, meowling and fighting, stalking along the fences, giving their shape to the horizon.

He was scratched by a cat as a child and his flesh bloated; he swole up large as a balloon. The Senator wonders if this explains why these cat dreams all his life have plagued him.

A single lamp burns.

There's my pretty intern, he says to himself. I know where I am now.

"Did you wash?"

"Yes sir."

"Under your arms?"

"Yes sir."

"Your ears?"

"Yes sir."

"You stink. You're a liar."

The girl kneels by the coffee table in the suite's alcove. She is keening, executing gentle wavering motions with her hands. Setting out her usual array of offerings — blessings, she calls them. Her blessings are composed of twigs, dry grass, white sand, broken sea shells, these oddments folded inside a green leaf.

"I heard you cry out," the Senator says. "What was that son of a bitch doing to you?"

"Ugg," the girl says.

"You are an extremely disagreeable young woman. Move your skinny ass over here."

"You'll hurt me."

"No, darling. I only want to stroke your pretty hair. Crawl in beside me."

"Please. I'm so sore."

"You do it, kitten. Do it now."

Three days. Already he is tired of the witless bitch.

Miss Chudd back in his native state is letting him down. These new interns she's sending him lack the grit. The wherewithal. They are not infused with the proper willingness. They have no respect for authority.

"Put your finger in my mouth," the Senator tells the girl. "Whimper some. No, dint I tell you? Leave on your clothes."

The suite where the Senator's meeting was shortly to take place was booked to the Friends For A Restored America — a Cutt creation. Head office Stantonville, Va. The Friends retained the Watergate suite year-round, initially receiving a special annual rental of $72,295.66, billed quarterly. Management has since significantly increased that rate. No discount, a huge damage deposit. To date, bills have been paid, though the Watergate manager, Mr. Jakovie, is wary. He had understood the Friends For A Restored America was an adjunct lobbying group of the Christian Coalition. Now he fervently hopes this is not the case. Nearby occupants, including those quartered immediately above or below the Friends' suite, complain regularly of the noise, the brawls, the obscenity. The manager is reluctant to domicile unsuspecting guests on the same floor, even in the same wing. Men and women have been assaulted, ridiculed, humiliated. Recently, a social services director from Racine, Wisconsin, was made to disrobe; she was hand-cuffed to her door; indignities were executed upon her person. The woman — Euphenia Linquist was her name — brought suit against the hotel, citing lax security, among a multitude of other charges. Mr. Jakovie recommended a substantial settlement, which he understood was accepted and duly paid.

In aftermath of the Linquist incident the manager issued orders that the Friends immediately vacate the premises. In the days that followed this eviction notice the tires on Mr. Jakovie's Honda were slashed, days later the vehicle set afire. His office was besieged with countless cancellations of bookings for its conference facilities from dignitaries high within state and federal governments, assorted corporations, associations. Dozens of phones calls were received from Congressional offices, all pleading the Friends' cause; letters, telegrams, e-mailings, faxes by the score, arrived from religious and/or patriotic bodies up and down the coast, protesting the hotel's "indefensible action" and outlining the Friends' considerable contribution to a revived America.

Mr. Jakovie hardly knew what explanation to give to these disturbing events; he was even more deeply distressed, one morning while sipping his coffee, to read of poor Euphenia Linquist's fate. In addition to suing his hotel the unfortunate woman had also filed civil suit against the Friends For A Restored America, a registered charity, and one Martin Lootz, described as a security officer closely associated with the organization. It was Lootz who while in a state of inebriation allegedly handcuffed Euphenia Linquist to the doorknob and issued the invitation to these unidentified others to make use of her as they wished. Criminal charges, for reasons that elude the Watergate manager, were never laid.

What Mr. Jakovie read in his morning paper was that Euphenia Linquist, who left behind three young children and a despairing husband, had been discovered on an isolated road in the dairy state, an apparent suicide — so local authorities said — by means of carbon monoxide poisoning. That the report of her death made it into the *Post* was doubtlessly to be explained by certain curiosities of the death scene. Her arms had been handcuffed to the steering wheel; below the waist she was naked; on the seat beside her body was a typewritten note which said: *I cannot live. I have betrayed my country.*

Mr. Jakovie was moved to telephone the Linquist family and offer his condolences. He learned that the victim had been receiving anonymous death threats, that their home had been vandalized, tires on her vehicle slashed, the vehicle set afire. These conflicting facts suggest an "apparent suicide"? Are the authorities nitwits?

Soon after the manager made these discoveries two men showed up in his office. The first of these was the Senator himself, a cane hooked over an arm, carrying a paper sack in one hand, a padlock in the other. The lock Mr. Jacoby recognized. It, or one very much like it, was supposed to be securing the Friends' door.

"Senator."

The manager was a courteous individual; he rose from his desk; despite his dislike, he offered to shake the Senator's hand. The old Senator was inclining towards feebleness. His color was pasty, the eyes bloodshot, his face a deformity of bloated wrinkles.

The Senator said, "Sir, I do not lightly shake the devil's hand."

The Senator said, "I gauge you are of the Jewish faith. You might have seen in the paper the other day where the Pope announced Jesus was a Jew? Did you see that?"

"Yes, Senator, I did."

"That dint do much for me, the papal enunciation. It struck me the Pope was being a tad indiscreet, maybe even anti-Christian?"

"Anti-Christian?"

"I thought — and said so to my colleagues on the Hill — next thing we know the Pope will be holding a seance. Showing off his play-dough creations. Learning arithmetic."

Behind the Senator was the man Mr. Jakovie recognized as Lootz. Lootz was fat and beefy, giving off a briny odor; he had the look of an outright imbecile, and Mr. Jacoby could not refrain from wondering why someone of the Senator's standing was so often to be seen in his company; Lootz had on an Orioles baseball cap, worn with the brim turned to the rear, just as Mr. Jakovie's son at Georgetown University did and to which he had the same intolerant response.

Lootz said, "Learning arithmetic. That's rich, Senator."

Mr. Jakovie said, "Senator, I don't want that person in my office. I don't want him on these premises."

Cutt said, "You like Mr. Jakovie's tie, Lou?"

"It's so-so. Tie's a tie."

"I'm disappointed in you, Lou. You don't see all the secret symbols for world domination in that tie? You don't see it, Lou? Those circles, those triangles? Those red stars? You can't see that tie's another of the secret Jewish conspiracy messages besetting the whole of our republic?"

"Yeah. Now you mention it."

Mr. Jakovie was an afficionado of Indonesian art. On a shelf alongside one wall was displayed a collection of carvings, ebony and bone, from Borneo. Male and female figures, nude, tufts of hair sprouting from elongated heads.

"You see those carvings, Lou? That African shit? Mr. Jakovie has an artistic nature: he's got carvings of black naked people out in plain view right here in his office. Genitalia, bosoms. He's a Jew loves blacks, you think? Or, nobody's looking, he plays with those carvings like a boy with his GI Joes? Can you believe that? But we're tolerant people, you and me. Aren't we, Lou? We can abide the odd, kinky perversion here in the nation's capital."

"What is it you want, Senator?"

"It is what you want, sir. You want to stay in business, I presume? You value your well-being, I presume. Here you see my friend, Lou, as nice a fellow as anyone would ever want to meet. Salt of the earth, right, Lou?"

"Yes sir. Salt."

"But matters got a bit out of hand with your Mrs. Linquist, a woman who disrobes right in your hallway. Says to a few good ole' boys, 'Who wants a poke?' And you know how ole' boys are. So here we are with this present misunderstanding got nothing to do with your secret kike commandments for world domination. You're blaming Lou. Sullying his reputation."

"Yeah. Sullyin' my fuckin' reputation."

"But I can understand that. Come over here, Lou. Stand in front of Mr. Jakovie. Mr. Jakovie wants to smack your face, let him smack it. Get all those evil poisons out of your system, Mr. Jakovie. Smack him. I promise you Lou won't lift a finger in retaliation."

That such nonsense could issue from the mouth of a U.S. Senator amazed Mr. Jakovie who remained seated, looking at his tie.

Lootz said, "Show him what you got in the sack, Senator."

"In a moment, Lou."

The Senator hobbled over to Lootz. He smacked him hard in the face. Then did so again.

"There you go, Mr. Jakovie. All there is to it. I got no resentments bottled up inside me, nothing at all, but already I feel better. You ought to try it. Here, use my cane."

"That's enough of this, Senator. I'm not going to change my mind. Your organization remains evicted from these premises."

"Then I think I'll just let Lou here have the cane, sir."

Lou, taking the cane, said, "You not going to show him what's in your bag?"

"Why, yes sir, Lootz, I am. In this bag, Mr. Jakovie, is ten thousand dollars. You can have this bag and we have your cooperation with the Friends, or Lootz here beats the shit out of you. Which will it be?"

"I'm not taking your money, Senator."

Then Senator Cutt left the manager's office and Lootz began beating him.

Mr. Jakovie arrived at the Watergate from a quiet resort in upstate New York catering to retirees; he has had little to do with men of the Senator's type. He longs for another assignment far removed from this lawless capital. He thinks perhaps a return to the friendly environs of upstate New York might be in order. He is dickering. He understands that wherever he goes his tie may pose a problem.

Meanwhile, in suite 3303 women of the profession come and go. Twice the walls and ceiling have had to be repainted. Twice the refrigerator has had to be replaced. One Samsung unit simply disappeared. Another was found pitched to an adjacent roof. The hotel no longer provides in-room bar service to 3303. This has meant that the ice machine by the elevator, repeatedly mutilated, has also had to be removed. Now the staff each evening takes up a large garbage drum filled with ice. By morning the drum is frequently empty. Water soaks the carpet. Ice cubes, unstrung toilet paper rolls, articles of clothing, earrings, government documents, litter the floor.

The door to 3303 on numerous occasions, from both inside and out, has been kicked in. The mattress has been sliced open. The chandelier is routinely yanked from its housing, the lamps shattered. The toilet bowl, for reasons that escape Mr. Jakovie, is often stuffed with newspapers. Windows are time and time again broken, stained with a viscous white substance which has a hard, durable sheen, difficult to remove. The television set in the mahogany wardrobe, the bedside digital radio, the prints of frolicking picnickers on the walls, the expensive arm-chairs, the heavy gray drapes, the gray bed-cover, have been removed. Long has Mr. Jakovie debated the merits of installing new carpeting; someone has apparently poured a circle of lighter fluid, or perhaps acid of some kind, on the current one; guests, he presumes, have danced a fiery circle in drunken frenzy.

The Filipina house cleaner who works these floors avoids 3303. She will not enter the floor itself without prolonged scrutiny of the hall. Passing the door, she scurries, crossing herself. Unbidden prayers leap to her lips. She thinks of pigs gone lame, of birds that suddenly become blind, of frogs turned into granite as they jump. Trees that drip blood.

Virginia Governor O.O. Orth and his entourage arrive at the Friends' Watergate suite shortly after nine.

"Where is everyone?" Orth asks. "Hasn't my day been fuckin' long enough? What idiot has left the shower running?"

Sliding back the shower door, Orth finds the Senator sagged over on a upright wooden chair in the tub, flaccid arms resting on white, bony knees. The Senator's flesh is a pasty white, his stomach in pleated folds. His breasts hang like ancient deformities, nipples ringed with sparse curling hair. Water sprays off his back, gurgling as it empties down the drain. The shower smells of mildew and rot. Towels are in a wet heap on the tiles. They smell.

"You the intern?" the Governor asks.

The girl stands to the Senator's rear. Bruises ring her long thin neck; apparently, the Senator bites. She is amazingly skinny. Emaciated. Crying. It looks to Orth as though she is the one who could use the chair. She is washing the Senator's bushy white hair.

"Goddamn, Senator," Orth says. "You move me to tears."

The Senator hoarsely instructs the Governor to close the goddamn door. He is letting in cold air.

"Well fuckin' excuse fuckin' me," the Governor replies.

But he closes the door.

He emerges from the bathroom, brushing at his suit. He snaps his fingers, an aide brings him a comb, and the Governor combs his hair.

"I wish someone would kill that sick bastard," he says.

"Real slow," a sidekick says.

Chuckles erupt around the room. It has already been decided that the Senator has outlived his usefulness.

Orth's crew has brought with them a tub of what once had been known as the Colonel's "finger-lickin'-good" Kentucky Fried Chicken. But the Colonel has been put out to graze, his image largely abandoned; now the chicken is simple KFC. The men talk about the chicken. Back then, one says, a tub of the Colonel's "finger-lickin'-good" chicken would set you back $3.95 for a eighteen-piece tub, biscuits and gravy included. Now a twenty won't get you near that tub, and as for the chicken, the gravy . . .

Brief debate ensues, having to do with declining standards, the scurrilous inflationary practices of international conspiracy Jewish bankers, poultry raising practices in which chickens live lives entirely under artificial light, denied sight of God's renewing darkness. The Jews are behind this, too. They weren't, why would they have all that shit about kosher food?

"Fuckin' A," someone says.

Lootz, this is, dressed tonight in his county Deputy Sheriff's too-tight uniform.

"You motherfucker, Lootz. Who invited your fat ass?" asks the Governor.

Now, now, it's too early for squabbling.

There will be no chickens in heaven, someone asserts. Two-by-two did God save the earth's creatures a first time; why should he do so a second?

What? No chickens in heaven? What, for godsake, does a man eat?

"Eat fuckin' gold off the streets."

"Now you talkin'."

The Governor occupies himself on the phone.

They are waiting for Jude.

"Hold down the noise," snarls the Governor.

The Senator hobbles through, folded over and shivering, a towel strung over his buttocks. He's bow-legged, the knees knobby, stomach distended, shoulders slumping, his feet over-large, bumpy, the nails knotty. The girl trails limply behind, her breathing snatchy, patting a towel to the old statesman's backside.

"It's cold in here," the Senator says. "Something stinks."

He snatches the phone from the Governor's hands, shakes it in front of the Governor's face. "That goddamn Zippo," he says. "He promises me delivery of the highrise on N Street in return for certain favors. Now I can't reach the fucker."

"Forget Zippo. He's dead meat."

"My son, that son of a bitch, has disappeared too."

Orth snatches the phone back.

"Your son's on a mission," he says. "Don't worry about your goddamn son."

The Senator's eyes cloud up. His hands shake. He looks confused. "Mission?" he says.

"What the fuck has he been poppin'?" someone asks.

The senator collapses on the bedside, knees splayed, staring at his kneecaps. He pats out a spot beside him. "Sit by me," he tells the girl. "Dry my toes."

He has hold of one of her arms, twisting.

"You're goin' to shit on the chicken," Lootz says to the assembly, "then stop eatin' the chicken."

A new party knocks, enters. Scans the room. He wears khaki trousers, a darker shirt, a black tie loose at the neck. He is perhaps five-eight or nine: not a big fellow. His shoes are highly polished, blond hair graying around the ears. A receding hair line. Dress coat slung over the right shoulder, around his slim waist a wide, brightly beaded belt likely of native origin. His face is deeply lined, making him appear older than he is. Forty, forty-five. Green eyes.

One of the Governor's men, working the door, says to the new-comer, "This is a private party, dint you know? Who the fuck are you?"

"Visit of the Magi," the man quietly says. "Come from afar."

The next second the man guarding the door seems to have tripped over his own feet: he's down, cupping a hand over his bleeding nose.

"Bud's the name. Be polite."

Bud gives a scant nod to the Governor, to the fading Senator slumping on the bed. He stares a moment at the emaciated girl kneeling at the Senator's feet.

"I wish," Bud hears the girl say, "yous stop pinchin' me."

Lootz says, "Hi, Bud!" He grins, waving a pudgy hand.

Bud ignores him.

"Nice belt, Bud," someone says. Bud's eyes slide his way and the speaker's smile dies. "Sorry, Bud. I dint mean nothin' by it."

Bud kills people. He is on loan from foreign soil and that is why he is among them. Should there prove to be the need. Bud is a legend. He will slice you wide open if you look at him the wrong way. People taller than Bud prefer to remain seated when in a room with Bud. When Bud has to look up at people a second or third time, when you see him flexing the fingers, narrowing his eyes in a special way, a room can suddenly empty.

Tonight Bud is drinking Coke from a can. Dainty sips. The Coke will last him all evening. The Coke is a good sign. When Bud is drinking Coke you know he's in a good mood.

Governor Orth abandons the phone to shake Bud's hand. To issue salutations. He hasn't seen Bud in a long time, not since the Governor was attached to the State Department in his younger, gallant, more glorious days when democracy was hour by hour being annihilated by socialist hordes and he was Ron's sunshine boy. Before — as he likes to describe it — the shit hit the fan and Ron hung him out to swing in the wind and America's values sunk another inch or two into the sewer.

The shower faucet has been dripping, the commode running. No one is aware of this until Bud goes in and shuts them off.

Bud can hear what other people can't.

Orth is on the phone again. "Zippo Giocametti trucks got to come through the weight stations, don't they? Impound his vehicles. Get Environment to close his quarries. Yeah, say it's a nesting area for Whooping Cranes."

He slaps down the phone, grins at Bud: "Jesus, it never stops. Me and you, Bud, we have to do everything."

"Kill the cats," the Senator is heard mumbling. "I said, 'Mama, you got to kill those cats.'"

The girl is having trouble getting the socks over the Senator's ropy toes, over his calloused heels. Her wet footprints are all around the room.

"Are they clean?" shouts the Senator. "Dint I tell you I want clean socks?"

"It's a muumuu," one of Orth's people explains. "What Little Miss Muffet is wearin'. Moo-moo, the cow. Something like that."

Everyone knows the Senator likes his interns in muumuu's or in his dead mother's old print dresses. The lacy chemise, the gauze hose. The Senator wants an old-fashioned girl who looks as stringy and shapeless as his mother did.

According to rumor, when the senator was a boy and his mother on her death bed the boy had heated a fire poker through the eye of the kitchen stove and driven the hot poker into the old woman's eye.

"Fuck off!" someone shouts. "That there chicken is my chicken!"

Bud watches the girl; he hasn't yet got the hang of her; he's pretty sure they come from the same place.

The moment he enters all eyes fix on Jude.

"Good to see you, Jude!"

"Was the traffic bad, Jude?"

"Step on it," Jude tells them.

He means their lips. They are to shut up. Jude moves slowly across the room, limping on his chrome walker, huffing for breath. Barrel-chested, spindly legs. The left leg is crooked; the foot drags. The harness on that leg makes harsh clanking noises. On both legs gleaming metal cages, support for Jude's decayed bones, extend from his hips to his boottops. The fatigue pants, the marine field jacket, are crisply starched.

"What's this shit? Cocaine?"

Jude has large hands, a gigantic burnished head splotched with tufts of pure white hair cropped low on the scalp. A skinhead, you might think. In the scalp can be seen various discolorations: ridges, roads, ravines. Jude's spine is crooked. Around his thick neck hang silver dog-tags inside the open collar of the pink golfing shirt worn beneath the jacket. That pink shirt is famous; sales of these pink shirts, nationwide, are sky-high. Jude just this year was seen on TV in that shirt, playing the kickoff ceremonial hole of the Master's course with George Bush. The Masters, and the black guy shocking the nation's golf enthusiasts by winning. A black guy, how can you explain this? First women on the course, now blacks! What's the country coming to? Jude's ball had sliced off into trees, as had the ex-president's. No one minded. It was cute, Jude and Bush, both slicing that ball. What wasn't cute was the black guy winning. *Qué va ya*, get out of here.

"Is this shit coke?"

"Not coke, Jude. That's plain table salt. Want some KFC?"

The girl has arranged small salt piles on the suite's every level surface, adorning them with sticks, sprigs of parsley, garlic chips, straw, fingernail clippings, strands of hair.

"Voodoo shit," Jude eventually says. "I like it."

Everyone relaxes.

"How you, Bud?"

Bud's back is to Jude. He does not turn.

"Killed anybody lately, Bud?"

Bud remains silent. He has taken a position by the window, has slid the window open so the cigarette smoke may escape. Bud's nose is sensitive, his temperament fastidious; he finds the smoke irksome, the suite's filth depressing. The Senator is right: it stinks in here.

"I need a word with you, Jude," the Senator remarks from the bed.

Jude waves him off.

The Governor says, "Someone get Jude a chair." He snaps his fingers. One of the Governor's aides hurries with a chair. "You like a drink, Jude? Let me get you a drink." He snaps his fingers. "Move it. Bring us ice." Someone races out of the suite, down the hall, for a bucket of Jude's ice.

"Ice?" says Jude.

It is clear from his tone that Jude is disdainful of ice. Ice is frozen water and who knows what shit is put into water? Jude pulls a pint bottle, Jim Beam, from a side pocket; he wipes the bottle rim with a shirt-tail, afterwards, with the palm of his hand. He takes a slug, wheezes, tilts the bottle to his lips a second, a third, time. Around the room other bottles emerge from a variety of pockets. Jude doesn't employ a glass, by cracky neither will they.

"Here's to you, Jude," the Governor says.

Here's to you, here's to you.

"Step on it," Jude says. "How come that gangster Zippo is still in biz? Dint you promise me?"

The room quietens.

The governor shrugs.

Jude's chair has been placed beside a tall rubber plant in a cracked ceramic pot. The plant has a ratty look. It has been spat into, perhaps pissed upon; the soil is layered with cigarette butts, broken glass.

One of Jude's own crew observes his distaste; the plant is hurriedly picked up, scurried out into the hall.

The man who has gone to get the ice returns. "The goddamn ice is all froze together," he says. "You need a goddamn ice pick."

"Step on it," someone tells him.

The man looks hurt; he wonders what he's missed.

Jude's attention has been on the girl. He hitches a thumb over his shoulder, indicating the door. "Give Cutie Pie a dollar, Cutt," he tells the Senator.

"I'm out of dollars."

"Send Tinkerbell downstairs to the coffee shop, Cutt."

Everyone looks at the girl's muumuu, at her red nose and wet stringy seaweed hair; at her skinny wrists, the long lean neck, the bony shoulders. The Senator's or Miss Chudd's pick? A few of the older people present know the girl's uncle, old Eddie Crisp, down on the coast. The Wilmington boy. Fast Eddie, the EatRite grocer, sure, you know Eddie Crisp, that ole' fucker. They know the family, then, family secrets, and steal looks at the girl to see if she carries any of the facial traits of that ole' EatRite fucker, her Uncle Eddie Crisp, who enjoys the honor of having had a wife and one child commit suicide. The wife by hanging, the kid overdosing: sure, you know Eddie Crisp.

Charter member, the Friends. Pays his dues, pays them promptly, does Eddie Crisp.

They follow the girl's whispery movements as she pads around the room, reshaping the salt mounds to her liking; she tinkles; what's causing that? Their attention shifts to the Senator as he says: "Screw yourself, Jude. I let her out of the room, she'll run off."

"Will she now?"

"She'll try."

"You won't run, will you, honey?"

Lootz takes hold of the girl's skinny elbows, lifts her, places her back down so that she's face-to-face with Jude.

"The man's speaking to you, lil' lady. Dint you hear?"

"Lootz," says Jude.

Lootz quickly releases the girl.

"The bad man hurt you, honey?"

"Who are yous?" she asks. Her voice soft, fragile, riding a delicate tremor. Dandelion fluff caught by wind.

Jude laughs. Everyone except Bud and the girl joins in. Bud looks at the Senator; he examines the dreamy, senseless girl. Then he turns his back on them and looks out the window, flexing his fingers.

"See. She won't run. Give Pussy the dollar, Cutt."

The Senator extracts from a pocket one of his trademark Kennedy silver dollars; he passes the coin to Jude, who examines both sides before pressing it into the girl's hand.

"Now give me one."

Laughter pervades the room. The Senator is renowned for his hoard of silver dollars. The rumor is that he so loathed the assassinated president of Camelot that he headed up a secret movement to buy up every Kennedy dollar minted. It's known that he has locked files in his office, jammed full of these dollars; another cache is buried down in Tarheel land at his trout farm.

The anklet bells sewn into the girl's shoelaces make soft jingling sounds. She clutches a shiny black plastic purse the size of an evening bag; Jude snatches the purse from her; the clasp opens with difficulty.

"Let's see what Tinkerbell has in here. Maybe she's wired. Maybe all you boys are wired. Maybe that chicken is."

Jude pats, slides, his hands over the girl's slender body.

"Jeez, she's bony."

The girl trembles, squinching up her eyes. Jude wraps his arms around her waist, presses his face into her stomach.

"When did you last feed this child, Senator?" he inquires after a time.

"She won't eat. Three days, I've not seen her take a bite. I believe myself she's too damned stupid to eat."

Jude rattles his crutches, laughs. "And here I been thinking these interns our dear Miss Chudd brings you were the cream of the crop. Your prime Southern nookie and you king of the hill. But you're telling me she's not even Honor Roll. Maybe not even toilet trained."

The girl's hands float down until they lay flat on Jude's head.

"Tama yama doo," she says.

Something like that.

"Yama llama ooo."

"What's she sayin'?"

"She's blessin' your head."

Finally Jude shoves her away.

"Goddamn freak," he says. "How old is this child, Cutt?"

"Seventeen."

"Bullshit."

Tinkerbell is thirteen, in the seventh grade at Neck School in the Senator's home district. She's on a field trip to the nation's capital. The Senator's intern, for godsake. Jude knows this. He knows her name, too: Little Butter she had been called as a baby in her Mama's womb. Then that Mama hemorrhaging and dying out on a country road, and a doctor with greasy hands, interrupted in his dining, cutting his meat with the left hand as he watches the Ed Sullivan show, hustling out to that road to cut open little mama's ripe belly. Little mama dead in a car crash, seventeen herself and too stupid to live. Out in swampy coast land, this was, or so Jude's resources have informed him: that doctor slicing with the same knife he's used on his table meat, then lifting Little Butter from the gore, jangling her by the heels and smacking the newborn ass.

She's lived. Jude thinks: Oh, there's too many of them have lived.

Jude knows all he wants to know about this ignorant, apathetic girl. He makes it his business to know. For instance, the Senator's penthouse, his U.S. mint deal. He knows everything he needs to know about the esteemed Senator, Otis Roy Cutt, and the use he makes of his fabled interns.

Bud leans on elbows out the window. The night is dark, as he considers the matter. Though rarely is it dark enough.

Governor Orth buffs up his white shoes. Silver buckles spell out "O O" across the tops. O. O. Orth is proud of those shoes. Looking up, he's startled to find Jude and the others staring at him. He shivers, glancing at the State Trooper by the door. The Trooper's face is set in a lazy glaze approximating a smile. Orth doesn't trust any of the spic-and-span bastards. Look at Clinton in Arkansas, those Troopers ratting on him. Though this doesn't surprise Orth. Life hasn't held many surprises since Ron turned sheep-ass, sticking it to him on the Contra deal.

Jude empties the girl's purse between his feet. The girl stares at the metal braces over his knees, at his leather and metal boots.

"Ugg," she says. "How did yous hurt youself?"

The room falls silent. Jude is known to be a sensitive fellow. He doesn't take kindly to such inquiries. They are all anticipating the one swat that will break the girl's neck. But Jude smiles; a fist gently clips her chin. His gaze fixes itself upon her own footgear.

"Look at that, Bud. Look how pretty Jingle Bell's got her shoes tied."

The girl wears dirty canvas sneakers. Green Day-Glo laces run through the top two eyelets; the laces encircle her ankles, climb the calf, there to be tied off in enormous bows. Small bells are sewn into the laces.

"The things people do," says Jude. "Don't it strain the mind?"

The comment is aimed at Bud's backside. How does Bud know this? He turns, inclines his head, says:

"It doesn't keep me up nights, Jude."

Jude laughs heartily. He rises, metal clanking. "Come here, Bud. Give your ole' war-buddy a hug."

When Jude in his clunking leg harness played the Masters course with George Bush, maneuvering over the manicured grass under a sweating sun, all of America cried. Imagine, twenty-three years locked inside a geek's cage! Yet there he was, Bush's arm on the hero's arm, making that nigger who would eventually win the crown wait a while. Shit. Tiger Wood wins the laurels, proof enough them niggers have been cuddled too long. Already they own basketball, football, track and field — now they're taking over the green?

Had Bush walked the Masters course with Jude during the election George would of buried that draft dodger who dint inhale.

Jude and Bud embrace.

The hug goes on so long the other men become uneasy. They squirm, joggle their feet, dart suspicious glances at each other.

Between Jude's feet, Tinkerbell's voodoo paraphernalia: a black powder compact, tufts of pressed grass, moss, rolled leaves, safety pins, string. Gnawed yellow pencil, rusting lipstick tube, lint, a frayed postcard depicting the Washington monument by moonlight. On the rear of the card between pale pencil lines has been written the word DALE in wriggly capital letters. DALE has been crossed out, DELL printed below.

"Who is Dell?" Jude asks. "He your boyfriend at home? Do you give it to him or make him beg?"

The girl stands slouched, shoulders bunched. She'd be tall, otherwise. She pulls at an earlobe, dabs a hand at her lips. Moans. Her eyes cross. A foaming drool flows from her mouth.

Jude shoves the girl away. "Someone get her the fuck out of here," he says.

Lootz pushes the girl into the hall. Slams the door.

"She's gone, Jude."

"You can pick them, Senator," Jude says. "What'd you give her?"

"Nothing."

"No sweet string of white powder? No Wonder Dust?"

"Not a thing."

"Maybe a few spools? Maybe Prozac."

"Nothing."

"You're a stupid prick though, aren't you?"

The Senator bristles.

"Bud," he says, "if you have a spare minute any time tonight, would you mind killing this son of a bitch?"

The Senator means it. He means it so much he can say it aloud to this room of litterbrains.

"I'll make it worth your time. Do it right here in this goddamn room right now and I'll let you write your own check."

Jude laughs, waggles his head. But you can see he's mildly curious. He's checking out Bud's response.

"Speak to my secretary," Bud tells the Senator.

"You forget, Senator," Jude says. "I been dead before. I was dead for twenty-three years."

"Would to God you had been."

The Governor intervenes. "Let's keep this civil. Aren't we all pals?"

Pals? What a strange word. 'Pals' is fuckin' kindergarten talk. Orth is new to the Friends. He's yet to prove he's the hot shit he thinks he is.

Jude is grinning. He won't pass up any chance he gets to rattle the Senator's cage. It has already been determined the Senator is horsemeat.

Cutt retires to the washroom, splashes water over his face. He's furious. He has run rough-shod over that acid bucket legal-eagle Chantelle Peru, in claiming credit for returning three vegetables from the wilds of Vietnam. Three. How much richer the world would be had they been left there. He has personally brought that son of a bitch,

Jude, back in his own plane. He has finessed a Congressional Medal of Honor for the jackass and arranged for him to deliver a three-minute oration before the Joint House. He's entertained the bastard at his own trout farm in Carolina, finagled a rent-free Air Stream trailer home for Jude to live in, sent military contracts his way, secured him secret monthly stipends payable through the U.S. Postal Service. He's arranged an arm-in-arm stroll with George at the Masters, wrangled a White House dinner with the metallic bastard decked out in Marine dress blues; hired a PR firm to tool the S.O.B. for talk show appearances on Oprah, with Jay Leno and that lacquered tower of shit, Barbara; personal one-hundred dollar a plate rubber chicken Christian Coalition dinners up and down the . . up and down the . . .

Oh, what the hell. What's he's done for this freak could fill a book. Never mind what practices Jude had been engaged in when the Senator unearthed him. Chantelle Peru, that hot-headed fancypants lawyer, had said to his face, "Don't pull this crap on the American public, Cutt. Don't. I'll have your septuagenarian ass growing daisies out of your rear end before I let you get away with this bullshit. Jude sold six-year-old girls into slavery, ran cat-houses, consorted with drug barons in the Orient. He's a psycho who kills people. Plus, despite your sumptuarial enticement of military brass, I have a court order for the release of documents showing the asshole was present at My Lai, that later on the fucker deserted. The fucker was not a prisoner of war. He was not a Forgotten Vet. I am going to stick you, Cutt, and mount your head on the spire of the Washington monument."

But who was Peru? Another bleeding heart liberal do-gooder with mush in her mouth; good for nothing unless you had her britches down. Old as he was, he could run rings around innocent tight-butt bitches like Peru. So he'd pulled it off, got Jude back from Vietnam, and been a hero himself. Koppel says tonight, Are there any more of our boys over there, Senator? The Senator says, Not in my opinion. I scoured every jungle in my Senate-mandated fact-finding mission. I walked knee-deep through a thousand rice paddies. I swatted a million bugs. I'm content Jude was the last.

"Thirty seconds, Senator."

"The cream of the crop, Ted."

Orth, polishing his Old Dominion cufflinks, wishes the meeting would commence. He wants to get back to Charlottesville before midnight. Things to do, people to see.

But you can't hurry Jude, now gnawing a chicken wing.

Other parties have arrived. Milling about, searching the suite for bugs.

"My people say it's clean, we can get down to business," Jude says. "The first order of business is Giocametti. The Friends will build the highways, run the quarries. Right, Orth?"

Orth nods. "Right. Remember he's connected, though. We don't want it messy."

A woman in a Tilley hat, crouched by the door, says, "We're workin' on it, Jude. But Zippo's out of the country."

The Senator is back again, sitting on the bed. He downs his bourbon, sneezes, extracts a tissue from beneath the pillow, loudly blows his nose. "I told you," he says. "You're to do nothing to Zippo until that N Street matter is wrapped up." He waggles the tissue at Jude.

"Wasn't there something about you and Zippo and a trainload of quarters from the U.S. Mint?"

"None of your goddamn business, Jude," replies the Senator. To Orth he says, "Why are you deferring to this tin can?"

Bud enters the bathroom, flushes the toilet. Picks wet towels from the tiles, drops them into the tub. The Senator's voice is droning on. The Senator's is not a voice that has changed much over the years, from that time down south when he delivered rabid TV and radio editorials three times each day over WRAL, the Voice of Free Enterprise. Roy Otis Cutt's launching pad into the Senate. The same paranoia, arrogance, drivel. The same lies.

"We got that Christian Theme Park deal to conclude," Jude says. "Bud?"

"I hear you," Bud says, bent over the sink.

Jude waits. Lootz pops his head into the bathroom, says, "He's washing his hands."

"Come in here, Bud."

Bud takes his time.

"It seems Vivian won't listen to reason. So we figure this one is yours, Bud. Bud?"

Bud steps out of the washroom, drying his hands.

"Don't sweat it," Bud tells Jude.

Their eyes meet. Neither wavers. Then Jude says: "Just one thing to remember. I'm the boss. You're the hired hand. Senator, you need to remember that, too. Lootz?"

"Yeah, boss."

"Show the Senator how he's to remember his business is our business. Senator, you weren't up to snuff on *Koppel* tonight. You dint inspire me. The Friends is an inspirational movement, Senator. Without inspiration a nation perishes. Theodore Roosevelt said that. Without inspiration, vision, a nation goes adrift. We fall asleep at the wheel. Lootz?"

"I'm just waiting yous to finish your speech, boss."

"I'm finished."

Lootz' right hand closes around the Senator's neck. He lifts the Senator from the bed with the choke hold, snatches the Senator's belt and cinches it so tight Cutt's tongue lolls from his mouth. The Senator is up in the air kicking his silk-clad feet, arms flailing.

Orth has gone jittery, his face pale. "Easy, easy," he says. "Let's take it easy."

Easy-peasey," Jude says. He smiles.

The discussion goes on — ragged, acrimonious — until the woman in the Tilley hat hikes her skirts, spreads her legs. Grins. "Anyone want a piece? Or are you ole' boys content with your KFC?"

The girl is in a booth by the cafe entrance, whimpering all but inaudibly, when Bud slides in. She doesn't notice. Beside the glass is the Senator's Kennedy dollar. She has been constructing small salt towers around the shiny coin. The salt has been laced with rice. She is busy separating rice from salt. Her towers, it seems, must be pure salt. She lifts her eyes, the wet eyes pass over and behind him, sweep the long room.

"Yamma damma do," she says.

"Cut that out."

Bud is pretty sure this child isn't crazy. He's pretty well certain that her scatty behavior is a ploy devised to keep the Senator at bay. Though he doubts this tactic has met with unqualified success. Insanity is said to run in the Senator's family. Maybe her craziness only makes the Senator feel comfortable.

Bud orders coffee from the waitress: a woman with broad hips, fiftyish, heavy thighs, high buttocks, hair a bright orange tied in knots tight to her scalp except over each ear where a rain of crimson braids fall — Ginger. A nice black woman. Ginger is divorced, lives alone. She has two sons and a daughter, all married, all far away. Ginger is into Bud for three hundred bucks, which makes her nervous.

"Anything else?"

Bud scans the menu. "Pasta Bolognese for my friend here. Hurry it up."

"How you doing, Bud?"

"Okay."

"Who's the crybaby?"

"God knows."

"My competition, huh?"

"No one is in your league, Ginger."

"You know how to cheer up a girl, Bud."

He's surprising himself. How often is he in such a a chatty mood?

In the Pueblo country out west during his frenzied youth Bud lived with a family that found him wandering the parched desert and took him in. He lived with this family for much of one year, in a cave on a high weathered bluff cut from soft red clay. Tables and chairs, beds, implements employed for cooking, for eating, were all carved out of this clay. They spoke a guttural language strange to the ear and followed customs he beheld as peculiar at the time.

Coyote Three Legs, they called him.

That was more than thirty years ago; he wonders how many out there are left alive. Water, food, were the greatest difficulties. Hot days, cold nights. He remembers best the uncommon light. Eerie silence so remarkably present one came to know it as company and spoke to it as an abiding friend. He can feel the rough walls against his fingers, sometimes; the cool floor against the soles of his feet. When the hard rains came it seemed to him that it was his own flesh eroding. On the ledge where yesterday you stood, today no ledge remained.

He was happy there.

They treated him well, as he recalls. He can't recall a time when a voice was raised. A raised voice, those people believed, could bring the roof down on all of their heads. He had believed this too.

He remembers one time in the Neck, both of them snotnosed boys, Jude pinning him down, holding a rock above his head. *If you rat on me I'll kill yous.* Bud can't recall now what it was he was not to tell or whether he did tell, or who there was who was so important that this person should not be told. Such memories seem peculiar now; they belong to another person's life. He can remember those asinine boys, those drab days in country that already was Cutt Country, but there it stops. It seems to him that that place, the Neck, was a much stranger place than the cave with the cliff-dwellers who spoke a strange language. Jude was a big heavy boy who had called him Runt, Jude being bad news even then. Though it wouldn't have been for long that Jude called him Runt — no more than a matter of days, hours, even; it would have had to be before Bud struck out for the vast unknown and lived his year as Coyote Three Legs with the Indians in the Pueblo country. In his mind Bud sees red flames, sees smoke, and he holds his breath waiting for the vision to clear. Smoking meat. That is what they were doing. This in another cave higher along the bluff. Reached by three rope ladders mounted on three different ledges. He can see the ladders, see himself and others climbing those ladders. See the narrow ledges, the hanging meat. A hundred feet below, the red river bed dry nine months of the year. The meat is on crisscrossed poles strung a foot or so below the ceiling. The meat is good, though it always tastes dusty and it is tough. There is never enough.

Thirteen, fourteen years old, he must have been.

He remembers snow, and the whole lot of them studying footprints in the snow and deciding whether the animal that made the footprints was a thing that could be trapped and killed and eaten or whether it was a thing that would kill and eat them. Rabbits, gophers, lizards, usually.

Ginger has long since brought the girl's food. Ugg, he heard his table companion say a while ago. "I can't eat this. I eat this, I'll be sick."

"Don't eat it, then."

In the caves, that lean winter when he was a boy, they ate gophers skinned and cut into giblets and boiled into soup. A hunter could hear a footstep through a hundred feet of clay. They could scale vertical walls with the ease of snakes.

The girl has eaten the food, scraped the plate clean, eaten the last speck of garlic bread. Sucked her fingers.

"Ummm."

I was right, Bud thinks, looking at her flushed face. All she needed was to be in a normal person's company for a while.

She says, "I saw yous — *you!* — upstairs in the Freedom Room. You were wearing those funny shoes."

Freedom Room?

"No. I remember now. That was someone else. You are going to do something awful to me, ain't you?"

Ain-choo, she says. Neck talk. How they talk down there. To the cliff-dwellers in the Pueblo country his must have been a strange language, too.

Bud weighs her question. He weighs it so long, his face in a hard smile, his teeth clamped, that the girl forgets he's there. She's reworking the salt mounds when he says, hardly more than a whisper: "You ever think of getting a new name? Changing your own into something nice?"

"Nice?"

He doesn't know her true name. But if this pseudo New Age disciple is from the Neck, he knows it is a name that can stand a change. The blacks are changing their names every day. Why not a helpless little white girl from the Neck?

"Tabita Banta. How about that?"

"Tabita?"

"Banta. Hey, Tabita Banta. Would you like dessert?"

The girl is losing her listlessness. She's getting her color back. Her breath does not come in snatches now. His fingers crumple the napkin, rearrange silverware, and her sight follows those hands. The eyes waver, they float, they circle the room, but she's coming back from the dead.

Why am I doing this? Bud asks himself. Good question, Bud.

"Our civics teacher, Miss Chudd," the girl says. "The field trips, from day one, that's all she talked about."

It has been a long time, twenty-odd years, but Bud remembers Miss Chudd.

"How did you come to share the Senator's refined company?"

"I don't know." *I-own-oh,* she pronounces it, three words transformed into one.

"Try to remember."

Her eyes squeeze shut.

"We were in his office. The Senator's office. He give us each a Bic pen. Like it's a big thing, them Bics."

Getting excited now, as she remembers. A bit of sparkle in those eyes.

"He give us each a signed photo of himself riding a pony when he was a boy. Him holding the saddle horn like he was scared to death."

"Yes?"

"Was an old woman with a fierce face in that photo. Holding the reins. 'That was mother,' he goes. The Senator. Then he pulls open a drawer. 'Gather around, boys and girls,' he goes. That drawer is filled with Kennedy silver dollars. "The Bay of Pigs fiasco, I almost choked his brother Robert to death," he goes. This snarl on his lips. Then he looks over us girls and points. Sixteen of us girls honored, uh-huh. He picks me."

"Then what?"

"Him and Miss Chudd whisper together. All the other students troop out. Miss Chudd goes, 'He's selected you. I am so proud!' She goes, 'You'll get a good mark, you don't mess up.' She goes, 'You just do what Senator Cutt says and mind your p's and q's and make Senator Cutt proud of our school. Wash your face each morning and evening and make up your face pretty and wear what he tells you.' He'll have everything I need, she goes. Lipstick and rouge and hair bows and pretty clothes. He'll see I make the bus when it's time to come home, she goes. 'This is a very great honor.'"

"But you missed the bus?"

"I don't know. I don't even know what day this is. He never even showed me the cherry trees, not a single monument. You ask me where I been, I'd have to say time has vanished. I put his yellow Bic in my purse but now it's gone too."

The meaty cop, Lootz, appears. Beckons. Bud has seen his approach: Lootz in the doorway rising on his flat feet, scanning the place, when they are right under his nose.

"Bud?"

"Yeah, Lou?"

"You're wanted upstairs."

Miles to go, Bud thinks, before we sleep.

"Tell Jude I'm busy."

He flexes his hands, drops them on his knees beneath the table. He looks away from Lootz to Ginger seated at a table folding cloth napkins for next morning's breakfast tables. Ginger looks subdued. She has had a long day and perhaps expects a longer night.

"Tell them I am otherwise engaged."

"Engaged?"

"Busy, Lou."

"Yeah. Well. You may be sorry, I tell them that."

"I've never been sorry."

"I hope you know what you're doing."

Bud always knows what he's doing.

"Yeah, well. Jude just wanted to know you could be counted on for that motel job. You fuck up that motel job, you'll be sorry."

"I'm never sorry, Lootz. Didn't I tell you to scram?"

There goes Lootz.

Bud signals Ginger to bring the coffee pot. Dessert for Tabita Banta.

"You want dessert, Tabita Banta?"

"Maybe a dab of ice cream. How come you git to name me?"

"It's your life, Angel. Name yourself."

"I don't know nothing about that name. I can't even say it."

"If you want to go back home to the Neck, I'm driving south tonight. You want to go, I'll take you."

Tabita Banta slowly shakes her head. "Ugg. I want never to return to that burg. It's bad as here. Maybe worse."

Bud nods. How many times did he say the same?

"I'll find a place to stash you, that's what you want."

"You won't do nothing harmful to me, will you, Bud? Bud?"

Sometimes on the bluff the Indians placed a smaller animal inside a trap in order to catch a larger one. A rodent to snag a hawk. Tabita Banta's eyes have the rodent's look.

He goes over to Ginger. For a few minutes they converse; then he's back.

"It's arranged," he says. "Ginger will take you in for a few days. Let's scram."

On the way across town, Bud driving, the girl weeps one minute, talks a blue streak the next.

"Them Friends, Bud, they's the grossiest bunch. Senator Cutt, he says I run away they will git me. He says I breathe one word my internship, I'm horsemeat."

Bud doesn't tell her what's on his mind: that pretty soon the Senator himself is likely to be horsemeat.

"Bud?"

"Yes?"

"That bug was on me, Bud. It was crawling out of its one part. It was all mucous and slime, crawling out of the husk or shell part. It was becoming some other kind of bug. Bud?"

"Yes?"

"I'm like that bug. Am I like that bug, Bud?"

"Yes."

"Where was I?"

"Jack Dreck."

"Jack?"

"Yes."

"Okay. Jack Dreck, his tight slick hair, his white bony hairless ankles, is reading the fine newsprint through splayed knees, going uh-oh, there's mayhem in Angola, uh-oh, them bikers over in Enfield are on the war path."

"Uh-oh, uh-oh" — on and on she goes, yapping that blue streak.

CHAPTER THREE

ZIPPO

Zippo Giocametti and his bodyguard and grunt, his best pal Pat Fish, were coming into Dulles on the morning Air Canada flight from Vancouver, B.C. They'd been out there on a family matter, what Zippo was calling a hit, although all they had done was shave a guy's locks, talk mean to him. The guy someone Zippo had never seen, scarcely heard of. Zippo had got it into his head the guy was mistreating his daughter, Doe — Dolores — so he'd booked the first flight out. That was Friday. Now it was Sunday, the two having stayed over Saturday night to catch the cheapo tickets. Zippo didn't believe in throwing away money, and as he said to Pat Fish, "What would we be doing anyway? You had a hot date? You wanted someone to admire your gold chains?"

Pat Fish had no objections to the lay-over. He liked the city, liked that cottage industry by the bridge, Granville Island or whatever it was called — liked the fish he'd had for dinner, and didn't mind at all clipping Doe's boyfriend's hair. He didn't see, though, why they couldn't stay at the Four Seasons, rather than that two-bit dump down on, what was it called, Englishman's Bay.

"You been a grouch the whole time," Zippo told him. "This the last trip I'm ever making with you."

"Call yourself a big gangster," Pat Fish said. "Cut a guy's hair! Man, you tough."

This was coming through customs, the woman in her cubbyhole saying to Zippo, "Sir, unless you're married to this man, would you please step back behind the red line?" Straggly hair, round shoulders, pouty lips, no lipstick, little black-dot D.C. eyes setting him straight.

Pat Fish at the booth emptying his pockets: wallet, keys, bag of airline peanuts, Canuck coins — dibbles and dabs of nothing the officer wants to look at. The woman glaring, waving the declaration form, saying, "You haven't been to a farm in the last thirty days, then how come you checked the *Yes* box?"

"I didn't say I was bringing in fruit," Zippo hears him saying. "All I said was I ate an apple up there."

"Well, did you pass it?"

Everybody and his brother a smartass.

Off to the side, a security guard, eighty if a day, feet spread, hand resting on the holstered pistolla, head angled to peruse the ceiling. Snoozing. Near him, a puddle of water, the roof leaking. Dripping this very minute. The U.S. flag so still you can see the cobwebs. The woman at last tired of Pat Fish's black face, stamping the form, thumbing him along.

Zippo breezing through, the woman sweet as pie.

"Anything to declare, Mr. Giocametti?"

"Only my good will. Only my noble intentions."

"Welcome home, Mr. Giocametti."

Like he's a big cheese. Like the country hasn't been the same since he left.

Joe Giocametti was gangsterlord of a multi-county strip that wrapped into and out of D.C., Virginia and the Carolinas. Zippo ruled the area through political payoffs, by and large, with only the occasional manifestation of modest violence to indicate his full potential and demonstrate that he was a rational being in a society already beset with sufficient grief to drive the average citizen insane. Zippo tempered his acts with mercy, with tact, realizing in any case that he could not compete with the atrocities unwinding daily in real life or on the nation's TV and movie screens.

The *underworld*, they called it. What a laugh.

Lately Zippo had been thinking he'd like to arrange an in-depth session with that beauty at *Sixty Minutes*, Leslie Stahl.

Set the record straight.

Better yet would be to fork over a few million for midnight infomercials over the major networks, in which he — or a hired gun more photogenic than he was, maybe that old *I Spy* guy who now did the "Grow New Hair" pitch — would move the American public to a better understanding of the criminal classes.

He had in mind printing up slick color brochures his audience could write in for. The brochures would offer thumbnail profiles on a day in the life of the typical criminal, define the gangster's customary cosy relationship with the police, the courts, with elected officials of your average city and state, in addition to providing more specific guidelines. Descriptions of how a prostitution ring worked, for instance, replete with show-and-tell features, charts, prevailing geographical fees, the historical context — together with statements from a ranking Republican — Newt, maybe — outlining for the common dweeb the benefit accruing to society from such meaningful and necessary depravity.

If depravity was the right word. Not having the hands-on experience, other than as arm's-length boss, Zippo figured he'd have to go with the opinion of experts. Let Leslie call the shots.

Waiting for their driver to show up, no bags between them except a catch-all from the duty free, this slung over Pat Fish's burly shoulders, Zippo says to him: "I'm telling you it will work. It's all image, you know. Rev up our reps."

Studying Pat Fish's face, giving him time to say, "Uh-oh, hold the phone, I got to go take a leak." But Pat Fish just spits.

"Say we follow this scenario. Twenty-four Hours in the Life of Pat Fish. What do you think?"

Pat Fish rolling his eyes.

"Say we start the day with you waking up. What's the first thing you do?"

"Take a leak."

"See? Already we've established the common link. Already we got the empathy thing going."

"Empathy? I wake up, I got no empathy with a single soul on earth."

"Think about it. Fame awaits you."

"I already been famous."

Back in his Martin Luther King days, he means.

"You think my infomerce idea's dumb?"

"Could be."

"You want me to shut up?"

"Could be."

"All right, that's your attitude, let me tell you it's a crappy attitude."

"What's the first thing you do, you get up, Zip?"

"Shoot all the help."

Now they are whipping along in the multiple-occupancy speed lane, the Beltway, Zippo on the look-out for what state troopers called the Fancy Dans: lone drivers who regularly stow a mannikin in the passenger seat, the dummy dressed like grandpa, cigar stuffed in the dummy's mouth, the driver likely nodding along to the thousand and one becrazed opinions airing on the G. Gordon Liddy talk show. West on 29 until they pick up 66, another three or four hours to reach his mountain digs. Rain coming down hard. The wipers slapping away.

Tie a string round the finger, Zippo thinks. Stop somewhere on the road, call Glo, let her know we're back safe and sound. Call

Chantelle, get an update. Call Cutt, tell him I've got a buyer for his Kennedy silver dollars. Give close thought to the upcoming coin heist.

Pat Fish rubbing knuckles into his eye sockets, toying with the window up and down.

"Why don't you take off your shoes?" Zippo says. "Relax."

"Don't want to."

"What, you got deformed feet? Take off your shoes!"

Zippo wriggling his own feet, the yellow socks, to show Pat Fish how good it feels.

The Caddy zipping along now, making good time. '52 Eldorado, fins, wire wheels, Brancusi bird flying the hood — best Caddy Detroit ever built. Fifteen beans it has cost Zippo to have it stretched, retooled. Odometer three times around and still on the original engine. Glo's baby, this Caddy.

The driver's head folded against the roof. Red hair. A stringbean. Not much more than a kid. Alonzo, that's his name?

"Gizmo to your left," Zippo says, taking pity. "Will lower that seat."

"Yeah?"

Feeling around, finding the toggle. It comes to Zippo, he's never seen the guy before.

"When did I hire you?"

"Two weeks ago."

"How much?"

"Two a week."

"Two grand?"

"Two hundred."

Pat Fish laughs.

"A raise was mentioned," the kid says.

"Why is that?"

"Once a crane is found."

"You do crane work?"

"It comes to cranes," the driver says. "I'm the world's authority."

"Remind me," Zippo says, leaning into Pat Fish, "why I need a crane guy."

"Coins."

Oh, yeah. The mint heist.

Twenty tons — two box-cars full — of U.S. quarters. At a rough guess, what, maybe thirty, forty million quarters? Put a mathematician on that, run a weights and measures test. Who knows how many quarters? He pulls the job off, which he has every expectation of doing, Papa Giocametti, don of the Jersey shore, brother Dominic in OJ Land — the whole horseshoe — they'll laugh themselves silly.

"Something eat your brains, Zippo? Where you going to stash, how you going to move, thirty million quarters?"

Like he hasn't already made the arrangements.

Drizzle drizzle. The rain a bitch.

Creeping along now, thirty-five, the highway clogged again. Zippo thinking he should have put in tinted windows when he'd had the interior spruced up. Glo saying, What, you're such a big-deal gangster you can't be looked at? On his back every minute since Doe was born, with these *gangster* digs. *Go straight, you son of a bitch!*

Zippo slapping Pat Fish's knee, a punch on the shoulder. A big grin. "Okay, quiz time. I'm thinking the worst Academy Award-winning pix ever made. What is it?"

"Forrest Gump."

"You got it. Okay, this one. Something *in the Sun?"*

"Raisins."

"Not *Raisins.* Try again."

"Duel."

"Not *Duel.* Adapted from Dreiser. *An American Tragedy."*

"Dreiser, huh? Poor white boy can't get the rich white girl, that's an American tragedy?"

"Take off your shoes. Something *in the Sun.* Come on. Okay, try this one. Laughton calls up Mitchum, he says, 'I have here a property about a thoroughly unredeemable shit,' and Mitchum says, 'Present, sir.' What movie?"

"*Night of the* Something."

"'Something' don't count. *Night of the* what?"

Pat Fish studying his nails.

The driver angling the rearview, framing Zippo's face.

"Yeah?"

"Glo says you're to stop, pick up something for dinner. Something you can cook yourself, she said. Pork chops, a sirloin, something like that."

"I'm supposed to go easy on red meat!"

"Yeah. Something like that. Also, I'm to tell you, 'water'."

"Water?"

"Yeah."

"You're kidding me! We still don't have water?"

"No sir. Not a drop except what's caught in the rain barrel. Your wife, I made her real happy with that rain barrel idea."

"A two-million-dollar home, I've got to put out rain barrels?"

They drive on through hard rain and soft rain. Through sludge. ATTENTION ROAD WORK ahead. Yellow flashers, red flags, barricades, trucks, dozers, cats, cement-mixers, asphalt-layers, packers: all Giocametti machines. Idle for the most part, waiting out the downpour.

A North American city you can erect overnight but the highways take forever.

A quarter-zillion miles of graft.

Zippo feels no shame. How things are done.

Hell, all but legit.

32-wheelers whipping by like transplants from Darlington Raceway. On the trucks' rear end, greetings: HOW'M I DOING?

Zippo thinking, hitting the mountains, of his big opportunities —
dealing in arms, military goods, being palsy with Noriega. Ethics, he
told the Colonel, O.O., told the Senator. The moral issue. No way I'm
joining the CIA in the assassination of good socialists down in Chile
or Nicaragua.

So there had gone his zillions.

At a fund-raiser last week the Governor himself, O.O. Orth, that
piece of self-glorified scum, has said: "Zippo, you lack the firm hand.
You don't got the blood-sucker mentality. You wouldn't last a minute
in my line."

Him saying that with the grease, the Gray-Away stink in his hair.
Tasselled white loafers, the silver O.O. buckles, metal clickers on the
heels, cheeks rouged for a camera gig.

Zippo responding, "Governor, you don't think I'm tough as you
because I don't wear your Ginger Rogers shoes?" Rye sloshing over
the Governor's fingers, the prick saying, glint in his eye, "Zippo, till I
met you I never known such a shitrag existed as a bleeding-heart liberal left-wing motherfucking gangster. I'd of said it won't possible."
All the Governor's shoe-sniffers guffawing. "I never liked you, *frocio*.
You're old news. Know what I'm saying?"

The Governor, what, issuing threats? Pat Fish meantime working
the ballroom, slipping envelopes into assorted pockets. Zippo's big
one already in the bowl on the head table. Donations earmarked for
St. Luke Charities, but everyone knowing St. Luke is right there in the
room clicking his white shoes.

Zippo isn't worried. They want gravel, sand, concrete, good
quarry work — they wanted roads, and name me one politician never
wanted roads? — they pretty much got to come through Zippo. They
want liquor splashed in their glass, their favorite hangout, it comes,
likely as not, from a Giocametti wholesaler. The nuts in the dish, pretzels, cocktail napkins, even the sawdust on the floor.

Zippo would like to have it unobtrusively slid into his infomerce that it is Zippo Giocametti money keeping a shelter for the homeless going not five blocks from the White House, and that his daughter put in a year on the Greenpeace vessel, Rainbow Warrior, hounding the French over their nuclear testing in the Pacific.

It would be worth doing it just to see Doe, Dolores, shit blue thunderbolts out there in her Vancouver Greenpeace office, slogging away at the strip-logging practices of the west coast forestry giants.

Still, after the French had rammed the Rainbow Warrior and the ship was being refitted by loin-clad guys away yonder on some god-forsaken atoll, who was it had arranged a go-between in Switzerland to wire the funds? There was no love lost between him and the French; he had only to sit down in one of Glo's fancy French restaurants to be reminded of that.

"Suppose I put this question to you," Zippo says to Pat Fish.

"What question?"

"How many women have you slept with? I mean, let's just suppose."

"Suppose what?"

"Suppose I put that question to you. What would you say?"

"You mean, after I say it's none of your business."

"Yeah. After that."

"After I punch your nose?"

"Yeah. After that."

"Sixty."

"Sixty? And how do you see these sixty? In your mind, I mean. Are they all there in a gang, or do they troop by your eyes one by one?"

"I've got them in a line. The line snakes all around the block. They been waiting all night in the dark for me to open my door."

"All sixty?"

"Give or take."

"Clothed or naked?"

"My mind wants them naked, they're naked. But a lot of these women, you know, don't like standing out there all night in the dark with nothing on."

"They're arranged by height, by age? By beauty? Intelligence? Or chronologically, say, by when you met them?"

"Oh, sure!"

"What you mean?"

"By when they come into my life. But now and then, all along the line, you'll hear one saying, 'Excuse me, I was here first.' Then that party will step in front. Spats, you know, breaking out all along the line. Now and then someone flounces her hair, says, 'This is the wrong line. I'm not supposed to be in this line.' Someone else says, 'What does this guy look like? I don't remember this guy.' Or: 'It was a mistake. I must have been drunk.' Another person saying, 'I was in love with this guy. I would have done anything for him. Now the name hardly rings a bell.' But most of them are quiet, going along with it, thinking, 'I could have done worse. I tell you, honey, there are some lines I'm ashamed to be seen in.'"

"The most recent woman you slept with," Zippo says. "Is she first in line, or last?"

"She's already in the room. She's been there with me all night."

"She's got out of bed once or twice, I guess. To look out the window?"

"Up and down all night long. Saying, 'Honey, who are all those women on your doorstep?'"

"Or maybe she looks out your window and what she sees is the long line of guys have been at *her* door."

"Sure. Could be."

"Okay, here's another question. Do these women look the way they looked when you met them, or how you imagine they look after all these intervening years?"

Pat Fish squinching up his eyes, kneading his brow.

"Damn!" he says. "Now you've ruined it. They are all gone."

"All sixty! Gone?"

"A few stragglers. But their backs are turned to me. I can't see who they are."

"So what about the woman was inside with you? Is she gone?"

"Wait a minute."

Pat Fish closes those eyes again. Wrenches up his face. Zippo laying down a fifty that says Pat Fish is going to find his room empty.

"I see some of her things," Pat says after a minute. "Yeah, there's her purse. Hey! She's put out yellow tulips in a vase!"

"But is she gone?"

"I think she's in the kitchen. I think she's making dinner."

"So go in the kitchen. See if she's in there."

Pat Fish opens his eyes, looks at Zippo a long time. Then says: "So now let me put the question to you. How many you got in your line?"

"Three."

"*Three?* You're calling three a line?"

"There's a whole streetful milling about. Those I've touched up, you know? Kissed. Well, a few I've kissed. Most, I only held their hands."

"Let me see I've got this straight," Pat Fish says. "You've got a streetful of women who have let you hold their hands?"

"Yeah. We both been blessed, right?"

Outside Menasas Gap, the Shenandoah close by, the driver swivels the rearview, says, "Gentlemen, I think we got a tail."

"What!"

Twenty-five years, easy-peasey, since Zippo had a tail.

A blue Jag. The Jag didn't go away. It hung a few hundred yards back, keeping other vehicles between them.

"Anyone packing?" Zippo asks.

Pat Fish, the stringbean, shake their heads.

"Try the glove compartment."

Nothing there except an assortment of yellowing documents, a collapsible umbrella, tins of Puffy cat food, a bent wire-hanger for when Glo locks herself out. In the bar fridge, Diet Cokes, Pepsis, Ting. Munchies.

"Let's lose the son of a bitch."

At sixty-five mph the Caddy engine begins pinging; at seventy, the front wheels wobble. Zippo only then remembering that Glo, a safety nut, had a speed-governor installed way back when Doe was a baby. Smoke billows from the hood. The Caddy is an oil guzzler. When last was it tuned?

"Jesus Christ," Zippo says. "We ruin this car, Glo will kill us."

At Riverton they take the 340 loop, which zigzags around the western border of Shenandoah National Park. The Jag stays with them through the elbow curves, the steep grades and valleys of Bentonville, Rileyville, Oak Hill, Luray.

"What's in the trunk?"

"Fishing poles."

"Under the seats?"

"Dixie cups."

No car phone. Glo opposes car phones. Showy opulence, she claims.

On the outskirts of Shenandoah, passing staggered billboards announcing FAMILY FUN TOURIST SPECTACULAR ONE HUN-DRED YARDS, the rear window blows out.

Yelps, everyone ducking, glass flying; cold wind whipping through the gaping hole, rain pelting their necks.

The side window goes by Zippo's head.

They are off the road. They are jouncing through a pioneer fence, mowing down laurel, mowing down a maze of hedge bushes cut to resemble horses, dogs, bears, giant chickens, giraffes, dinosaurs. Onwards through the mudholes of a common hog pen, hogs squealing, running, tree limbs flashing by. Up a grassy embankment, dodging boulders, Alonzo Smith's knuckles white on the wheel, fighting to get the fishtailing Caddy back onto hardtop.

The rain pelting in. The wind killer-cold.

Then, miraculously, they are back on hard surface, the Caddy groaning, pinging. Slowly picking up speed on the slick curving road, as the Jag closes in for the kill.

"Shit," Smith says. "I never could do this."

"Do what?"

"Movie stuff. That three-six-o. I flip every time."

Already slogging the pedals, thumping them as for a hoedown. Spinning the wheel. Zippo and Pat Fish holding on, crushed together one way, now slung another. Up-ended. Everything a blur: Zippo's shoeless foot in the icebox, cans skooting back and forth. The screech of tires, burning rubber, the car rocking, skidding. Sure as hell, they are going over.

When Zippo unclenches his eyes they are barrelling back the way they had come. Still in one piece. Releasing the breath, sucking in another. Metal drags the highway — their tail pipe, maybe a fender. Glass shards poke at the backside, the elbows; Zippo looks down: all this while, how long, his zipper open. How come you guys didn't tell me? he's about to say. Then noticing a long slither of glass impaled in the driver's neck below the right ear; the kid flicking, flicking at it as though it's a bee sting. WINDING ROAD, the signs say. STEEP GRADE. TRUCKS USE LOWER GEARS. Deep valleys to either side, water gushing down the mountainside, the Shenandoah River roaring along below, the wet road a slithering snake.

Pat Fish sees it before Zippo does: the Jag square in front of them, coming fast. Virginia plates. A rental car, Tri-Star. Who has ever heard of Tri-Star? Two people hunched in there.

Alonzo's face set in a snarl. He's taking the whole of the road, holding the Caddy tight onto the road's the yellow lines. The Jag will have to hit him or leave the road.

They each see the driver's astonished face, fear etched there beneath a floppy Tilley hat. A woman, god knows. Hefty, oldish, her mouth wide open. The guy beside her in a yellow slicker bracing himself, screaming warnings — in that flash of time before the Jag simply slides away from the Caddy's nose, floats off into the blue, sails out over the tree tops down the steep, befogged mountain as if in uncertain aim for one or another of the many alpine rooftops insecurely perched below.

"*Quién anda,*" says Zippo.

Who goes there.

CHAPTER FOUR

VETS

Friday, the tail-end of spring, was a hot day in the nation's capital.

Wally, doorman at the high-rise on N Street where Senator Otis Roy Cutt was soon to breathe his last, all morning long had been dragging his chair from sunshine into shade. Wiping his brow, shouting obscenities at passersby, making life a hell for jittery old John Fudge across the street hosing a nest of oleander bushes on his postage-stamp lawn.

To residents entering Wally's building, some loaded down with shopping bags, Wally said, "What, your arm is broke? You want to bring back servitude of the lower classes? Open your own door."

He was union, Doormen's International, a media celeb, no way they could sack him so long as he didn't stab a knife into a resident's chest.

Often a tempting thought.

What Wally liked best about the job was the constant parade of stretch limos lumbering along N Street — senators, congressmen, lobbyists, bankers, and the like reposed behind black-tinted windows. Once or twice a week he threw out a handful of tacks just to let the big shots know he couldn't be pushed around.

Noonish, leaning back in his chair by the front door, Wally got excited. Here came the President's limo, riding low, the tires needing air, flags streaming fore and aft. Eight cars, all told, three to the front, another four trailing.

Wally sprang out to the curb, hoisting the chair as though he had in mind flinging it through the President's windshield.

"Yo, One!" he shouted, running alongside. "Up yours!"

The procession whispered by, no response from the Secret Service tag-team paid to protect number one's Razorback butt. The SS people knew Wally, looked forward to seeing the nervy bastard out there each day insulting the nation's commander-in-chief.

They'd arrested him once. The publicity this generated had ended careers. Never again.

Just after one o'clock, a white van, *Giocametti Industries* painted on the sides, dropped off a load of Italian tiles, shovels, a trolley, sack after sack of ready-mix cement. Behind the van purred another stretch limo. The limo halted. Out of the rear doors popped two men dressed in army fatigues, lugging tool boxes. They were middle-aged, inclining towards obesity, their chins scruffy. The two promptly began shoving each other, making noise.

"I carry up the fuckin' tiles! Dint I tell you? I carry up the fuckin' tiles, you carry up the fuckin' cement!"

"No way! You carry up the fuckin' cement!"

"Lardass!"

"Prick!"

Not caring who heard them.

Old John Fudge, hiding behind his oleanders, thinking they might kill each other on the spot, wondered if he shouldn't call the cops.

When the tilemen turned their venom on him, shouting, "What you gawkin' at?" Fudge scrambled inside.

Wally missed the drama. He was at Pancho's Bar around the corner, on his lunch break, downing a free Guinness and munching on pretzels. Pancho, another celeb, had the overhead TV tuned to *Wrestlin' Fever:* Gay Predator vs. The Masked Espagnol. Espagnol's trainer or manager, attendant — a black woman in stiletto heels, skimpy costume owing a lot to Wonder Woman — was stalking the ring apron, smacking at the Predator with a straw broom. The crown of peacock feathers wafting above her multi-story Afro hair was more than the cameras could handle; the folks with the zoom were contenting themselves with the cleavage, the trio of snakes slithering about her beautiful neck.

Wally and Pancho had seen brooms just like hers in Vietnam.

"Them two bruisers been eating steer rods," Pancho said. "I bet they got peckers like burnt match sticks."

Steroids, he meant.

Now Stiletto was trying to kill the Gay Predator with her snakes.

So Wally was slacking off, shooting the breeze, improving his mind, when the killer tile guys got into the building on N Street.

Senator Cutt, their target, didn't arrive until hours later.

"You seen Ms. Peru lately?" Wally asked Pancho.

Chantelle Peru, their lawyer, Wally meant. Wally and Pancho had recently joined in bringing a forty-million dollar class action suit against the federal government for leaving them in Vietnam twenty-three years past the war's end.

Senator Cutt, chair of the Senate Armed Services Committee over recent decades, was one of those named in the suit.

Pancho said, "Naw, I've not seen the divine Ms. Peru lately. She been avoiding me. You?"

"This morning she comes flying by, a piece of cake in her hand. Up like her hand's a platter, you know, the cake on that platter."

"I hope she offer you a bite. Let you lick that cake right off her hand."

"I wouldn't pass it up, even without the cake."

"Man, you in love."

Chantelle Peru had an apartment on the seventeenth floor of the condo on N Street.

The killer tile men were already at work up on eighteen as Wally and Pancho concentrated anew on the mattress-thumpers. The tilers had snagged a black boy off the street to trolley up the tiles, the cement.

Two o'clock.

"Yo, Sister! Spare the time?"

The heat is a dilly, record temp for this date in the year. So reports the U.S. weather office. But are the weather people to be trusted? Alien beings have taken over the U.S. weather office. So Pancho the barman has been insisting to Wally, doorman *par excellence*. Wally has no dispute with this opinion. "You gotta consider, though," he tells Pancho, "the positive influence on society of negative thought."

"Yeah. You gotta."

"Without negativism, how you even going to recognize yourself? Progress comes to a halt."

"What I've been saying."

"On the other hand — "

"What other hand?"

There they are, two o'clock, the sun beaming on their faces as they commune on the broken pavement outside Pancho's bar.

"Like, I still might maintain," Wally insists, "a Happy Hour improve your business."

"Why confuse matters? You and me, we are our own Happy Hour. You want to hug me or we just going to stand here?"

It is an embarrassment, two deranged Vets with wet eyes hugging in public view. Retaining the embrace so long one might surmise they have fallen asleep. Wally in the seedy gray doorman's overcoat with the tattered gold braid, gold buttons, the frayed hem, Pancho in jungle-war fatigues, stringy-haired, flesh a rough purple, as if fired by brimstone.

"Our situation ever improve. You think?"

"We die, Pancho, everything improves."

"So we don't die, everything remains the same?"

"Not what I'm saying."

"Whatever you're saying, I know you are a man of your word. You've convinced me."

"Exactly! Exactly what I was saying."

Wally ambles back to his post around the corner at the building on N Street, thinking: That Pancho. A good guy, my best amigo, but, man, is he hard to talk to.

"Up yours!" Wally shouts to lumbering limousines. His knees grazing bumpers, daring wheel men to run him down.

"Fat Cats!" he shouts. "Go out and get honest employment!"

Ambles is an imprecise word for how Wally moves. Something is the matter, an observer might presume, with the man's appendages. His feet strike the pavement tentatively; splay off into opposing directions. Similarly, his arms. Wally's limbs, that is to say, seem not to know where the rest of Wally is going. He walks on the sides of his feet, rolls them; high-top boots unlaced, tongues flapping. Where can a man find such boots? These boots cushioned, reinforced with steel bands, custom-made, as are Pancho's, to a surgeon's specifications.

Twelve hundred bucks the crack, those boots. VA hospital cut-rate price.

Even so, Wally's feet seem to slide, to stumble. Soft ankles. Let's look at those ankles. Does the man have ankles? No ankles. Perhaps this is why Wally walks always in a near crouch. Or is his spine also impaired? In the long doorman's coat, Wally is quite the sight; people gawk; he looks a misery, he's frightening; but Wally is celebrated. The Fat Cats dare not tangle with Wally. Twenty-three years in a cage, you want now to give him more grief?

The elderly retired gentleman across the way from the building on N Street, John Fudge, retiree from the aerodynamics industry, has come out a second time today to overwater his oleanders, his postage-stamp patch of city green. Wally has Fudge's attention, as often he does. The doorman is a scary son of a bitch. Unpredictable, often obscene: this Fudge knows from experience. But sorely crippled. At times, late afternoon, Fudge has seen the doorman disintegrate before his very eyes. Wally's bones seem to be at war one with the other. The head jerks, limbs twitch. One shoulder rides above the other. The hands are constantly slapping at air. How come? What has been done to him? Fudge is a devotee of *Aerodynamics Quarterly*, *Black Hole Messenger*, of *Qfwfq*, the industry wind and waves journal; he's missed *Time*'s cover story, the *People* feature, the *Post*'s double-page spread on Wally, Pancho, and Jude: "Return of the Invisible Warriors." With each step the man's knees quiver; he seems on the verge of collapsing. He's eternally licking his lips, boring a finger up his nose, into an ear. Slapping his brow. Scratching. The unshaven face is scarred, lit with yellowish patches. Scar tissue, skin grafts. This suggests, to the old gentleman's mind, that at one time or another a plastic surgeon, not a very good one, has had a go at him. Perhaps several simultaneously; doubtless, if the result is any indication, with conflicting opinions. Even the eyes, those awful eyes, deep-socketed, always a flaming red, dart and leap about as though looking for a place to settle. With unsettling regularity, to Fudge's way of thinking, they settle on him.

"Yo! Waste our last resources, why don't you?"

The man holding up the street's traffic, screaming this inanity at Fudge. "Rice! You're putting in *rice*?"

A lunatic. Possibly the victim of a car crash, a fire, an unfortunate deformity at birth.

Indeed, Wally has his eyes on the old fart, Fudge. Why won't the geezer exchange a simple greeting? Act civil. What's the matter with everyone?

Nam. Little by little Wally knew less and less what country he was in. He did not know the country he was in.

What time is it? he would ask.

Half past ten.

Always when he asked himself what time it was he would answer half past ten. He would see women kneeling in the rice field, clearing weeds, their heads tied yellow, and he would say, It is half past ten.

He invented a new system of months, giving those months strange names: Fortunado, Sibelius, Walpole, Mary; first twelve, then fifty, then five hundred strangely named months, but always, whatever the month, time was locked at half past ten.

I will be home, I will be in love, I will have my first child, I will become an old man, I will die at half past ten.

Nam, he lived through the entire year 1492 without dramatic incident. 1360 was not a good year, though he had suffered worse. Through the whole of the period 1562–1574 a boy named Shakespeare lived in a thatched house on the other side of Wally's rice field. The boy would call across the field, "What time is it?" and Wally would call back, "Idiot! It's half past ten!"

When Wally was especially anxious or vexated by the sight of curious movement in the rice field or if the women at work there had stubs for arms, were missing a leg, he would say, I *think* it is half past ten, though I could be wrong.

The year 1000 BC he thought up the word chivalry, the word charity, the word idolatry, the word corn; that entire year he thought of little else except the many cathedrals of meaning contained in those four words. In the previous year 1640 there had been other things but in the year 1000 BC there were just those things.

The war would end, he would go home, at half past ten.

"What time is it?" he would ask.

"Everything points to its being half past ten."

For weeks without end his cage door in the rice field would remain open and Wally would look at the door and look at the door and ask himself how it had come to pass that the door had opened without his having noticed the door was open.

Often Wally would awaken and someone would be in the mud beside him and when he moved to touch this someone she would say Why are you touching me? — with the result that he ceased his attempts to touch her and lay on his side with his cold back against her back.

What is the time, dear friend?

Half past ten.

The day Chantelle Peru showed up he was not surprised in the least; he thinks it was half past ten or half past ten or possibly it was half past ten.

Pancho says it was the same with him, though not the same, because Pancho, Pancho says, was not where he left him and anytime he went back to see where that old Pancho was there was another Pancho there, not a party Pancho wanted anything to do with.

Who are you? Who goes there?

I didn't do the half past ten. I did the fingernail.

"By your leave, General," Wally says. Dropping down heavily into his rickety N Street street chair. Slipping his mangled feet free of the sweltering boots. The socks wet, toes a mystery. When was it he lost his toes? Was it land mine, mortar fire, or rodents in the rice field? In war or peace? He could use a stool to prop up these thrashing legs. Why hasn't his man Giocametti provided him with a stool? Let the good soldier rest his stumps. Perhaps a stool fitted with plush red velvet cushions, topped with golden fringed canopy to shade me in my hour of need? Ah, Wally thinks: my insatiable needs! To think of needs, of comfort, in these perilous times. Across the street, a stooped old man is passing, bewhiskered, pushing a wire cart. Wally is up from his chair, yelling: "Have you written to the Swiss banks? Have you yet collected a cent?"

Wait.

Oh, happy interlude! Oh, *"Hark! Who goes there?"*

That dish Chantelle, Ms. Peru, just now flying from an unlicensed cab, giving Wally the quick eye, the nimblest of waves, the briefest flash of thigh, as she rockets inside.

He'd like getting to know in lip to lip sync, in precious harmony, the affable, the brilliant, the loftily eccentric Ms. Peru. Chantelle Peru, it must be said even if he is the party to say it, is quite the piece.

Oh, yes, Ms. Peru, Wally, your humble doorman, loves you.

Would a classy, learned woman like Chantelle Peru, ex-Congresswoman's assistant, vegetarian, fashion plate, she of the mini-skirts, custom-cut suit tops, sexy leotards, purveyor of exquisite aroma, of silver bracelets and wampum-beads, of fine Italian purses, finest Italian shoes, First Nations arbitrator, last-ditch Death Row defender, Counsel to Women For Equality, Counsel For the Abolition of Corrupt Electoral Practices, Counsel to the First Lady's Committee for the Repatriation of American Soldiers Abandoned in Vietnam — would she? could she? — smile on him?

That woman going there, shooting for the elevator: the one with the ear-cut chestnut hair, the well-turned legs, the deliciously trim feet, the bewitching hips, the white teeth, the friendly mien. Dark eyelids, eyebrows trapped in eternal surprise, long lashes, a sleek nose, ears decorated with dangling silver fish, knee-caps that have tantalizing faces genetically engineered into the tawny skin. Sweetest of all, Ms. Peru: your lips, your eyes, that smile. Your intelligence. Oh, Ms. Peru. I adore you.

Well, why not? Wally asks himself. Isn't this America, land of the free and the brave?

Over vast distances, through air that became water, water that became flesh, did not Ms. Peru find him? Did she not slog through unending rice fields past the very gateways of inhuman breath? Mud up past her knees, mosquito bites over each inch of skin, didn't she? Come? Didn't she?

Ms. Peru, defender of the faith, keeper of the light.

Oh, Ms. Peru, wilt thou beside me sing?

Wally's love enfeebles him. With Ms. Peru in his orbit, Wally submits to wave after wave of exhilarating exhaustion. Breathing becomes laborious. His every bone aches. Each rasping breath is a labor of love for the divine Ms. Peru.

It is so hard, Wally thinks, to love. It takes so much out of me.

Yet he would die for even a pat on the head from the illustrious Ms. Peru. I love you, Ms. Peru. Let me shine your shoes. Let me smell you.

But just once could those lips touch mine?

Wally tilts back in the rickety chair, the sun hot on his face, his eyes closed. Ms. Peru, he thinks: let me dream of you.

So it is that, for a moment, the woman's voice he hears calling his name, calling with more than a little anxiety, is the property of that dreaming mind. He clinches his eyes tighter, seeing out through twitchy lids . . . twenty-three years of undulating rice field. Ms. Peru is walking a shaft of reddish light over those fields, calling to him in his cage: "Yoo-hoo! It's half past ten! Time to go home!"

A hand is roughly shaking him. Perfume and hand become one, both attached to beautiful Chantelle Peru.

"Wally! Wake up! We've got to help this boy!"

Boy? Then he sees him:

Sweet? Is that you, Sweet?

Ms. Peru is out hopping in the street, squirrelling between oncoming traffic, shouting, "Taxi, taxi!"

I worship thee, Ms. Peru.

"Sit down, Sweet," Wally says. "Let the honkie investigate."

The bleeding boy wants to run. But he sits.

One of Sweet's eye has survived the massacre; the other is already closing. Puffy lips, a wide gash in the lower divide. Teeth lined with blood. The blood is coming from the gash, as well as from the boy's nose, which is clearly broken. A flattened ear. But Sweet is holding up. Not for nothing is he his mother's son.

A white limo pulls in, Ms. Peru trotting alongside; the limo halts, idles, in the UNLOADING ONLY stripes outside the N Street door.

Ms. Peru, back again, is down on her lovely knees beside Wally, assessing the harm done to the bleeding Sweet. Wally is distracted. He would freeze this moment, as on the budget VCR in his room. Hold there forever Ms. Peru's divided knees, the hiked mini, the comely thighs, the face locked in heart-broken concern.

"Tiles," Sweet is saying. "Them assholes tilers up there, they done it."

"The meter is running, counselor," calls an impatient voice.

John Fudge, across the street getting an eyeful, recognizes not only the man's voice but his face as well. He has seen that face, heard that voice, on numerous occasions. Most recently at televised Senate hearings convened to consider the controversial nomination to the Supreme Court of William Streicher. Fudge has promised himself never, never to advance beyond his own curb, but he would like a real-life close-up look at the man said to be shaking the dirt from the high court's traditional roots. Fudge is deeply impressed by the persuasive powers of the skinny woman on her knees in the mini; that someone of Streicher's elevated status would consent at her command to assist an anonymous black boy, to Fudge's mind, warrants inclusion in *Qfwfg*.

"He's going to need stitches," Ms. Peru announces, flying up. "Wally, can you go with him? Oh, honey, your poor lip."

Sweet slapping her hands; better to die than have whitey tend him.

"*Pro bono*, pal. We find who did this, we'll murder the son of a bitch."

In Streicher's limo the boy sits a sullen lump between Wally and the famous judge. Not goin' to no Emergency, he's said. Don't need no doctor, he's said. You can forgit that shit. Goin' to the Gate.

"Gate?"

"See my brother. See the Digger."

"Digger?"

Streicher's back is turned to them; legs crossed, wearing those black one-size-fits-all stretch socks, a dark-blue lightweight suit, one of those funny French caps, what you call them, berets, on his head. A heavy-hipped man, beautiful hands, a hirsute face. Glasses. On his lap a stack of papers, his nose inside *Jones vs. Duke Power*. Champagne on the drop-table, a wrapped sandwich, corned beef, from Seymour's Deli.

"The Digger. He see to my welfare."

These honkies, they've surprised Sweet with their Good Samaritan act, but booger that jive. It was honkies assaulted him in the first place. Well, they live to regret it, all he can say. His brother the Digger be settlin' that score. Anybody mess with Sweet, here come big brother Ish the Digger.

"Judge?" Wally says.

Streicher is deep into *Jones vs. Duke Power*.

Slashing a Bic pen across a yellow legal pad so hard he's ripping the pages.

"Judge?"

Streicher sips champagne, his sight afar, that right hand slashing. Not hearing a word.

At the Watergate, right away there is Ish. He's out front with another man, Ish dwarfing the second party, the two of them, what, counting money? A big fistful, counting it out on the street in broad daylight beside two holly bushes, feet on the red carpet, Ish carrying the day in his black silk shirt with the flying collar, the gold chains, red silk Arabian Nights trousers. Cool. He's cool. Across the way, a dusty panel AT&T van, what, taping Lewinski? Ear phones on the mother?

"Ish, Ish, Ish!" the boy in the limo singing.

Judge Streicher blithely carrying on. Not yet has he looked up. He has no interest in where he is. Nothing exists in the world other than *Jones vs. Duke Power*.

"Don't worry, honky. I not let Big Brother Ish harm you."

Ish the Digger, squatting down, taking a gander into the big limo. Frowning, those eyes enlarging; now coming on fast.

"Sweet?"

Not so much as a quick by-your-leave to the renowned Justice Streicher.

Sweet stepping out, brushing the judge's knees, trampling the Court's papers. Already, Sweet, his shoes not yet striking ground, is spilling out the whole story. Tile guys, fuckityeah, panel truck with the name *Giocametti* on the side. "Over on N Street, Ish. Yeah, over on N."

Ish shifting his eyes to take in Wally twitching on the back seat, the judge with his racing Bic. Leaning in through the limo door, giving Wally's hand the brother's soul greeting, saying: "Couldn't believe my eyes, Sweet and you and the judge here, pulling up together in this bitty vehicle. You seeing here a fellow vet, my man, oh yes. Now s'pose I was to ask you, good brother, what could you tell me about who it was done this shit to Little Digger's face so's I can rip out the perpetrator's guts?" Stepping back, closing the limo door, saying to the judge, "Not only *seek* but *seem* to seek justice, ain't that right, Judge? But that little Frenchie hat got to go, man. Y'all be cool now."

Ms. Peru leans a slim hip against the lobby wall, legs crossed at the ankles, legal pads, documents, obscuring her face. The elevator isn't moving. It has been stuck on eighteen since God knows when. A barrier mounted on the stairs advises against entry. The black boy's blood sprinkles the steps, the walls. Sacks of cement, tiles, grouting powder, are stacked on a trolley by the elevator's closed door. Noises echo along the shaft: obscenities, shouts, a tape deck's raucous din.

Waiting with Ms. Peru are Norm and Muriel Goering, whose one-bedroom apartment is on thirteen, and Fat Albert Ale whose place is on nine.

This trio, a convention of eccentrics, Chantelle Peru does not count among her favorites.

For the past several minutes Muriel has been flooding the ears of any who will listen. "Norm has seen action too, you know. Norm fought the Nips on Guam. But I've yet to hear of anyone bringing a forty million dollar suit on Norm's behalf. No, people will go to bat for crazies, for freaks like that deadbeat Wally; they will take hard-earned tax dollars out of my pocket, but otherwise —

Norm puts a restraining hand on his wife's arm: "Remember Ms. Peru is left-wing, dear."

Over her shoulders Muriel carries a yellow parasol stamped PROPERTY OF THE RITZ HOTEL.

The effrontery of this vastly amuses Muriel Goering.

"— Now it's pickaninny juvenile delinquents dripping blood right and left. Frankly, I think Mr. Giocametti should be informed. The police — "

"Shut up, Muriel," Norm says.

"My shoes are soaked with sweat, just look at them. You have blood on that lovely blouse, my dear. By the Potomac today, as I was sitting on a bench resting my feet, a pigeon tried to nest in my hair. Can you imagine? This elevator — "

"Oh, dry up," Chantelle Peru mutters.

Chantelle Peru isn't really listening to this chatterbox. She is furious at the whole of Capitol Hill for its foot-dragging on the Invisible Soldiers issue. For the Hill's insistence, against reams of evidence, that all American soldiers who had wanted to come home had done so. Any left over there, the line goes, are poppy-sniffing un-American dope addicts, hoodlums, the dregs — remaining by choice. She has today resigned as Counsel for the First Lady's Committee because it, too, has only wanted to spread snake oil over the debate. She has told the First Lady not every event is an occasion for the docile or ceremonial or platitudinous or cupcake smile. Dolly Madison, she told Hillary, according to legend had at least sewed us a flag. "Remember Martha Mitchell. The Attorney General's wife was not allowed to pick up a phone."

Pick up the phone, Hillary.

Hillary, of course, is already in hot water for picking up too many phones.

Chantelle Peru has decided she is leaving government. Working in this burg is about as rewarding, as socially effective, as running water buckets into hell. No one can say, she hopes, that Chantelle Peru has tucked in her wings in fear of a tough fight. Wally and his friend around the corner, Pancho, are to her mind living proof that the past four years have not been total folly. She has gone there and found them. She has negotiated their release. *She* did it. Not that pig's breath, Cutt.

Now that turd, Ale, crowding her elbow: "I thought the case the Senator made on *Koppel* was most convincing, didn't you, Ms. Peru? Ms. Peru?"

"Well, you're a hare-brained idiot, aren't you, Ale?"

Get out of my face, Ale.

Music blares. Echoing down the elevator shaft, a deejay's rollicking voice: Now for all you shut-ins and shut-outs, you get-up and get-abouts, here's Rude Dude's hot new disc-wisk, "Baby Be Bad To Me."

Twang, twang, twang.

> *Baby be bad to me*
> *if you want me to be*
> *good to you*

"This is outrageous," says Muriel Goering.

"It bugs you, Muriel," says Norm, "then go up and make a fuss."

"Don't think I can't. Don't think I won't. I can stop that trash up there the same as I've stopped yours for thirty years, Norman Goering."

Chantelle Peru feels hot, she feels loopy. When last did she eat? It comes to Chantelle, shocking in its suddenness, that what she most wants in the world this minute is ardent soliloquy, passionate avowal. She wants to be up in the Arctic, on a boat made completely of ice, decked out in a long doorman's coat, in boots, a fan blowing cool wind over her naked shoulders. The Hill, playground of the inept, paradise for smarmy Fascists, is getting to her.

The elevator door rattles. Gears engage, chains thump and clank, but the elevator does not come down.

"Your lot," Muriel says, hefting her parasol, "can wait for this elevator as long as you like. But someone must do something to stop this outrage. I am going up there this minute and tell those swine responsible that this is a respectable building and such shenanigans will not be tolerated. They might rough up a black boy, but who would harm me?"

There she goes up the stairs, switching the fanny, flouncing the white-gold hair, click-click the heels.

Goodbye, Muriel Goering. Hello, Death.

CHAPTER FIVE

BUD

The Neck, Bud figures, is no more than a three-hour shot south from D.C. on I-95. Then east into hog-wallow country. He's glad to see they've pushed the interstate speed limit back up to 65. That means 75, five below that if you want ease of mind from the Troopers. The Accord rental is on Cruise, seat elevated, window lowered, a good breeze hitting his face. It has got coolish. He'll be there by four, beating daylight by several hours. He wishes his arrival could be a touch later; it would give him a kick to hear roosters crowing. He wonders whether the place will have got any bigger. Probably not. The Neck was dying even when he was growing up there. He's seen worse places since that time, though not many.

The by-pass around Richmond is a big surprise. The roads are all different now. He once hauled juke boxes to jive houses up and down U.S. l, up and down 301 and state roads 248 and 86 and 52 and all of those. Up as far as Petersburg to the North and Monk's Corner, South Carolina, going the other way. He'd hire black boys with naked feet, fellow pellagra sufferers, wormy circles in the skin, to help him load and unload. Yessir, boss, and no sir, boss, although he was only fifteen himself. Buy the boys a soda pop, give them a reject 45, a dollar or two, for their trouble. Five cents a song the jukes had cost, bonus tune if you dropped in a quarter. He supplied the small table models as well. Sit in a booth, flip the leaves, punch in A-12, G-22, whatever. Little Richard, Fats, the Platters, but mostly country. The white boys, Como, Bennett, Bing. Then Elvis, his hip-checks, foot-slides, knee flutters, and Elvis is on the charts, tune a month. Now and then, in joints that hadn't remodeled in forty years, you could still come across his old machines. A dairy bar outside Pittsburgh, he always drops in there. Slides in the quarters, orders a Reuben. Antiques, he guesses those machines are now. Music for your own private booth, the sound pretty awful. It was a girl who usually dropped in the nickel; lean her elbows on the table, moon over some sweetheart. Dream of other lives, other places. Dream Elvis was singing just to her. Elvis doing what the blacks had been doing for thirty years in their clubs, their road-stands, natch. But give the man credit, why not?

Of course, he'd been marketing other goods as well: gambling games that proprietors hid under the counter, hid in back rooms, these the real money-makers. Blue movies and porno black-and-white comics in which Dagwood put it into Blondie or Popeye the Sailor Man downed his can of spinach and suddenly had an erection stretching through every panel. A telephone pole, for godsake. I laks what I laks, Popeye saying. The bad guy — Blupo? — looking a lot like that fatso Lootz, now that he thinks of it. Smilin' Jack, Brenda Starr, the whole gang, sometimes all together in a backroom orgy. A nice old frumpy woman getting into the act as well, although now he can't summon up her name. Mary Worth. Yeah, Mary Worth. Incredibly raunchy, old Mary.

Inconceivably stupid stuff.

Dick Tracy, prick square as his jaw. Archie and his gang, they all got into it.

Bud hasn't decided yet what line he'll take with Miss Chudd. She is probably nearing retirement age by now, although his sense of the matter is that she's going strong. A friendly chat to begin with. See where Miss Chudd is coming from. See will she wilt. He doesn't expect wilting from Miss Chudd.

He's crossing the state line before he knows it. Recognizing all the dipsy towns the illuminated signs proclaim. The region has grown a lot since he worked the area. Dodging cops, haunting dirt roads, since most of his clients were off the beaten track and he didn't yet have his driver's license.

It could be any one of a hundred such interstates. Twenty-five years since he's been back here.

A lifetime.

Idena. His girl-friend of sorts, his mistress he supposes she is — he wishes he'd had a minute to pop in on Idena before leaving D.C. Haul in a few groceries, surprise Idena with some of those new CD's she's been wanting. Eat one of Idena's waffles, the woman dearly loves her waffles — catch up on another of Idena's weird reincarnation stories. Back in ancient Egypt, she hadn't had waffles. Nor in that other incarnation, Idena the slave in the Mississippi cotton fields. Yes, quite a piece is Idena.

He wonders who it is left in the Neck might remember him. The cops, certainly. Well, let's hope I run into them.

Bud shooting past the big trucks, letting his mind drift back to Ginger, figure out if her safety worries have merit. Just by chance, few weeks back, past midnight, Bud saw Ginger in a supermarket. An EatRite, now he thinks of it. He had thought at the time, what, she's following me? Isn't that Ginger? He tracked her down the aisles, noticing that her shopping habits were much the same as his. Ginger didn't fritz around. She headed straight to the aisles that had what she had come in for, no dillying, dallying, no impulse buying. And her aisles pretty much the same as his, except that this particular night she needed tampons, such as that. At the checkout he asked the clerk, Do you know that woman? The clerk, black, goateed, young, looked scared.

"Long shift, Bro?"

Bud's conviviality didn't relieve Goatee. A sign hanging the way they hang them in the quick-stops, WE EMPTY OUR SAFE AT NIGHT.

What time? Bud asked himself, and laughed. In the old days, when life was difficult and every day a revelation, he'd survived by robbing more than a few such places. Maybe the cashier sensed that. Maybe he was psychic like Idena.

Ginger bought a tabloid, one of those spacy papers published for morons, so Bud bought a tabloid, too. She had looked for a while at a novel on the Silhouette Sizzler rack. He had thought for a minute she might slide the book inside her jumper or drop it in her purse, but Ginger put the book back on stand and went through Goatee's checkout clean.

$6.95 he shells out for the Silhouette romance.

She got into one of six cars parked in the giant lot, the most rundown, the one rusting heap out there — just the wheels Bud had decided would be Ginger's. The car didn't start right away. A quiver, the starter catching, then dead. Ginger grinding that starter. Bud took bet she'd end up flooding the engine, killing the battery, but apparently Ginger was wise to the crate's tricks. Faded blue Cutlass, bald tires, boot held down by wire. Ginger'd probably been proud of that car once. Probably it was one she and her ex had owned. Probably Ginger had driven her children in that car when they were little. To the playground, the beach, to their grandparents. Now those children were grown up and scattered, as was the husband, and what did Ginger have now except her ratsuck Watergate job and this old heap?

He followed her home, curious to see if she lived in the kind of place he had decided she would. The speed limit is fifty-five, she goes fifty-five. Thirty-five, she drops down. Minute she sees the posted notice, she hits the brakes. Angela Davis, Ginger ain't. Black neighborhood. Poor, run-down. No grassy lawns, no picture-window facades out here. He spots a low cinder-block single-family unit ahead, midway the street, sagging roof over the front door, rusted chair, he says to himself, "There's Ginger's place." All the houses out in this development are cinder-block, low, bumping each other, the earth gravely, the yards weedy, trees straggly, streets randomly lit. Rooms to rent, No Smokers, No Alcohol. Not *all* black. A few doors down from Ginger's house, eight or ten big bikes out in the yard, Harleys, mostly. What, a biker gang hangout?

Trash cans out. Collection tomorrow.

Ginger parks on the street, locks the car. Twenty-six seconds it takes even a mediocre guy to unlock a car, but hers, a piece of junk, in this ratty neighborhood, she locks.

There she goes. Shoulders sagging, no bounce in her step — the woman is weary.

Inside, first a snack. She hits the fridge, sucks in the cool air. Ginger Ale for Ginger, crackers, Vienna sausage. No plate, just dine there at her two-seater table on a paper napkin under the naked over-head bulb. Smack-smack, now isn't this good! Won't this little snack assure me my good night's rest?

You gone sit here stuffing yourself all night, gal?

After Ginger undressed, washed her face, she watched television briefly, a yellow throw-cover hugging her shoulders. Before bouncing up from the divan, flinging her arms. Muttering something, likely, "Enough of this shit, gal." How Bud figured Ginger talked to herself when alone:

Enough of this shit, gal!

Put an egg in it, gal!

Shit, gal, are you pregnant? Shake them thighs! Go brush your teeth.

Issuing instructions to herself. Little built-in Mama ever on the job, telling her what to do.

Now into bed with the tabloid, splash of rye decanted into a jelly glass. A last cigarette.

Nothing too good for you, gal!

She wore a long gown for sleeping, of truly hideous design. Bud liked her for that. Ginger knew the gown was ugly but she felt cosy in it and here she was by herself in her own place, no one to approve or disapprove; she could do what she desired. Ginger flipping the tabloid pages with a sullen face, moving her lips, tracking the lines with a finger. Occasionally rolling her eyes; once, laughing out loud.

She looked at the black window at one point, looked straight at Bud, straight into Bud's eyes for a long time, although of course she didn't know that. She checked that the alarm clock was set, fluffed the pillows, flopped over on her stomach. Reached to get that light. Then she slept.

Maybe she slept.

It was uncanny, Bud thought, how close Ginger's evenings were to his own . . . before he hooked up with Idena. Something else, that Idena. All that Egyptian tomb mumbo-jumbo — Idena, Princess of the Vault.

He got into Ginger's car without difficulty, placing the romance novel on the front seat beside a box of tissues she had there. He was pretty sure the book was the same one she had examined in the store. He read the first few pages — pretty good. White female executive comes to Northern Woods Lodge, is dually attracted to fabulous Paul Bunyan type guide and to wealthy charmingly enigmatic Sebastian Cabot whose smoky eyes are ever undressing her.

Finding the book might scare Ginger, but once she got over the shakes she'd be tantalized by how the book got there. Ginger could use a bit of magic in her life.

Later on, back at his hotel, he had looked for the page in the tabloid that made Ginger laugh. He couldn't find it; nothing in the paper made him laugh. SECRET EVIDENCE UNVEILED: ALIEN CRAFT BLOWS UP OKLAHOMA FEDERAL BUILDING.

His stashing of Tabita Banta, Little Butter, at Ginger's, how will that go? will they sit on the same settee, paint each other's toenails?

Bud pulls into the Neck two minutes before four. WE WELCOME YOUR BUSINESS, the Chamber sign reads. CUTT COUNTRY & PROUD OF IT.

BIRTHPLACE OF THE FRIENDS.

Population 800.

The burg has grown.

It takes him thirty seconds, no more, to drive through the Neck's business district. Creeping along, beams on high, speedometer barely registering. He can't believe he's actually here. A half-dozen unpainted wooden buildings, two-storeys, that have the sag of a hundred years. Not built that well in the first place. Wooden sidewalks elevated a foot or so above the street — from the old days when it was decided something should be done about buckboards splattering the ladies' skirts. The street is paved now; they've added blinking caution lights at either end. No street lighting as yet. Chairs which come daylight will be occupied by old codgers line the boardwalk. Cuspidors, tin cans, adjacent to each chair. The ole' boys will mutter to each other and spit into the cans, wipe their mouths on the hand's backside, watch the world go by. The same as they did when he was a boy.

Cutt Mall exists now a mile or so out of town, likely on Cutt land; otherwise, the Senator's fifty-year Senate seat appears to have brought little in the way of prosperity to his constituency.

Bud half hopes a patrolman, someone from the Sheriff's Office, will pull him over, ask what he's doing. If they say one word not wrapped in civility, they will regret it. Maybe he won't kill them. Maybe he will leave them with their pants around the ankles, tied to their cruiser hood like prize deer. He can name more than one party they did this to back in ancient times, including his once-upon-a-time dad.

There's the Chew Shop. He'd had his first drink, used his knife the first time, at the Chew Shop.

The little town has put in gutters along the road down to the old school. Cutt School. They've had to add an extra wing now that blacks are being bussed in. Portable units as well. The Otis Roy Cutt Gymnasium, newish red brick. The class of '86 has presented the school with a plywood sign painted in the school colors, installed on the school lawn. Miss Chudd's institution. A Community Chest thermometer reveals that the Neck has raised two thousand dollars towards its goal of ten. The flagpole is new. An enterprising Necker has stationed a hotdog wagon across the road. But the playing field is still pebbled and the trees dead.

The graveyard still backs up against the place, although Bud has seen a newer cemetery sprawling north of town.

The state, he's noticed, has seen fit to designate Cutt's birthplace a historic site. Abigail Chudd, Pres. He's driving by where he thinks Jude grew up: dingy two-room frame house on a stone-post foundation, aluminum side-boards, rotting window frames, a wide porch. It looks the same as it did on the NBC special, *America Sings,* profiling the Invisible Vets. The place is a wreck and not yet a national monument — inhabited, from the look of things. Rusting tricycle in the crab grass, lard cans, sofa, wringer washer, on the porch. Jude isn't out there in the grass now, with his grunts, his pile of stones. Grunts, by and large, got you by in the Neck, those days.

Returning through town, up what used to be Main but is now Cutt Street, Bud stops to take a long look at the Chew Shop. The guy he knifed was roly-poly, with stumpy legs, smoking Chesterfields. The knife in the guy's fanny, the fleshy part hanging wide of the stool. A funny place to stick him, Bud thinks now. The guy didn't get it, thought he'd been stung. Jumping up, slapping at his rear end. Blood on his hands, blood cruising down the leg, leaking out over his shoes.

Bud has to show him the knife. He has to say, "I don't think you're going to do anything about it, do you? I think you're going to go home, get the wife to pour disinfectant over the wound. Don't you?" No misgivings, no fear of reprisal either. He isn't pumped up, especially. The guy's smart mouth has got him pricked and maybe next time he'll watch his mouth.

Mrs. Chew comes around the counter to see what the guy is making such a fuss about. She sees the blood, she says, "Goddamn, Horse, you have a miscarriage? Are you done? Shall I get the mop for you?"

You wouldn't have taken Mrs. Chew to be a prostitute. The dime-store blouse is maybe a touch tight, the breasts pointy, her make-up a touch heavy: that would be the only indication. Otherwise, she has on the same flaring-skirt, the same wide belt everyone favored at the time. Breck Girl hair, or maybe a Tony home job that she did herself. Maybe a bouffant.

He'd like to see Mrs. Chew, who had been pleasant to him. It would be interesting, a challenge, to look up someone he wasn't obliged to leave dead.

Lift the latch, come right in.

Bud gets to hear his roosters after all. Barking dogs, clucking hens. This from Miss Chudd's porch rocking chair, when the sun comes up. Behind billowy curtains in a front window at the dilapidated frame house across the gravel road one of Miss Chudd's neighbors is checking him out. Any minute now Miss Chudd's phone may be ringing: Do you know there is a black man on your front porch?

People get up early around here. They go to bed early, too.

Miss Chudd will accept black boys and girls in her classes if she must, but the grinning black boys holding aloft lanterns and watermelon slices still occupy pride of position in and among her lily ponds. A Dutch Girl, midst rows of daisies, dispenses her eternal seeds. The street hedge has been pruned. Dogwood blossoms are out. A giant pecan tree overhangs the garage, dropping its black branches onto the roof. White-washed rocks and pink flamingoes steer one through the wooden gate, past the new Lincoln in the garage, along the mossy path towards Miss Chudd's front door. Rose vines climb the four porch posts, fragrance adrift in the morning air. Green window shutters permanently anchored to the walls have ducks, rabbits, waddling geese cut into the wood. The façade has recently had a face-lift of aluminum siding; around here they like the product. Never Paint Again. Bud has seen the billboards coming into town. A thick straw mat set by the front door offers the greeting, WELCOME AMERICA FIRST. Flags flap from standards mounted in the corner walls: the Confederacy, the Stars and Stripes.

Funny, though, how this entrance appears unused.

The real story is to the rear. Miss Chudd has bought up the neighbors' properties, flattened the shacks in which these neighbors' sons and daughters were born — expanded her estate.

There, within a sculpted roll of lawn spreading down to a rise of longleaf pine in the far distance, a long wall of climbing kudzu, Miss Chudd has her swimming pool, pavilion, bathhouse, gazebo on a distant hill strewn with heather, lilac. Morning glory blossoms bloom from the imported shrubbery, itself in bloom.

The pool is shiny black marble.

Miss Chudd is asleep on a high four-poster bed in the new addition. At one time the bed boasted a canopy, but Miss Chudd, for whatever reason, has had the canopy removed. A foot stool with brocaded cushion makes her ascent into bed a breeze. A huge black Jacuzzi with multiple depths occupies an open stage to the right. From the Jacuzzi Miss Chudd, should she have a mind to, can look out over the Neck's entire southern exposure: over the kudzu, the pines, the rise of corn and cotton fields, to Cutt's birthplace.

Before retiring, Miss Chudd drapes her next day's wear over an armchair. White Flokati rugs of a varying size adorn the highly-glossed floor. Wouldn't these carpets, once in a while, throw Miss Chudd for a loop? A television set the size of a small car occupies one wall. In the closet, furs, an extraordinary number of boxed shoes. Pant-suits, blouses, size 18. Preponderance of stripes, zig-zags, triangles. Miss Chudd will have put on weight.

By the bedside, a saucer contains two fig newtons over which ants are crawling. That was dinner? Telephone. Sleeping pills. Water glass bearing her lips' imprint. In the water, her teeth. Clock with a loud tick. Reading glasses in rhinestone frames. Crumpled tissues. Does Miss Chudd have a head-cold? Puffy pink slippers aligned on the floor await Miss Chudd's morning reentry into the world.

Miss Chudd snores.

Her hair rolled. A yellow spot on the pillow where her mouth — it does so now — leaks.

Bud watches the woman sleep. Looking for a twitch in the lids, the eyes to pop open.

Miss Chudd has worked late. Atop the comforter, a calculator, accounting pad — a plain cardboard box filled with cash. Miss Chudd, Bud has determined, is Paymaster to the Friends. The week's contributions?

He takes the box with him.

In the office: three telephones, fax machine, copier, shredder. Miss Chudd needs a shredder? She needs three phones?

On sawhorses, a mock-up of the proposed new Christian Theme Park. Cutt photographs in abundance. Cutt and Miss Chudd over the years: arm-in-arm at the seashore, Miss Chudd in a fifties bathing suit, smiling from a hammock. Miss Chudd, a baby in her arms, Cutt in the background. They've had a child? Cutt with Presidents Bush, Reagan, Ford, Nixon — all the way back to Eisenhower. There's Jerry Falwell, Pat Robertson, and Cutt, each with a hand over the heart. There is Jude with Clinton, receiving his Congressional Medal of Honor, Miss Chudd attending. Photographs of Miss Chudd's famous field trips. Tributes from eminent people. History's ledger of dead cronies: Strom Thurmond, George Wallace, Bull Connor, KKK Grand Wizards. There's Clinton's nemesis, Starr, the Special Prosecutor, with rod and reel seated on a keg by the Senator's trout pond.

A filing cabinet holds hanging files, scored by year. Personal remarks, entered in Miss Chudd's own hand, offer thumbnail portraits of each student ever to come under her wing. *Puts out . . . Rude . . . Catatonic.* Bud is not surprised to find he was himself absent a good deal of the time. But she had him rightly pegged. *A stupid boy. I frankly see no reason why the state should expend money educating his kind.*

The intern files are starred. In the old days Miss Chudd was content with a single group photograph; now there are individual shots, some in the nude, apparently taken by secret camera in the girls' gym changing room. Each file has been updated over the years: clippings of wedding and birth announcements, noted events, obituaries, the like. She demonstrates a definite preference for attractive females. No Jews, no blacks, no natives, once in a while the odd long-lashed boy. Thirty-seven interns through the years. Twelve of these, according to Miss Chudd's records, are now dead.

An astonishing rate.

Under the desk blotter, a snap shot of Jude in Nam, crouched as if to spring, bare-chested, ammo slung, weapon at the ready, grinning down at dead people in a ditch. *Dept. of Defense*, the stamp says. *Not for circulation.*

Sun-up, Bud is out rocking on the porch.

Rise and shine, Miss Chudd.

As smart as Bud is, Miss Chudd is smarter. This comes to him minutes later, still in the rocker, still playing eyes with the neighbor behind her curtain. It comes to him that he is seated in a rocker outside an empty house. Miss Chudd has got the neighbor's phone call, or not got it, but she's gone. Not in the Lincoln, for she would have had to come by him.

He's inside in seconds and sees the proof. The bed covers flipped back — Miss Chudd has skedaddled.

She's good, all right. She didn't panic. She'd played possum without a twitch.

He hears sirens.

In the kitchen Bud flips on the stove's six electric eyes, upends oil over them; splashes, sets fire to the curtains, the trash beneath the sink. He is exiting the back door, his hand on the knob, when someone calls, "Freeze it right there, Skunkbreath!"

Two of them.

"I thought she'd flipped. But the old bitch was right. Bud's back."

"Dint he say he would?"

It's been twenty-five years but Bud has no trouble recognizing the voices. The pair has put on weight, they look a hundred years older and a thousand years more stupid, uglier, meaner.

"What you got in the box, Bud?"

Bud spins as the first one lunges, the nightstick aimed at his head. The next second the man is sprawled on his back, holding his throat: Bud has the cop's night stick, his hair, the man's Police Special.

The kitchen is burning. Flames are climbing the wall behind the stove, the smoke thick, churning through the open door.

Then the second one's down also, Bud shoving the gun up his nose.

"Repent or die," Bud says.

"Don't hurt us, Bud."

Grovel a while.

It doesn't take long to mount the two cops on the Lincoln's hood. Miss Chudd even has rope hanging from a hook to help him along. He strips the pair, secures them on the bonnet side by side.

"I believe I saw you do this to my dad," he says. "Of course, you ole' boys were young studs then, sowing your wild oats. As I recall, you then came in, tied my sister to the bed, took your turns. Then set fire to the house. Am I hallucinating? Maybe it's all nasty delusion, some movie I saw."

He's pulling away from the curb just as flames are licking through the windows, jumping through Miss Chudd's roof; one of the Neck's volunteer fire-fighters, his pickup squealing around the curve, almost slams into him; a fire-engine siren blocks away sounds like a train leaving the rails.

An elderly black man sits on a stump, taking no interest in Bud's approach. A dog labors for breath by the old man's feet, too old or malnourished to rise.

After a time, the old man says, "Are ye blind like me, or are ye blind in your own way?"

"In my own way," Bud says.

After a time, the old man says, "Have ye seen my dog?"

"She's there by your feet."

The old man pokes about with a stick.

"I worry about that dog," the old man says.

"She's an old dog," Bud replies.

"That she is."

"Older than you?"

"Pretty mite to it. Do you know, I believe that dog never mated. I believe she is an hermaphrodity-type dog."

"It takes all kinds."

"Ummm-huh."

The old man rocks a while, then reaches out a shaky hand and scratches the dog's head. He lifts the dog's ear and blows in his own breath.

"Did Lucy wag her tail?"

"Yes sir. She sure did."

"Well, there you go."

Bud crouches beside the old man until the sun breaks red above the tree line.

"I'm going to step inside the grounds now, and set fire to the Senator's birthplace," he says. "You don't mind, do you?"

"Naw sir. Me and Lucy don't mind a bit."

So Bud did that.

CHAPTER SIX

ZIPPO

Glo naked, her head full of lather, when Zippo comes in. Raking those long fingers into the scalp. Bent over at the hand-painted Mexican sink, pitcher of creek water nearby. Their well dry or a break in the line, plumbers no help.

"All we can tell you," the old timers advise, "your well goes dry, you dig a new well."

"Where?"

"I reckon as how it would be better you dug where there was water."

Glo wants her water. Weeks now since she's soaked in a hot foamy bath. Weeks since she could say, Get in here with me, scrub my back.

Glo probably out there herself much of the weekend with a wire hanger, divining, dowsing. The wand quivered, she'd say, "Dig here." It quivered again, "Dig there."

Gangster World.

Eyes closed, really going at that lather.

Kiss the pretty neck, let her know the warrior is home.

"Mmmmm. Who's there?"

Like it could be anyone chancing to pop in.

"Zippo? Wait till I rinse."

Wriggling hello, nice to have you home, with that artful behind.

The shampoo lilac-scented, good enough to put in a martini. A martini he'd like. Just now, he's too tired to find the mixings. Nine, ten o'clock, he's pooped. Jet lag plus being shot at — dead people, the cops, the waiting, the why.

Most especially the why.

Zippo throws himself flat on the bed, gives the grit in his eyes a moment's rest. He's stripped off coat, tie, shirt, maybe his shoes. He can't think. Did I take off my shoes?

The Jag sails out over the mountain, crashes through trees and bush. Daylight, a let-up in the rain, they will bring the bodies out on chains, pulleys of some kind. *Have to find Rupert. Rupert, round here, is the pulley expert.*

Maybe a helicopter, they can spring one loose. Or pontoon the whole shebang down the river. *Hell, we got to find it first. You'd think it would of burnt, wouldn't you?* The sheriff's office, the highway patrol, the Shenandoah police still out there.

A shotgun, you say?

A woman named Tilley, you say? Oh, I see. Tilley is the hat? Ummm. Uh-huh. Tilley?

Zippo can see this Tilley woman in his mind, months back, sitting in a beautician's chair, perusing the magazine ad, saying to the hairdresser, "What do you think of this item? Will it do anything for me?"

Doe, she's sometimes decked out in similar garb, safari jacket, hiker boots. The L.L. Bean man, west coast, he's Doe's bag. The rustic Dan'l Boone look. Either that or Sally Ann, St. Paul, Goodwill — the toesack look. Hour-glass waistline, long legs, but Doe's got to hide it. Stow those good looks under a basket.

The bouncy cop — Lootz, that his name? — said, Now what I'd say, we got us a bunch of rich folks playin' chicken. You won't playin' chicken, were you?

Giocametti, Lootz says, Now where did I hear that name?

Johnny Law not bothering for a long time to look at the Caddy's blown-out windows, the glass-strewn seat, but why should they when it is all so obvious: rich folks playing highway tag, hot-ass drag race that got out of hand. "Just remain in the vehicle, gentlemen. We'll take your statements directly." One a week, mostly kids, mostly pie-eyed, shaggin' these mountain roads, Lootz saying. Sawin' off tree limbs, plowin' into snowbank, river bank, some geezer's front porch.

Something peculiar about Lootz, to Zippo's mind. Like the man has a vested interest? Or is it just he's stupid, or is it both? *Dint I tell you? Stay in the car."*

The officers making them walk the yellow line; then the breathalyzer turns up, was on Lootz' back seat the whole time. Astonished when they come out clean, the bubbly long absorbed, His driver, Alonzo, surly with the deputy, incensed by the idea that anyone would think he drinks. Hasn't touched a drop ever, he said. Don't want it, don't need it, never intend to. A promise he has made to some sweetheart, maybe to his dead mother, long ago.

An odd bozo, this Alonzo.

But for the stringbean they'd be dead.

Must remember to jack up the bozo's pay. Lay on a bonus.

"You're saying you never saw these people in the Jag-wah before? It was a Jag-wah, you say? A couple, you say? White, Caucasian, hatted female — Tilley? White, Caucasian male, age — oldish — Commonwealth of Virginia tags, Tri-Star rental, firing a shot-gun?"

Pat Fish ready to take a swing. No love lost between Pat Fish and the law. Too many lawmen in his time whacking his skull, saying, Hey, boy, hey, jig, hey, coon. Hey! I'm talkin' to you.

Troopers' search lights sweeping the valley. The few brave souls attempting a descent cracking their skulls, their kneecaps. Tangly, slippery, down there. Crawling back up, huffing, letting everybody know not even lizards can traverse that bitch. It's rain forest, Blind Man's Bluff — buttermilk sky — down there.

The car itself nowhere to be seen.

It sailed out, touched down, tumbled, sailed off again, wallowed about, plunged, took off the corner of someone's roof, took down power lines, leap-frogged the lower switchback road, flipped into craggy peak, swished by ole' Charlie Merritt's turnip patch, ripped apart John Mayhew's outhouse, shot through Widow Syke's clothes line, took down more trees, careened off rock — disintegrating by the minute, but still going, still tumbling. Three, four thousand feet.

Nine calls the Shenandoah office had.

"Find its wheels, hubcaps, maybe the victims too, over in the next county."

A pair of dogs brought in to sniff for drugs.

The treatment all a good deal heavier, less polite, less sympathetic than might have been expected.

Lootz — that his name? — acting the big cheese. Like he's surprised, had expected something else. Not happy at all when that hat business comes up. One of the troopers overheard saying, "Who's he? Who shot in that dumb cracker?"

Now the light dims in the bathroom. Glo pitches herself down beside him.

"You look wiped. What, the airline short-change you on caviar?"

It's okay now, her holding him.

"How was the trip?"

"So-so."

"You see Doe? Dolores?"

"No."

"See Nasty Boyfriend?"

"No."

Brief hesitation there, which she's wise to. But bypasses for the moment. She sits up, combs the tangled hair.

A minute goes by. Her seated on the bed, combing that hair, flicking that water.

He peeps open one eye.

Yeah. Looking at him.

"What happened? You're soaked. You fall in the river?"

Zippo grunts.

"Where's Pat Fish? He go to the cabin?"

A nod.

"What happened? Talk to me."

Zippo wants to ask has Doe, Dolores, called, but lacks the energy. He feels nailed to the sheets.

All his life never so much as a splinter in the behind; now he's climbing the hill someone starts blamming away at him.

"No, Doe hasn't called. But a thousand others have. You didn't check your messages? Why are you so late?"

Flicking that water.

"Should she have? Doe, I mean. What have you done that you think she might?

"Nothing."

"Nothing?"

"Not a thing."

"You and Pat Fish flew all the way to the west coast, didn't see Dolores, didn't see Nasty Boyfriend? Did nothing? That's what you're telling me?"

Grilling him.

"What, you went to a movie? I'm betting you fly out there, skulk about, pick Doe's lock to see if she's sleeping with the guy, she isn't, or you find out they've patched everything up, all is lovey-dovey, so the two of you decide you'll do the next best thing, which is go to a movie."

Gearing up. Soon she'll pounce.

No, he opens his eyes, she's at the closet rummaging the rack. Two bits she selects the dingy, shapeless robe.

Yep.

"I hope you stopped at a store. We don't have a scrap of food in the house, not so much as a limp carrot. Your people in every minute, raiding the fridge. Don't tell me Lonnie didn't relay my message."

"Who?"

"Lonnie. What was your impression of Lonnie?"

"Lonnie?"

Can't get his head around the most simple thing she's saying.

She strides to the bed, sits; again flicks that water.

"What's the matter with you?"

Up again, heading off into the bathroom. End of talk, she's started the blowdryer.

No, back again, smearing cream over her face.

Zippo's flesh stings. Everywhere a hand touches skin he finds pinpricks of glass.

"I've got it. You and Pat Fish, you're in this groovy B.C. bar, walls with floating fish, you meet these two stunningly gorgeous women, you both fall desperately in love. You hit the sack, fuck your brains out, get up in the morning and have a double wedding. Now you're back here wanting a divorce and can hardly stand up. How close am I?"

He laughs, a rumble in the chest. It suddenly occurs to him he has a headache.

"I poked my head in at the Greenpeace office. Just to see had the French, the Gulf Oil dickheads — had they firebombed Doe's workplace."

"Dolores."

"Right. Dolores."

"She's not our little baby any more."

"Right."

Her free hand caresses his knee. Creeps up his leg.

Now that hand — things about to get interesting — snatched away.

"Lonnie — 'Lonzo? — told me this wonderful . . . wait a minute."

Now he knows who Lonnie is.

She's jumped up. From the bathroom, brushing her teeth, the Lonnie tale taking off.

"This morning? I had Lonnie doing the laundry. God, I like that guy. His hair, you notice his hair? Strictly terrific. One of those big red woodpeckers. Woody. 'What's up, doc?' Wasn't that Woody? Anyway, he says, his sister, ten years she's been driving around with their father's ashes in a Toyota Hatchback. Unable to decide where to park those ashes, so she drives them around. All the time talking to those ashes. She says, 'Daddy, now we are passing your old bait and tackle shop. There's the new fire station. Now we are parking at the A&P. Anything I can get you?' Like that. Keeping her Daddy — her Daddy in the ash state — up to date on everywhere she goes. This sister — "

Zippo feels his eyelids locking. Another minute, he'll be asleep.

"Now the Hatchback, a heap, fifteen years old, it needs junking. Twelve cents the hundred pounds, she's had offers. You listening?"

"Yeah. Edge of my seat."

Glo at the sink, spitting. Set to floss those pearlies.

"All right. Sure, she can move the ashes into the new used job she's got her eye on, but still there's the Hatchback been Daddy's home all these years. Thinking she just can't *move* him. Mindful of how upset he'd be. Her saying, 'Daddy, there's the new Plantation Bowling Alley. The new Blockbuster Video. Isn't it ugly? And over there? Where the tire retread shop used to be? Up there past it, you used to eat your grits, your country ham. Flirt with Fujiyama, what's-her-name, your old flame? Up there the wrecking yard, I'll drive by, let you have a gander at your old blue Fairlane, you want me to.' Zippo, you with me?"

Zippo wonders how he can work into the conversation that he and Pat Fish and Stringbean could be dead.

"So. You know what?"

"What?"

"She wants Lonnie to bury the Hatchback. Some time when he's working the heavy equipment. A short ceremony over the spot, 'Dearly beloved, we are gathered here' . . . you with me?"

"Mmm-huh."

"A duet, the two children Lonnie and his sister to sing that old Red Clay Rambler tune, 'Hard Times Come Agin' No More.' You know that song?"

"Un-huh. A great song."

Glo hums the number, does the horn, the banjo, to see he's got it.

"Then sister says, 'Daddy, it's so long now. You were a good Daddy, poor as sin, but my bosom sidekick through to the end.' Isn't that beautiful? Don't you love it?"

Zippo thinking, I ever do a movie, I'll get that in.

Zippo wants to get it all in, including Glo in the open robe telling him the story. No way he can see getting in that pair going off the mountain, though.

In bed, Zippo pooped, she's still rattling on:

"Did an excellent job on the laundry."

"Pardon?"

"Lonnie. The laundry."

What, she's in love with the guy?

"Didn't mind a bit toting up creek water. Sorted the colors and whites, didn't overload. Knows fabrics. 'I'd recommend this be done by hand, Glo,' he says to me. 'You got any Zero?' Strictly an Okay guy. You know what else?"

"Umm?"

"Sometimes the sister, riding Daddy around?

"Yeah?"

"I wish you wouldn't say 'yeah.' 'Yeah' is rude. Sometimes she'd turn her head and there Daddy would be."

"A ghost, you mean?"

Glo thumps the pillow, rolls over — not slowing down her tale a minute.

"Two of them."

"Two ghosts?"

"Un-huh. Her Daddy sitting up high in that back seat, his arms around the shoulder of this other ghostly presence. Some woman, I mean. Sometimes his old flame Fujiyama, sometimes another one, looking very cheap, you know. Like even in the ghost world they have their one-night stands. He'd be pointing out the sights to this woman just as his daughter has been pointing them out to him. 'See there, honey? The Nehi Bottling plant. Nine years I worked as a bottler there. See that hillside behind it? Those houses? I was a boy, there won't not a lick there but chattering birds.' Can you believe it? Doesn't it blow your mind? One night, she's out showing her Daddy the sights, she looks at him, he's in the back seat waving at someone. 'Who you waving at, Daddy?' she asks. Then she sees them. A whole city of dead people, they've all come out: all of her Daddy's old cronies going about their business, but waving back, so happy to see him."

Zippo gone thirty-six hours but it's like Glo hasn't had anyone to talk to for a year.

Get those dead people in his movie. Shoot that scene in infra-red.

Zippo thinks: Maybe I'm in shock. Maybe it's just now hitting me.

Years ago, before Zippo met Glorianna, he'd been trying to make time with a woman worked a gypsy con — dressed in these net tights, a seal-skin dress, red tennis shoes, red snake-hair wig, this mumbo-jumbo cape. "Read your fortune, Good Lookin'? One gold piece!" Zippo forks over a twenty, she instructs him to hold the wet tea bag. Yes, in your hand. The other hand he is to place on her knee.

Like this?

Like that, lovey, but not so high.

She falls into a catatonic trance, goes: You are in the time of the wolf.

Wolf?

Time of the zebra cat. Late spring of the fox. You are having a sorry passage through life, wrestling to get in touch with your karma. The Fates. Is this so?

I been reading Camus, existentialism, that what you mean?

You are finding only barred gates which you must pass through. Moats you must swim. The moats are eel-infested and you cannot swim. Can you swim?

No. A beach right out front of Papa's door my whole youth. But, to fix him, would I swim?

Squeeze the tea bag. Are you squeezing?

I got this puddle right by my shoes.

Quiet. I see . . . your future now. You will get cut off in life by the quick arrow of circumstance —

Quick arrow?

Don't interrupt. Happiness will elude you because zephyrs from the protoplasmic plane have usurped your soul and rot is eclipsing your . . . Hold on. Look up there on the bookshelf, third row from the bottom, you'll find a message meant for you personally.

Which book?

It doesn't matter which book. Close your eyes and reach.

So he closes his eyes, reaches.

Which page?

How do I know which page? It's my control telling me what to tell you. Wait a minute. My control says turn to page 219.

Zippo is reaching for the page when suddenly everything has gone dark and someone is swatting his head with a book.

"Leave me alone!" Glo is shouting. "What are you doing? Why are you after my book? Talk to me."

"I'm in the late spring of the fox, Glo. Can't talk."

You're going to dream, Zippo's thinking, why not get some good out of it.

"Fox? What are you talking about?"

"I'm here thinking. Who would want to rub out me and Pat Fish?"

"Lots of people. Why?"

He tells her the Caddy is shot up, falling apart, she won't let him sleep all night. She'll be out there in her ratty nightgown blaming him for every dent.

"Fine. You won't talk, I'm turning off the light."

He wonders has he ever told Pat Fish about that bridal party at the Jersey seashore, years ago, where he first met Glorianna Ditchpern. Brother Dominic strutting about in a peacock tux, arm-in-arm with his tootsie bride, her shellacked hair, cleavage you could walk into. A tall woman with spectacular eyes, Glo herself, sidling up next to him, saying: "I caught the bouquet. My hand up, since I didn't want it to hit me in the face, and there I was, holding the damn thing. What's this I hear about you people being gangsters? Taking people for rides?"

Glo, driving by in her beat-up Bug, spotting a glitzy wedding on the seaside estate, decides she will pop in, sip the Moet. Check out how gangsters get hitched.

How he met her, Glo crashing his brother's wedding. Beside him, fluttering those lashes, asking, Are you one? Kind of tagging along beside him so Papa Giocametti's goons won't throw her can out.

Someone else, perhaps his mother, saying, "Coney Island, used to be you could ride. I miss that. Darling, who is that perfect stranger holding your hand?"

"Made entirely of licorice," Zippo says in his sleep. Off dreaming again, thinking *The Gold Rush*, Chaplin's boot. Next he's dreaming a dead woman's leg protruding from a sack of potatoes. Which movie? Quick!

Glo shaking him.

"God a mighty, Zip! Put a lid on it!"

His snores, a flock of geese, she's always saying.

Zippo struggling up, flapping his eyelids. He makes out Glo high on the pillows, lamp behind her illuminating that huge bundle of hair. A wide haystack, the way that hair always is after a shampoo. Streak of gray in there, thank you kindly, where the rinse didn't take. Shiny ears. Someone tell me why women don't grow hair in their ears.

Emma abob on her tummy.

Up to page six, he sees. Whipping through that text.

"Dolores called," she says. "Few minutes ago. Man oh man, is she mad!"

Zippo jerking awake.

"She know I was out there?"

"Let's say she's suspicious. Something about a friend losing his hair."

"Whatayaknow!"

Glo boring her eyes into his the longest time. Then saying: "It wasn't serious, you know. A crush. She'd have been over it in a week."

Closing *Emma*. Swatting him with it.

"Now, goddammit, Zippo, if she goes back to the prick out of sympathy, some stupid loyalty thing, I'll wring your neck."

Reopening *Emma*, flipping back a page. Page four. Now she reads *Emma* backwards?

"You ought to check your tape," she says. "Yak yak all weekend long. There's an anonymous caller, keeps asking did you make it safely home."

"Safely? He used that word?"

"Yes. Like he didn't expect you would."

That minute, the phone rings.

"You get it," Glo says. "I'm engrossed."

Zippo examines the number displayed on the phone's call-screen before picking up. Not a number he knows. D.C. code.

Zippo makes a sound in his throat.

The voice says, "You there, Mr. Giocametti?"

Guy with a soft slushy voice, like he's attempting a Peter Lorre imitation.

"Yeah?"

"No injuries? No broken bones? No buckshot in your face?"

Zippo's mind going, What is this?

"Ah, well. Another time."

Zippo silent, looking through the window at drizzling rain; water pooling on his new gaboon-from-Africa window frames.

"We missed you this time. Next time maybe we give you what Cutt got."

The line disconnects.

What did Cutt get? Was that O.O. Orth with a rag over his mouth?

He dials Pat Fish.

"You in bed?"

"Didn't I sleep on the plane? Why'd I be in bed?"

"You feeling okay?"

Zippo, over at the south window with the portable phone, looking downhill, can see through the drizzle the cabin lights. He can see Pat Fish seated at the table, feet slung over a corner — oiling, it looks like, his pistolla. The big Sig. Probably the first time he's had that Sig Saur out in years. Looking up, throwing the friendly wave.

"It was O.O.," Pat Fish says, "why would he need a rag over his mouth? Down here, they born with that rag."

"You're saying the guy threatening us wasn't O.O.?"

"Threatened *you*. Me, I been innocently sitting here cleaning my Sig. You tell Glo yet?"

"No."

"Didn't think you'd have the guts."

"I could say we skidded, ran into a ditch."

"Could."

"Think she'd go for it?"

"Nope."

"So you're saying I should tell her the whole story."

"You ever had to tell anyone the whole story about anything, Zippo, the functioning side of your brain would have a seizure."

"Why you oiling the Sig?"

Pat Fish shrugging, aiming the Sig.

"Where's our boy Alonzo?"

"Out in the woods."

"In this rain? What's he doing?"

"By me. He taps on the door a while ago, asks me did I think anybody here ordered a pizza. Then he's gone."

"Pizza?"

"Saw headlights coming down your driveway. I believe he went to investigate."

"He's a good boy."

"Un-huh. We are all good boys."

Zippo goes to another window, shades his eyes. Sees nothing. Rain slapping the window.

"You know who it is?"

"How would I know? He the one went."

"Well, Jesus Christ. What kind of bodyguard are you?"

"In retirement for the minute. I get riled, though, watch out."

From the hallway closet, no umbrella in sight, Zippo pulls on a tight raincoat, pulls rubber boots up over his bare feet, Glo's knit wool cap over his head.

A second out of the door, the sensor lights flash on. High intensity beams, four hundred watts. Anyone wants to shoot him, now's the time. He stands still a minute they'll go out.

There.

Walking, he feels tiny beads of glass trapped in his buttocks. The boots going squeak squeak.

Zippo hasn't got around yet to having a security system installed. Sensor lights at strategic doors, that's about it. An electrified wire at the tree line to keep out stray animals. But Glo won't have that, an innocent deer, cougar, lynx, a nice bear, getting stung. So she's clipped the wire. Wants that wire fence replaced with split rails in the old Virginia style. Years ago when he first bought the land, he had in mind a nice quarry to the side of the house. God knows it's rocky enough. A Cub Scout troop wanted to storm the place, they could. Key in a bed of moss in the potted fern by the front door in the event Doe, Dolores, makes a surprise visit home.

Not so much as a No Trespassing sign.

WELCOME, it says right there on the mat.

Gangster life.

It's dark out. A black night. The rain not let up a bit.

He hears a rustle in the bushes, hears someone say *"Qué pasa, Zippo?"* — and all but jumps out of his skin. Alonzo emerges from the darkness . . . in pajamas, covered with mud.

"There's a van," he's says, "up the ridge there. Two men with spools. They got a tap on your phone."

Zippo and Alonzo scramble up the slick hill, hands out to ward off invisible limbs, stepping on mulching leaves, sticks, deadfall.

Snakes? Zippo doesn't like snakes.

"There it is."

Way off there, a black spot in the blacker night.

"This way," the kid says. Like he was born here.

They circle along a black ravine, Alonzo leading, apparently able to see in the dark.

Pretty soon they have a clear view of the intruders in the van. A man in a flannel shirt, his face lit by a propane lantern, bent over the recorder, ear phones over his head. The other man sits on a tilted stool, flipping through a magazine.

"Why the light?" asks Zippo. "Why is the door open? What kind of surveillance is that?"

A voice to their rear startles Zippo.

"Man on the stool's a smoker. The other guy isn't."

Pat Fish, with his Sig. He's up by Alonzo's elbow now, wanting to know did Alonzo hear him coming.

"Yeah, I heard you," Alonzo says.

"Didn't."

"Did."

A cigarette's bright tip arches into the night. The man on the stool rises, stretches. He says something to the guy with the earphones, who grimaces, shakes a fist back at him.

"Who are they? Feds? State?"

"FBI," Lonnie says. "I crawled up under the chassis, heard them talking."

"Anything interesting?"

"Nope. Like, is the van stuck? Like, why didn't we bring a keg of coffee? That kind of crapola."

The three of them falling silent for a minute, considering the matter. Then Zippo says, "What do we do?"

Pat Fish says, "Shoot them with my Sig Saur? But I'd hate to, since I just cleaned the thing. We could catch a mountain lion, throw it in there."

"Pitch in a grenade?"

"We got grenades?"

"No."

"How about a rock?" the kid says. "They'll think grenade, come flying out of there."

The smoker reclaims his stool, lights up again. Swats his face. The other guy can be seen snatching off his ear phones, doing a jig. Swatting the same as the other one did.

Zippo's trio is swatting also. Mosquitoes whine by their ears, taking out chunks.

"I wanted a zapper," Zippo says. "Glo said no." He's moving downhill, arms out to stop a fall. Going home. "Let them sit. Listen all they want. What we got to hide?"

"One round from the Sig Saur," Pat Fish says. "Make them Feds lose their supper."

He fires.

Then all parties are scrambling.

"The title of that Lizzer, Monty flick?"

"Yeah?"

"*Afternoon in the Sun.*"

"No way."

"*Sun Also Rises.*"

"Git outta here."

"*Sun of the Misbegotten, The Sunshine Boys, Sunset Boulevard?*"

"Wrong again."

Zippo, Pat Fish, Alonzo conversing on the bighouse porch, looking up at the sky. One reason Glo has wanted to build up here, that sky, the stars. But all is rainy scum tonight. Sky, trees, the hills, all black.

"I got it," Pat Fish says. Your American Tragedy masterpiece. "*A Place in the Sun.*"

"You win the prize."

"Burl Ives was in that," the kid says. "I always liked Burl."

"Not a chance. You're thinking *Cat*. Where he plays Big Daddy."

The three of them scrunched up together on the porch swing. Eighty acres and they have to sausage themselves together like the Andrew Sisters on one mike. They can see on the rise, deep in the trees, the bounce and swing of vehicle lights, hear the rev of the Feds' van. Hear the occasional curse. The van stuck, time and time again reversing, sliding, advancing another foot.

"Those guys going to need chains," Lonnie says. "A tow."

Later on, silence; the hillside falls into blackness again.

"I think they going out on foot," Pat Fish says. "I think we've inherited a vehicle."

"So," Zippo says. "Where were we?"

The rain has quit. Moon and stars are out. He looks up the valley, past a crumbled log house said to be a Confederate General's birthplace. General Surrender or Die, the yard man has told him. *He was brave, huh?" "No. Smart. He surrendered."* On a rise can be seen the slabs of a family burial plot, ages old. Colonial columns, a porch that wraps around the house's front side. Urns, plants, bushes galore. It's a big house, certainly, set on rolling acres, mostly wooded. Inner courtyard, gabled cedar cathedral ceilings, bountiful clear glass windows cut in a multitude of shapes, angles. A bitch cleaning those windows, huff and puff. Heated courtyard swimming pool, empty at the moment save what the rain has dropped in. Nights, the pool full, he and Glo will slip off the duds, light a few candles, jump in. In the courtyard they've got palm trees foreign to the geography, all coming along: *palmas kerpis, palmas kerpis grandes, palmas viojeras, palmas sica.* Bougainvillaea, jasmine, wisteria, lilac, dwarf dogwood supposed to grow no more than four feet high, blossom profusely twice a year. All coming along, except for those blossoms. Fountains, Italian angels, water gods, lion's paw benches; a sculpture garden. There's a Henry Moore piece he's got an eye on, for that garden. In the garden an incredible black marble chair in the shape of a woman, the spine of that woman twelve feet high. You can sit in that chair, settle your feet beside hers, your knees beside hers, reach behind you, stroke the rounded buttocks. Up above you, the woman's face looking down at you, her draped hair, her mournful eyes, the mouth open in indignation, surprise. Delight or pain, you're rarely sure which, all depending on how light strikes her features. A little item Pat Fish commissioned, executed by a former

Atticus brother turned celeb, unveiled six months back on the occasion of Glo's fiftieth. The roof open that day, snow coming down, two dozen gorillas in bathing suits dangling hairy legs in the pool, playing splash and tag, pool volleyball like a gang of six-year olds. Glo bursting into tears, hugging Pat Fish's neck. In and out of that chair all night long, Zippo himself rolling in the cake, leading the song.

Two million he's poured into this project. Not a patch, of course, on Papa's Jersey Shore mansion, Dominic's showplace in Coral Gables, Bill Gates' crazy palace out on Lake Washington.

"I mean," says Pat Fish, "we ought to wake up Glo, clue her in. Bring in the brains of this outfit."

"Bring in Glo? Wake her up? No thank you." Zippo amazed at this idea.

"Look at him. Man won't even let his own mind in on the truth."

"For instance," Zippo says. "Give me a 'for instance.'"

"For instance, one, the past year you been divesting the company of its assets. Keeping Glo in the dark. Two, you not even been business-like about it. You been pissing everybody and his brother off."

"You're talking the bookie operation. That what you mean?"

"One thing."

Pat Fish cluing the guy in on the ins and outs of secret Giocametti business, like he's now a member of the family.

"Zippo decides gambling, the bookie operation, is not his cup of tea, now it's how governments are milking the citizenry — casinos, lotteries, the like — so he *divests* himself. He closes the doors, passes out fat severance envelopes to the stooges, walks away from four, five million a month."

The kid whistles.

"Not that much," Zippo says.

"Man's decided the two-point, four-point spread, Bulls over the Pacers, don't interest him no more. *The Red Lantern* he'll jabber on about till his cereal turns soggy but a bookie wants to know will he cover a fifty K bet Jordan goes triple-double, he can't trouble himself to talk to the man."

"I covered it," Zippo says. "We took the man's fifty K."

"Just closes the doors. Tells everybody to go home. Tells them he'll see them in Sunday School."

Pat Fish warmed up now, hitting his stride.

"Losers out there carrying his markers a year, I say to him, 'Zippo, you want these welchers leaned on? You want our guys should break a few arms, establish the example?' He dishes me shit about Sisyphus, shit like that, the man doomed through eternity to push a rock up a hill. 'Go easy,' he says, 'Life is hard.' Zippo hears a sob story, crackhead mother comes in walking the rafters, she mentions her baby needs a jar of Gerber's, he's peeling off the C-notes."

Zippo laughing, getting a kick out of Pat Fish who never passed up a subway beggar's hat in his life. A hundred bucks a week it costs him just for squeegee gangs working traffic lights.

The night cooling, the breeze quickening. Zippo thinking, I sit here much longer in this wet raincoat, Glo's wet hat, I'll catch pneumonia.

Pat Fish saying: "Man clears out a KoolEd warehouse, retail $69.95, he's going to give the shoes to that shitfirm PatSquat at twenty cents the unit. His nose wasn't inside *Emma*, he didn't have to check out *Smoke, The Gold Rush*, Garbo, the hundredth time, he could be hustling a deal with Wal-Mart, up the profit a thousandfold."

Alonzo waggling his size thirteens.

"Dominic, down there in South Florida with his Zulu gang, his anti-Castro, alligator-shoe platform-heel freaks, ready to wring his neck. Last week Dominic sends up two shooters, dandy dudes in white suits, open-collar Latino shirts, so much gold around their necks they make Shaquille O'Neil seem an urchin. We're at the A&P carrying out eggs, melons — that shit — gone there for the Specials — when the shooters decide to hassle us. They say, 'Dominic wants to know what the fuck you're doing, did you get religion, you got guava jelly eating your brain? Your dick fall off?' So I got to ask the head dude to hold my melon. 'What?' he says, 'hold your melon? Hold your own black-ass melon.' So I got to break the one shooter's arm, spit in the other one's hairpiece, crack his *cajones*, before they catch on that up here politeness counts. Meanwhile, seeds, melon rind, sticky juice, all over my shoes, my Durango jeans. Zippo wiping his hands like he's done all the work. See what I mean? Trouble. Not just from Dominic either, he the least of our worries."

Frogs croaking, crickets cricking.

That rain-swollen creek going to town now.

Far away, sound carried by wind, a trucker on the highway hitting the air brakes, the rig's wheels screeching.

"Too much divesting?" says Alonzo.

"That's right. Man's becoming so legit I can't take a leak I'm not expecting the late Mother Teresa, the Pope, all the favored disciples, at my elbow asking can they hold the pan. Cat houses? Nudie clubs? Divested. Long gone. Saint Zippo here now buying his girls cockatiels, yappy dogs, giving them free apartments, free enrolment in book clubs. I know three personally, ladies of the night, he's put them through college. Sends their kids to summer camp. Nudie owners, bag men, politicos, lawmen and women robbed of kickbacks, all ready to fit us up with concrete shoes. A thousand crooks he's single-handedly put on the bread line. Meantime, you're asking who sent out Tilley Hat? Well, name that tune."

Zippo smiling in the dark, pretty pleased with Pat Fish's recital. Happy with the pace of these divestitures. It will make Glo proud, bring Doe back into the family fold. But he's cold, wet, and hungry. Shivering. Not a bite in his belly since that plane.

"I'm going in to eat something," Zippo says.

"See?" Pat Fish says. "Can the man take criticism? You can't even talk to him. No, Zip, my nervous stomach, I couldn't touch a thing."

Pat Fish grinning, like he's got a secret stash. "So. The criminal classes up in arms. The FBI thinking Zippo goes out of business, they'll be downsized. Governor O.O. wants his balls on a plate. The Senator, too, waxed off at him over this Invisible Soldiers jive. All of them mad."

"Which senator is that?" asks the kid.

"Senator Otis Roy Cutt."

"Cutt? The one has disappeared?"

Zippo and Pat Fish look at each other.

"Say again?"

"Yeah. Was in the paper. This Cutt guy missing. Three days ago, Friday, I think it was."

"Missing, you say?"

"Yeah. Violence suspected. What's his name, Saddam Hussein, Kadafy, might be behind it, the paper said. Fate undetermined."

"Okay," says Zippo after a time. "Where are we?"

Pat Fish leans out, speaking to Alonzo across Zippo's lap: "Did you hear him? Man wants to know where we are."

"Un-huh. I heard him."

"Like you go, 'Who goes there?' he's now got to go, 'Where are we?' Like those are the two defining questions of our age, see what I mean?"

"Un-huh. I see where you're coming from. You guys turn in. I'll hold the fort."

What Fred MacMurray said, 1948, in *Apache Law*, before Victor Mature and 50,000 Indians swooped down from the hills.

CHAPTER SEVEN

TILERS

Friday, I think it was, the boy, Alonzo, had said.

Friday it was, is now, near three, Wally back at his doorman's post and here comes the House Majority Leader's limo. The driver nods, winks, slows, as Wally slogs alongside. The window is down a crack, cigar smoke wafting. Wally smears his face tight against the crack, shouting, "Boondoggle! Trade mission! Secret Swiss account!" Hot sparks fly; expletives are heard; Texas Congressman Himmler's red face is briefly seen; a flurry of hands, ashes, hot sparks. The Congressman is stabbing his cigar at Wally. Hooting: "I got him! I got the bastard! Got him good!"

The building lobby is aswarm with residents incensed at the elevator's prolonged capture on eighteen.

Muriel Goering went up but she has not come down. Muriel Goering has not been heard from for over an hour. This is unusual; Muriel Goering normally makes herself heard. Ask Norm.

Several of those milling in the lobby are willing to bet that they have heard a woman's scream.

Ishmael Digger has sought out and found Chantelle Peru; he is this minute talking to her. Chantelle is captivated. His vast size, his ego, his rage, all this impresses her. She likes his manner. She is telling Ishmael to lay off the soft soap. That she hopes his little brother Sweet will be fine. No, she has no idea what is going on. It appears that there are tilers, goons, really, renovating up in the Senator's penthouse suite. Apparently they are the party that beat up on Sweet. The police have been called, several times, in fact, but have not troubled themselves to respond.

"Senator?"

"Yes. My understanding is that Senator Cutt was to take possession of the penthouse today."

They have drifted out into the street to escape the lobby's noisy throng.

"Who is this Giocametti? Sweet said a Giocametti truck delivered the tiles."

"Zippo's truck. Forget Zippo Giocametti. He's our angel, the lawsuit. A prince of a fellow."

"He's innocent, huh?"

"A new-born baby. God knows how he's made it in the rackets."

"Thanks," says Ish. "I'm in your debt for a good turn."

"Thank you for the flowers."

Ms. Peru has in her arms a huge bundle of fresh-cut flowers of an exotic variety. Orchids, Agapanthus, Bird of Paradise, like that. She expects there will be others every day for the next little while.

"Would you like to accompany me to Pancho's Bar for a quick drink?"

"Pancho's is around here?"

"Right around the corner. If you're sure your business can wait."

"I put it on the back burner a few minutes," the Digger says.

They head off.

Wally can press a tack up to its head through any portion of his hands, and feel no pain. But his fingers have felt the heat of Ms. Peru's flesh those times when he has said, "Yo, Sister! Spare a Vet the time?"

Sourly, he watches them go.

Up Avenue N rumbles another black limo. The passenger window slides down as the vehicle floats slowly by Wally's chair. Senator Otis Roy Cutt's gnarled face, the froth of thick white hair, his white, capped teeth, fills the space. "Mongrelized piece of shit!" the Senator yells. "Get away from my building! Go back to the jungle, you useless veg."

Wally sees the face as a blur, but instantly knows the voice. Wally loathes Cutt. He would disembowel Cutt. *Cutt! Cutt! Unkindest Cutt of all! Why don't you expire, Cutt?* Before Wally can get his feet inside his boots, his torso under control — before he can subordinate his limbs or even think about taking a machete to Cutt's brains — the Senator's driver has turned into the ramp leading to the underground garage. The limo descends, disappears.

Old Fudge across the street shakes his head in a bewilderment of disbelief. Cutt is in his eighties, a vile person by all reports; he should know better than to make such a public spectacle of himself. But the doorman's behavior is Fudge's major concern: the man's limbs shake as in a dance. The ankles fold, the arms flap. He's down on his knees, as though fighting for breath.

Fudge worries. His own father shook this way, blood trickling from his ears, on the day he died: the doorman should be in a hospital. He should be under close medical care. Cutt, too: he's a genuine nut-case.

Through the bowels of the condo parking lot goes Cutt's limo. "Stop the goddamn car," the Senator tells the driver. "Let me out. No, not here! By the elevator, you ignorant bastard. Then get your ass out there and look for my runaway. Who you think I mean? My intern, goddammit! And wash the car. It stinks!"

The Senator alights, hobbles on his cane to the elevator. Punches the button. Waits. What's wrong with the elevator? A minute, he waits. No elevator. Is everything falling apart? The whole damn country? It is more of this left-wing liberal do-gooder rot, what else? Put the cock-roaches on an island, float them off to Red China. *"RED China, Mr. President."*

So, okay, he'd old, he may die from the exertion, the bush-beaters are ever driving his flesh, but so be it: he's not dead yet; he will take the fucking stairs.

There he goes. Up, up, up.

The tile men up on eighteen are ready. They've hashed it out, come to an agreement.

"Yous ever a school boy, Al?"

"I went a while. Why?"

"Eighth grade, I think it was, Miss Chudd has our class studyin' this piece."

"Miss Chudd? Yous had Miss Chudd?"

"That bitch, yeah."

"Yeah, me too. How about that? But what piece? What the fuck yous — ?"

"Prose, I think she called it. In this thick fuckin' book."

"Prose? Fuck yous sayin'?"

"'Cask,' I think it was called. 'Cask,' something or other. Yous listenin'?"

"I dint knock your head in yet, did I? I'm listenin.'"

"Well, look at me, I'm talkin' to yous. So Miss Chudd she reads this shit to the class, see? Bunch of morons, throwin' spitballs, showin' off for the girls, but I'm there, payin' attention. I got to pass that class or it's no more football."

"Git to it, okay. Do I want yous fuckin' life story?"

"Yeah, up yours too."

"So what happens?"

"In this prose thing?"

"Dint yous say so? Ain't that what yous fucking tellin' me?"

"She reads it aloud, see?"

"Yeah?"

"Like we's too stupid."

"Yeah?"

"What it was was the one guy is pissed off at the other guy been jerkin' him around. Insultin' him, like."

"In his face, yous mean?"

"Yeah, the guy's a prick."

"The other guy, the one yous tellin' me about?"

"Yeah. So the guy invites the prick over, gets him in the basement. To show him this special rotgut he's got. Wine, yeah, some kinda wine, yous following me?"

"I'm not sure. I think yous lost me. You can't tell a story worth shit."

"Fuck is wrong with yous yous can't follow a simple story?"

"Just tell it, all right. Fuck I'm listenin' to yous for?"

"They get down there, they shoot the shit a while, see? Like the guy tellin' the shit, the author, can't just tell yous what the fuck happens, no, he's got to string the shit out, throw in all these hotshit wrinkles."

"Yeah, fuck that. Get off the pot, right?"

"Right. So what does the guy do?"

"Which guy?"

"The one I'm tellin' you about. The one was insulted."

"How did the other guy insult him? Yous not mentioned that."

"I'm supposed to remember how the man was insulted? How? Why's that matter a shit? He called him a stupid prick, okay? He called him a lardass son of a bitch, that suit yous okay? So what the guy does is — "

"He sticks him with a knife? Shoots him? Sticks his head down the commode?"

"What commode? Did I mention a commode? No, what he does is seal the guy up. Seals him up alive behind this wall."

"Seals him . . . ?"

"Yeah. Neat, huh?"

The two of them looking about at the wrecked walls, the bags of redimix, the trowels, the tiles. The idea slowly dawning . . .

A woman spread-eagled on the floor, big pool of blood beneath her head.

"What'd that fatty say was her name?"

"Muriel, I think."

Looking to see will she move.

"She had an insultin' mouth."

"Fuckin' I'm tellin' yous? I never heard the like."

"So what do yous think?"

"What yous mean what do I fuckin' think?"

"Do we cask both their butts?"

". . . Yeah. Yeah, I think yous fuckin' right."

"The Senator spill the beans on that coin train, we git his Kennedys, then we grout his fuckin' mouth."

"Fuckin' A. Cask the fucker."

CHAPTER EIGHT

BUD

Motel Bud. Here you go, Bud.

Bud guessed the pretty redhead behind the desk had got out of bed to answer his ring. She had on a worn housecoat, loosely tied, satin mules on her feet. Behind her was an open door to the room or rooms she likely called home. Bud could see a table lamp and a sofa and a throw-cover on the sofa, a pillow which still held the imprint of her own or someone's head. Oval rug on the floor, fatherly figure in an oval frame on the wall. In the lamp's glow, a white ceramic bowl with a twinned ceramic spoon inside.

"Those cards are not free," the redhead was saying. "These are." She pointed to a stack of postcards on the counter beside a large jar with a handwritten sign attached: DONATIONS FOR NEW CHEER-LEADER UNIFORMS, the sign said. In the jar were a few quarters and seven or eight one-dollar bills. The jar looked as though it had been there for some time.

The free cards showed an expansive parking lot, a rank of rooms three stories high, the ancient motel sign attached to the outer wall of the small office space they now occupied.

"If you don't want to buy that card, then don't fool with it."

Edgy voice.

She was speaking of the postcard Bud held in his hand. He had taken the card from the revolving rack on the counter.

Bud could hear someone moving about in the room behind the desk. It would be the redheaded woman's husband, he guessed. Maybe the cheerleader-daughter, needing a new uniform.

"Sure, we got rooms," the woman said. "They haven't closed us down yet. You can have the royal suite or the honeymoon, or regular." She had a habit of tilting her head when she spoke. She also liked clutching the housecoat tight about her throat.

"Cable TV, hot water, whatever you want."

She turned her head to regard a large wall clock in the shape of an Alpine chalet, down to the artificial snow on the roof.

Six a.m. Outside, it was already getting light.

"Check-out is eleven," the woman said.

Her expression made it clear that she did not trust him on this. "Sharp. Probably you think the few hours you have left isn't worth the cost. But I didn't ask you to stay up all night, did I?"

She inclined, Bud had noticed, towards the quarrelsome.

Bud put the postcard back on the rack.

"I'll pay in cash," he said.

"How did I know that? Do you need any help with your bags?"

Bud said he didn't have any bags.

"How did I know that?"

The room assigned him was a third-floor southside, overlooking the highway and the parking lot on view in the free postcards. He could see his own car parked there now in slot 316, the space the woman had said was his. Very few other cars were in the lot. Most of the rooms he had passed getting to the third floor had felt empty. Maybe guests had left before daylight to beat the morning traffic. Maybe there were no guests.

His hostess was waiting for him, standing outside door 316, whirling Bud's key on a finger. He had told her he could find the room by himself, but apparently she hadn't believed this. She was still wearing the green housecoat, the floppy satin mules, but had combed her hair and dabbed on lipstick, not expertly.

"You took your time," she said brusquely, unlocking the door. "Go on in."

The room was long, actually at one time two rooms, from which a dividing wall had been removed. One could stroll through the room to the motel's north side, which Bud straightaway did.

Down there was another parking lot, completely barren of vehicles. That side, like the other, had a wall-to-ceiling window, with a sliding glass door out to the balcony.

"Don't go out there," the woman said. "Keep that door locked!"

She spoke from inside the bathroom. She was in there flushing the toilet. Then Bud saw her turn on the sink taps and examine the water as though for rust.

Furniture was sparse: two single beds shoved together, window drapes, no end tables, no lamps, no pictures, one straight-back chair not built for comfort.

A TV cable protruded from the wall, but there was no TV.

The telephone was on the floor.

The bed was unmade. Bud was taking a good long look at that.

The carpet was a gray weave, threadbare in spots. Mildew had attacked it along the four walls; it had ugly stains where liquids over the years had spilled. Bud couldn't tell how recently the carpet had been vacuumed, since the weave was made to hide dirt.

Opposite the bath was another door, bolted, a metal plate nailed where a doorknob normally would have been.

"Why shouldn't I step out on the balcony?"

The redhead had come out of the bathroom. She looked at him as though she'd never seen him before.

"What?"

"What is wrong with the balcony?"

She didn't appear to find anything irregular about the room's sparse fixtures, the absence of the TV, or the unmade bed.

"Why would anyone want to?" she said. "What is there to see?"

She was right. The view beyond the forbidden balcony and the empty northside parking lot consisted only of a range of scraggly trees within a fenced-off area in which were heaped thousands upon thousands of used automobile tires over vast acres.

The air was misty, not yet burned off by the sun.

"That tire dump was my father's," she said, taking a position beside him.

"Now it's mine," she went on, her voice higher. "My father always said those tires would be worth money one day. What do you think?"

Bud looked over his shoulder at the unmade bed.

"They shred them," he said. "Sometimes they use the shredded rubber in the building of highways."

"Not around here they don't." She snapped that out, as if she thought it was his fault. Then she spun about, sitting down in the room's one chair.

"We haven't had a fire yet. I suppose I should be grateful for that."

Bud gave a vague nod. He was looking at the imprint of lipstick on one of the white pillows.

On the floor beside the bed was an overturned glass, a tissue box with nothing in it, an empty pint bottle of Wild Turkey. An empty package of those French cigarettes in a blue wrapper with white smoke wafting about.

The woman crossed her legs. She pulled the housecoat over to cover the bare knee as Bud stared. The satin mule dangled from the toes of the raised foot. A frayed band-aid adhered to the exposed heel.

"I have an acquaintance who owned a tire dump like mine," she said. "He had a fire in his yard that burned for two years. That was after the fire department and National Guard had a go at putting it out."

"I've heard they are hard to stop," Bud said.

He was still roving his eyes over the lipstick stain, the Wild Turkey, the phone. He wanted to sit down but was reluctant to sit on the unmade bed.

"Adolescents set his fire," she said.

"Why?"

"I guess because they had nothing better to do."

She ran fingers through the red hair, then looked with apparent distress at her nails.

"I worry every night they are out there setting fire to mine. I've got signs up saying danger, these premises protected by vicious guard dogs. But you and me and the gatepost know I don't have any such dogs. Who would take care of them and feed them? If I had such dogs, what would keep those dogs from attacking me? Or say I had those dogs and one night someone snuck into the yard, or a drunk found his way in there, or a child, and the dogs attacked. What is it would keep those parties from suing me, winning every penny I've got? Tell me that."

She seemed extremely angry at these possibilities. Talkative.

Bud yawned.

"I suppose you're sleepy," she said. "Don't mind me."

Then she laughed. She had a pretty laugh, one that completely transformed her face, making her look far more youthful than the forty or so Bud took her to be.

Bud poked his head into the bathroom. He flushed the toilet and briefly let the sink taps run. The water was clear. It was also very cold. A soap wrapper lay beside one tap, the small deformed bar decomposing in the drain. In the waste basket were discarded miniature shampoo and conditioner bottles, together with numerous crumpled tissues. Bud could see smears of make-up on the tissues, along with more lipstick. A white towel nestled in the corner, still damp. Another hung on its holder untouched. The shower curtain on the rod over the tub was missing most of its holders. It had a rip along that side where the person showering would open or close the curtain, mildew creeping along the bottom seam.

The shower walls were tiled, the floor linoleum, much of it cracked.

"Why am I doing this?" Bud said aloud.

Then he came out.

The redhead was standing in the doorway, which they had left open. The sun was up over the trees now and he could make out the shadowy outline of well-proportioned legs under the housecoat. Freckles climbed the nape of her neck, disappearing under the red hair. Her feet were bare. She had left her mules by the chair. Her other heel didn't have a band-aid.

She was looking away at the horizon, arms folded.

"You're going to catch cold," he said.

"Why not? I've caught everything else."

Bud squeezed by. Leaning against the balcony railing, he looked down at his rental car in slot 316. The car was dusty and mud-splattered.

He could see a portion of highway, the traffic thick now, people rushing to work, tires humming. A state trooper was parked by the overpass, alert for speeders. Bud could even see one of the trooper's knees and the nightstick on the seat beside him and the trooper's hand thumping ash into the floorboard.

"He likes that spot," the redhead said. She had drawn up beside him. Bud could feel her heat. "That's where he has his coffee and donuts, and reads the paper, when he isn't parked in my driveway."

A bird perched upon a wire took flight, and Bud waited to see would other birds follow.

The woman swayed a bit, their elbows touching. Bud had a strange thought. The woman was going to pitch herself over the balcony. So he looked at her. He found her looking back at him, in a gauging way. Then he had a stranger thought. No, the person she had in mind pitching over the balcony was someone else, perhaps him. Then she removed a Gitane package from a pocket, lit up, and the thought vanished.

"You should wash that car," she said. "I would hate the thought of riding anywhere in such a filthy automobile."

"The interior is clean."

Bud turned and looked back into 316. His eyes went to the bed, then to her satin mules by the chair.

"I think you signed in with a false name," she said. Their elbows touched again. Bud was certain this time that the touching was intentional. It had nothing whatever to do with sexual interest, however; Bud was sure of that.

"I don't have any reason for thinking so. It was nothing you did, certainly not your paying in cash, but somehow I knew it."

Bud didn't say anything.

"I think it was how you were looking at that stupid postcard. You were trying to distract me."

The postcard Bud had been looking at was of a dog dressed up as though for an English fox hunt, sitting on a white potty. What a relief, the dog was saying.

It was certainly a stupid card.

Now another bird was in the sky, but this one had come from a place far off. It was no more than a speck, and it was not coming any nearer.

"Not that I care what your real name is. If that is what you were thinking."

"I wasn't thinking anything at all."

The woman's hands slid along the railing. Then they were snatched up and the housecoat again tight at her throat.

"I would like to sign false names my own self. I would like to be another person. What do you think of that?"

She tilted her head, waiting for an answer.

Her eyes had a green sheen; her eyebrows and eyelashes were a slightly deeper red than her hair. A range of freckles crossed the bridge of her nose, more of these along her throat and the backside of the hand clutching the robe.

Sometimes her skin showed more freckles, sometimes less.

"Maybe you have become another person without being aware of it," Bud said. "Maybe becoming that other person is something you don't have to worry about any more."

His remark made no impression on her. Bud wasn't sure she was listening.

She was looking past him.

A chambermaid had appeared on the balcony, pushing a house-keeping cart towards them. The chambermaid was another redhead. When the chambermaid saw them she stopped. Her hands shot up to her face. For a moment she had a stricken expression. Then with a small cry she whirled away, disappearing down the nearby stairwell.

Bud looked back into his room at the unmade bed.

"That was my sister," the woman said. "We do not get along."

"Why not?"

She strode away to the housekeeper's cart, returning with sheets, pillow cases, towels, soaps, and bottles identical to those Bud had seen in 316's trash can.

She had hips you noticed, above long legs and a country girl's wide strong feet.

She wheeled into the room without a glance.

Down at the overpass the trooper had got out of his car. He was leaning into the open door, fanning his trooper hat, wiping his brow. But he did this too long and Bud realized the trooper was staring at him.

From somewhere below another man appeared. He crossed the parking lot, walking with a crimp in the left leg, obviously heading for Bud's car. About eighty, wearing a long, baggy black suit coat, frayed at the elbows. Baggy trousers winched beneath a protruding beer gut. Athletic shoes with holes cut into the sides. On his head a black-knit pullover seaman's cap. He had a pinkish face, the skin mottled. Needing a shave. The old man circled Bud's car, peering through the windows. He stooped briefly at the rear-view mirror to pick something from his teeth. Then stationed himself at the car's rear, lifted a writing pad from a side pocket, a pencil from another. He gnawed the pencil end, then wrote something down on the notepad.

The license plate number, Bud assumed.

"What are you doing?" Bud called.

"Fuck off," the man replied.

It seemed to put the man in a huff that Bud had dared speak to him.

The trooper was still looking Bud's way. He stood with one foot in the car, a radio mike up to his mouth.

Bud could hear two other people talking on the level below. He leaned over the railing but saw only the shoes of whoever it was down there. Women's shoes, female voices.

"That's my car," Bud called.

"I don't care shit whose shitty car it is," the old man said.

He pressed a finger against the side of his nose, blew, and a long string of snot went flying.

The old man put away his notebook; in no hurry, making grumbling noises, he moved on out of sight, favoring the left leg, the way he had come.

The trooper's actions were more bizarre. Both arms were on the vehicle's roof; he had his pistol aimed at Bud. Even with the traffic noise, Bud could hear him going, "Pow, pow, pow!"

Now a second trooper was pulling in behind the first.

The women below had fallen silent. Bud bent to see if they were still there. He didn't see any shoes this time.

He reentered 316. He had thought the woman would be making up his bed. This was not the case. She was sitting calmly in the chair, linen stacked up on her lap. She was smoking another cigarette, a hand in one pocket over the pack. Or over whatever else she had in there.

"Julian takes the plate number of every guest," she said. "Pay no attention to Julian."

She blew smoke out at him.

"Who is Julian?"

The woman shook her head a few times. She glanced up at him through the smoke, flinched as though she had been struck, then again turned her gaze inward.

Bud looked at his watch. Almost seven o'clock now. He scraped a hand over his chin, silently studied the redhead, then went into the bathroom. He turned on the light and looked at his face.

"I will have to speak to him, though, or he will be calling a tow-truck."

"Why?"

Bud was washing his face.

"I don't know why. I've never known why Julian does what he does."

She spoke in an exasperated voice.

"He damned well better not have my car towed."

"Oh, they may not come. It depends on which firm he calls. Sometimes he disguises his voice."

She was mashing the cigarette into the carpet.

Then she lit another one.

"Smoke?" she said.

"I don't smoke."

She slid the blue Gitane packet back inside the pocket.

Bud wiped his face with the clean towel from the rack. He looked a moment at the shower. What he wanted to do was get in there under hot water. He felt tired. This surprised him; he was never tired when on a job but now he was tired.

"I don't want to talk any more about Julian," the woman said. She sounded tired, too.

A small entry space had been cut into the bathroom ceiling, replaced with a board. Bud stood on the tub ledge to push the board aside, then got a grip with both hands, hoisting his head up inside the opening.

He didn't see anything except rafters, wires, joists, insulation, ventilation pipes. A secretion of dust.

"I've been through those rafters a thousand times," the redhead said. "It was my hideout when I was a child."

"Why did you need one?"

"Every child does. Some like it so much we just go on hiding."

Bud couldn't tell how serious she was.

"There's a leaky toilet somewhere on this level," he said, dropping back to the floor. "I've heard it since I arrived."

"That will be 310. Why don't you go fix it?"

"Fix it?"

"Don't you fix things?"

When Bud came out of the bathroom he took in her slumped shoulders, the sagging housecoat, the contours of her breasts. She glanced at him, then sat erect. He was himself naked except for briefs and shoes. Had removed toiletry articles from his coat pockets and placed them by the sink. Had hung his shirt, coat, and trousers on the door hook.

"Only a few hours until checkout," she said. "But maybe you didn't come here to sleep."

He stood a while at the room's north side, his back to the woman, looking out at the tire yard. Mist was gone now. The tires seemed to stretch for miles, mountain upon mountain of them. Narrow service lanes twisted about through the rising field, past dusty trees. They were quite large, those trees, old-growth pine, all overwhelmed by the endless tires.

In places along the cyclone fence surrounding the area the weight of tires had toppled the fence; elsewhere, the tires had swum out over the fence to form piles on the near side. A few had rolled out into the parking lot.

"I wish I had dogs," the redhead said. "Maybe about twenty. Maybe a man-eating tiger as well."

"The tiger would eat the dogs."

The woman, subdued, laughed a hollow laugh. She scratched at something high inside one leg.

Up by the gate leaned a small ancient shed Bud had not noticed before. The man Julian was there, sitting on a tilted chair, with binoculars up to his eyes, looking back at him.

"You have a nice build," the woman said.

Then she swiggled about in her chair, peering into the bathroom, looking up at the ceiling. Bud hadn't replaced the attic board.

"I wonder whether anything has changed up there," she said.

"Up there nothing ever changes."

She extracted a tissue from a pocket and blew until her nose was red. Then she pushed the tissue back into the pocket.

"I'm not signing anything," she said. "If that's what you had in mind."

Bud approached the bed, smoothed the sheets, and sat down on the side. The mattress was firm. He kneaded his brow for a moment, folded his arms over his knees, then bent forward, closing his eyes.

With the door open a cold breeze was blowing; he could feel it on his shoulders; he could hear the highway traffic every second going *whoosh, whoosh, whoosh.*

"Why don't you take off your shoes and relax?" she said. "It is your room."

Because he hadn't liked the look of the carpet he had kept on his shoes.

Bud slid off his shoes.

"We used to have a shoe polisher in the lobby. I can't imagine what happened to it."

"Maybe Julian had it towed."

The woman reached down and brushed something from an ankle.

Bud regarded the rumpled bed. The sheets looked extremely clean. Near the stained pillow, shoved partially beneath it, were several more crumpled tissues.

"Do you know anything about guard dogs?" asked the woman.

"What's there to know? They snarl, they bite. They have to be fed. No. I don't know anything about any kind of dogs."

"What do you know about?"

"Not much."

For some little while neither spoke.

Bud could feel grit on his feet. He wished he hadn't removed his shoes. Then he plucked a bar of soap from her lap, went into the bathroom, and stood for a long time under the shower. There was plenty of hot water.

He came out, feeling restored, the towel wrapping his hips.

The bed remained unmade. So far as he could tell she hadn't moved.

"Look over there," the woman said, raising a hand. "Used to be there was a wall. But my father had all the inner walls removed in every room on this floor."

Where the wall once had been the carpet had been extended in fabric of a different weave, a slightly different color.

"I don't know why he did that. Do you?"

"No."

"Why don't you go to bed? I'll tuck you in."

There was nothing flirtatious in how she said this.

"I'm surprised that a man who uses an assumed name would be so fussy about an unmade bed. Why should a man like you care about a little lipstick stain on a pillowcase?"

"I don't."

"If you want your bed made, ring for a chambermaid." She pointed at the phone. "I am not a chambermaid."

"Who is Julian?"

"Let's just say Julian one day, like an old dog, simply drifted in." She smoked a while, then said: "As with us all. We drift in, we drift out, then we are heard of no more."

Bud nodded. He retrieved the tissue box from the floor and poked the pillow tissues into the box.

"You could care less about any of this, couldn't you?" she said. "What concern is it of yours whether my father did or did not remove walls years and years ago in another era?"

"How long ago did he do it?"

"Twenty. Thirty. How could I be expected to remember?"

"You'd remember if you were hiding in the rafters while it happened."

She didn't reply. She was sitting erect, knees together, looking at him with loathing.

Then he wondered if he hadn't dozed off, because he opened his eyes to find her standing very close to him.

"Sinewy, I think might be the word," she was saying, looking him in the face. "Your build, I mean. Although sinewy is far from being one of my favorite words."

"No?"

"A snake is often described as sinewy."

"Not by me."

The phone rang. Both of them jumped.

Neither made any move to answer it.

"That will be Julian," she said. "He will be in my kitchen, wanting breakfast. He will be wanting eggs done over easy, with sausage and fresh tomato slices on the side. Parsley, too. He likes a sprig of parsley, to make the plate pretty. What do you like for breakfast?"

"It wouldn't be Julian," Bud said, "unless he has put down his binoculars and run very fast."

"Then I don't know who it could be. To tell you the truth, I'm surprised that phone is even hooked up."

She had sat back down in the chair, lacing her hands together over the linen. Her fingers were ringless, the nails roughed and unpolished. On the underside of her left wrist was a gauze pad, spotted with blood.

"I rarely eat breakfast," Bud said. "I like the parsley idea, though."

"Do you eat it? The parsley?"

"I eat everything put on my plate."

"For fear if you don't you will be punished?"

"I never think about punishment."

The woman was studying his body without embarrassment. Nor was there any sign of interest, beyond the looking.

"You have a much more dangerous appearance without your clothes," she said. "I thought you would have marks on your body, cuts and such. Even a tattoo or two, but I don't see any."

"They are all inside."

The phone rang again. This time they didn't jump. He could feel the phone's vibrations through the mattress.

"Shall I?"

"It's your room."

Bud picked up the receiver. He heard a woman's distraught voice say, "Vivian? Vivian? Is that you?"

Then he put down the phone.

"It was for Vivian."

"Isn't that too bad," the redhead said. "Vivian has missed her phone call."

She sounded almost vivacious.

Bud went outside through the still-open door. It was cool now with the morning breeze, though warming.

The two trooper cars remained by the overpass.

A panel truck had pulled in behind their vehicles and now the two troopers and a third figure, paunchy, wearing a red billed cap were huddled on the road shoulder. They were laughing about something. All three had turned to look his way when he showed up on the balcony wearing the towel. The man in the billed cap looked vaguely familiar.

One vehicle after another whizzed by, most of them exceeding the posted limit.

Bud's car was still in its 316 spot.

A tow truck, yellow lights spinning, was coming down the ramp from the overpass. But it didn't turn in. He watched the tow truck until it was out of sight, then reentered 316.

He slid between the sheets, arranged the pillows to his liking, leaned back, and looked at the redhead who had been watching him.

"Surely you don't sleep in your underpants," she said.

Bud merely looked at her.

A slow smile was working its way over her face. When she smiled she had a way of looking wonderfully happy.

Then she stopped smiling.

"Let me tell you about this room. Would you mind?"

Bud thought about asking her to turn off the bathroom lights, but didn't.

He had closed the outer door.

The sheets felt clean and cool.

He was already drifting off, his eyes closed.

"We had a killing," she said. "A man in this room was stabbed, oh, I think, thirty-two times."

He felt the mattress give as she sat on the side. Then he heard cloth rustling, the bed moving, and realized she was changing the pillow slips.

"It was a vicious killing," she said. "By all reports. Here, how's this?"

She was restoring the new pillow to its place, her hand on the back of his head lifting as she slid the pillow beneath him. He could feel the heat of her body and smell the faint scent of her sweat. Her breasts were just above his face, as she made adjustments to the pillow. The robe open. A flick of his tongue would have touched a nipple.

"There," she said.

Then she was away again, pulling the housecoat up around her neck, striding into the bathroom with his towels, his little motel pack of hair products.

He was wide-awake now.

"Why was the man killed?" he asked.

"Why don't you tell me?" She reentered the room, closed the drapes over the north and southside windows, then resumed her position on the bedside.

The room was quite dark now.

"Like you, he registered under an assumed name."

"There must be a lot of that going on."

She regarded him as from a distance, her expression grave.

"Did he pay cash also?"

"Oh, he had lots of cash. He made sure we all saw that. He had it all in a big brief case."

"Thirty-two times, you said?"

"According to the coroner. You really should take off those underpants. I can't stand it when a man sleeps like that."

Before Bud could stop her she had slid an arm between the sheets, yanked down his briefs, and flung them away onto the carpet.

Then she went to the north window, kicking his briefs towards the wall; she looked out at her tires. She had both hands deep into the pockets, pulling down the ugly housecoat.

"Developers are hungry for this land. Everyone involved could make a killing."

"So sell."

"Houses, hotel resorts, lakes, golf courses. All in a nice Christian village like that one Jim and Tammy Bakker had down in South Carolina. And just minutes from the new interstate. Although that's secret. No one is supposed to know about the governor's new interstate."

The woman picked up the Wild Turkey bottle off the floor, uncapped the bottle, and drank any final drops that might have been there. She recapped the bottle and dropped it back to the floor.

"Here where I am standing is the spot where the victim was stabbed. Perhaps you can see the blood. Well. They say you can see it. As for me, all I can see is grime.

"Who stabbed the guy?"

"What a good question. Let me ask you one. What time is it?"

"About nine."

"Will you excuse me? I'm going to take a shower."

She stepped out of the housecoat.

"Have a good look," she said. Then she went into the bath, closed the door, then Bud heard the shower running. She wasn't yet under the water, however. Her red head poked out:

"Could I use your toothpaste? Your toothbrush?"

Bud got up to see what the troopers were doing. He counted eight trooper cars down there now, some with their flashers going.

His car was still in the 316 slot.

Up on the overpass were three yellow fire trucks, the big ones.

He went next to the room's north side. The woman he had seen earlier pushing the chambermaid's cart was out in the tire field. She was splashing gasoline over the tires. The old man, Julian, if that was his name, was doing the same. Way up on the rise was a third figure, younger looking, perhaps the cheer-leader daughter, with her gas can.

He could smell the fumes in the wind. He couldn't imagine why they believed they would need so much gasoline.

He looked through the redhead's robe pockets, thinking there might be a knife, but there was only the Gitane package, a lighter, and eighty-five cents in small change.

A little later, the woman walked naked out of the steamy room. She stood by the bed, dripping water.

"I thought you might be asleep."

He was sitting in the chair, legs crossed.

"With so much going on?"

"There can't be anything going on that hasn't been going on for a long, long time. Do you know what all of my father's old property is worth?"

"In whose hands?"

"In the hands of those who want it."

"How much?"

"I've turned down thirty million."

"Why are you doing this?"

"Why are you?"

"In my father's time, you know, he had guard dogs. About a dozen. There was a kennel back there then. My father was the only person able to come near those dogs."

"You have a dog obsession."

"When my father died, he died of a heart attack in the tire yard. My mother saw this and went running to help him. Do you know what happened?"

"The dogs ate her alive."

"Yes. Then someone came and shot all the dogs. But a few escaped up in the hills. All these years they have been breeding up there. Some nights you can hear them."

"I guess, up in the attic, you saw all of this. How long did you hide out up in the attic?"

"Three days. Then my sister chopped the ceiling apart and brought me down. They washed and dressed me and made me go to my parents' funeral."

"Because, around here, that was the decent thing to do. Otherwise, people would talk."

"In the Civil War this property was a slave pipeline into the north. My family's acreage stretched for — well, I don't know. About fifty miles."

"How far does it stretch now?"

"All the way to whoever is paying you."

Bud went back to the tire window to see what the gasoline people were up to now. He didn't see anyone. The gasoline smell was very strong. This side of the motel building was perhaps fifty yards from the fence. How much of the building would go when the explosion came was anyone's guess.

Then he looked to the other side to see if Julian had managed to get his car towed after all, and what the fire brigade and troopers were doing.

She was sitting on the side of the bed, rocking herself.

A helicopter flew over and Bud took a guess that it was Orth, Virginia's law and order governor. This wasn't a hard guess because he could clearly make out the state seal.

"You should have accepted their offer," he said.

"Fuck their theme park. They ruffled my feathers. They went up my bad side."

She was in between the sheets now.

"I feel chilled. You could hold me for a minute."

Bud held her. She was so cold she was shaking.

A minute went by, then she said, "Is this what you do for a living, Bud?"

He dressed standing at the foot of the bed, the shower water still running.

Then he put his toiletries into a pocket.

The woman was on her back, a pillow squared off beneath her head. Her skin was cold, though it was a different kind of cold now. He couldn't see that he had left a mark on her.

He pulled the sheet up over her face.

He went down to the parking lot where his car was and raised the trunk. Miss Chudd's box of money was still where he had stowed it.

He returned to his room, wrapped the sheet tightly around the woman, slung her over his shoulder, carried her down the stairs to his car, fitted her into the trunk, slammed the lid. Then got behind the wheel and drove off.

No one waved goodbye.

At a state rest stop he pulled in to use the telephone. First he called Ginger's number and got Butter.

"Bud?"

"Yes."

"When are you coming to get me, Bud?"

"Pretty soon."

"Bud?"

"Yes?"

"Come soon, okay."

"Okay."

Next he called Idena. He held the phone extra seconds before dialing the last number. He never knew what country, what century, Idena would be in.

"How's my astral traveller?"

Idena said, "Bud Bud Bud."

She said, "I see you in a park-like area. Lots of cars and trucks. Whooshing sounds. The interstate? I see death all around you, Bud."

"Play fair."

"I see a motel. Heaps of . . . what *is* that? Why would there be so many tires, Bud?"

"I don't know."

"Bud Bud Bud."

"Calm down."

"Will I see you soon, Bud?"

"I'm on my way."

"Do you miss me, Bud?"

"I miss everybody."

CHAPTER NINE

VETS

Up on eighteen — Friday the thirteenth, mid-afternoon — the tile guys are getting ready to apply the finishing touches to their wall. Senator Roy Otis Cutt, bound by ropes to a white wicker chair, is watching them do it. Muriel Goering's nude body hangs on a nail driven into a two-by-four stud; her killers have inserted a wire mesh screen in front of her hanging form, have poured kwik-dry behind the screen, smoothing down the surface with a nice professional finish. Pretty soon the surface will be hard enough for them to dab on the tile adhesive, dress the wall with the smart Italian tiles. Grout and wipe Giocametti's tiles, rehang the portrait of General Lee astride his white horse, and at last stand back and admire their show-place wall. They have said so themselves: never have they done a better job.

"Hey, Senator, what you think? You like it?"

"What I think, we ought to get a fuckin' bonus."

"Dint they say two?"

"Yeah, they said two. But one was to be a skinny thing just outta the egg. This old mouthy bitch was hefty."

The gods have, for the moment, spared Little Butter, the intern, Tabita Banta.

"Work on the head a while. Some of that hair is coming through."

"Yous tellin' me what to do? Dipshit, I'm tellin' yous, yous tellin' me what to do, yous better watch it."

"Shut that yap. Turn up the radio. I can't hear a fuckin' note."

"Well, yous right there. Maybe the Senator, he wants to phone in a request."

"'Oh Lord, I will see you on high.' Maybe that the one he want."

The pair ignite in riotous laughter. They've worked together before. They are bonded at the waist.

Norman Goering was the kind of a guy couldn't resist telling you how many suits he owned, how many pairs of shoes and what size. If he got a splinter in his fanny, he'd tell you that, and go sour if he couldn't show you the spot. A hangnail, he'd have to show you how deep it went. How often he went to the toilet; he was constipated, what antacids he took. He'd tell you when he had last got it off with Muriel, her favorite words, how she liked it best, how long it lasted, how age hadn't slowed him down one widget. "Hell, I've sped up. I pull the trigger, there she goes." This coin, he'd say, showing you a piece of change from his pocket — "This coin, you won't believe it, Gypsy Rose Lee picked this dime up off the stage floor at the Zanzibar, Toronto, Canada, with her you-know-what."

A real cracker-box, was Norm. More in his toot than any of those stand-ups you saw on the late shows.

While Norm was at the N Street building reminding a neighbor, Chris Rosenkrentz, that he, Norm, had been an MP on Guam during the war with the slit eyes, that his unit under Admiral Nimitz had liberated the whole chain of islands in that slag end of the world and pitched the slit eyes back into the sea, saved the world for democracy from shining sea to shining sea . . . while he was telling Rosenkrentz that they then discovered on Guam a colony of four thousand slit-eyed females pressed into servitude for the carnal pleasure of the slit-eyed Nip navy — "all double-bunking in these two-storey barracks, the whole shebang then turned over to us liberators to use for that self-same purpose, the best nine months I ever in my life had!" . . .

while Norman next went on to fill Rosenkrentz in on some of the relevant details peculiar to the occupation of an island with four thousand female slit-eyed sex slaves — Norm getting more and more irritated at Rosenkrentz's interruption of his recitations of sexual prowess with these slit eyes, at Rosenkrentz's repetitious questions re Norm's wife — "Aren't you concerned about Muriel's safety? Don't you worry about what could be happening to her up there?" — while Norm was affirming that Muriel was a big girl who could look after herself and getting back to juicy tidbits about the good times he and his MP buddies had had with the slit eyes — "You said bend over, they'd bend over, you said lick it, they'd lick" . . . then getting pissed off anew when Rosenkrentz said, "Well, you know, don't you, Norm, that the Japanese government is finally after fifty-five years paying compensation for forcing those girls, their own citizens, into slave sex-labor, and if you and Nimitz and the whole Seventh Fleet then used these women the same way, it might look like these women have a case against you and our government as well, which they can take to the Hague . . . " — while Norm was reliving his war experience with an enthusiastic recitation of the fabricated and the true and demonstrating a marked indifference to the transactions under way upstairs on eighteen —

— "Use the fuckin' notched trowel to put on the fuckin' glue."

— "Fuck the fuckin' notched trowel and you too!"

. . . While Norm, that is to say, was shooting off his mouth in the lobby, Chantelle Peru was strolling the sidewalk with Ishmael the Digger, regaling him with tales of her criminal patron, that genius of hyperbole, Zippo Giocametti.

"Zippo says to me one day, first time I met him, he says, Ms. Peru, I feel like I've taken the last curve. Like I'm heading for home. Not that I feel old, mind you, just that I'm feeling *older*. You ever feel that way, Ms. Peru?

"Un-huh, I say.

"Like even on a sparkly day, your heart catching the glitter, you can feel it, right?

"Un-huh.

"The racing time, the night that cometh, you following me?

"Yep.

"So what I've been thinking, he says, before I get past that last curve, I ought to do something decent for a change. I don't mean a penny here, a nickel there, chiselling my way past the gates. I mean, something decent. Just for a change, know what I mean?

"Un-huh.

"Like, I tap my good side, see what's in there. Like I'm cutting the plug in a watermelon, you understanding?

"Yes sir.

"Not just *thumping* the melon, see, but cutting the plug.

"Yes sir.

"Which, looking at you, is a thing I can see you've been doing all your life, am I right? Like you've seen from the beginning our responsibility don't end with just screwing everything up, like is Cutt's bag. Like, say, we come to earth with these grappling hooks attached to the ankles and the black crow of doom riding the shoulders, but at some point we can get out the hack-saw and tell the black crow of doom to go lead its own life, right?

"To get off *my* shoulder, right? Like I'm saying to the bird, 'Who invited *you*, who told you, you son of a bitch, that *you* had a free ride? Excusing my language. Pat Fish here, you see him? — already he's tipping his hat, excusing my language.

"I have no difficulty with your language, Mr. Giocametti. It is a nice hat, Mr. Fish. Most becoming.

"At that point, Mr. Giocametti is taking his first deep look at me — the first time he's taking a personal interest in me, in who I am, because Mr. Fish isn't wearing a hat.

"Then he starts his engine again.

"Like, say, you ask yourself the question 'How long doth the body rot when it be in the grave?' — without even seeing the emphasis is on the *if it be not rot already*, like. You following, Ms. Peru?

"You're a student of William, Mr. Giocametti? A devotee of Alas Poor Yorick?

"You don't need to look so surprised, Ms. Peru. By the way, you got a great face, Ms. Peru, you don't mind my saying.

"Thank you.

"Plus a body we won't get into, though I think you can see Pat Fish here has been expressing his approval since the minute we walked in. Don't tell me you didn't notice.

"Yes, I noticed.

"Anyway, it comes to doing the decent thing, upsetting the applecarts of the gods, so to speak, I have been asking myself to what good cause I can drop a few bucks, which is what brings me to your desk, you know what I'm saying? Because Pat Fish here, reading the paper the other day, the *Post*, I think it was, he reads aloud to me the case of the *invisible thousands* of our military personnel left over in Vietnam, Cambodia, according to what *you* are saying in the *Post*, and not dogshit anyone right up to the president is doing to bring them home. You remember that, your *Post* quotes? Cutt, the Senator, saying in the same *Post* it's all humbug, him and his committee having looked into the matter and twice already rejected the drafting of an appropriation to bring the invisible boys home. And you implying, no, outright saying Cutt is a liar and a son of a bitch would sell his own mother to anyone else would give him a Kennedy silver dollar. Did I read the *Post* story right? Wasn't that what you were saying?

"Close enough, Mr. Giocametti.

"So Pat Fish puts down the paper, he does this jig in the middle of my kitchen floor, saying here's to Chantelle Peru, may she live forever, and nail Cutt's crooked butt to the cross with her every breath, excusing my language.

"So excused.

"Ms. Peru, so here we are. Pat Fish and me having poured over the issue of what we *personally* might do to help you out with your crusade. Wasn't that how the *Post* boy, Woodward, put it? Your crusade?

"Well, you know what they say about *him*, Mr. Giocametti.

"You mean what his wife said about Bob and Venetian blinds?

"Yes sir. Among other things.

"Look at her blushing. I believe, Pat Fish, the star reporter might have come on to Ms. Peru, what you think?

"I have a busy schedule, Mr. Giocametti.

"Right. So moving along now. You got troubles with Cutt, Clinton won't listen to you — does he? . . . the entire Congressional force has a deaf ear, your First Lady's Committee on the Return of The Invisible Thousands is foot-dragging, merely a sop till the issue sogs down. You got a stone wall with the silent voice of the silent majority, with the War Department generals, the American Legion, the Vets of Foreign Wars, all doing doodly-squat and more than content to keep that door closed, am I right?

"To lock that door, Mr. Giocametti. To lock it tight."

"Now that look on your face, we came in, you're saying, Well, my goodness, who are these hoodlums? We know you will hop on the phone the minute we leave, quiz your contacts, likely did so the minute your secretary set the appointment. So you will discover, or have discovered, certain things that scrunch the brow. Like, me, connected, a hand in this, a hand in that, son of the big Jersey warlord Papa Giocametti, brother of that badass Dominic down in south Florida. Or take Pat Fish now, a good-looking devil, killer with the women, will keep you on the dance floor all night, but is he Sidney Poitier? Is he coming to dinner with Tracy and Katherine? No, Pat Fish there is not Sidney Poitier, he has put in his time with Alabama chain-gangs, he has held residency up New York State way, an Attica graduate.

"So you know this about us, you are saying, Who goes there?

"And the minute I slide my certified check over your mahogany you're going to get a splitting headache trying to figure it out. *Why? Why? Well Well Well, isn't this the strangest thing!* That is what you will be asking yourself.

"But you see Pat Fish there winking at you? I'm going to tell you a thing or two re Pat Fish.

"This isn't necessary, Mr. Giocametti.

"No, you're right, it isn't, and like you I'm eager to jump to the chase. I mean, here we are, the reel is winding and people are shaking their heads, thinking in a minute they are walking out of this movie house because nothing is happening. What I'm saying, Did we pay good money to listen to all this chit-chat? All this boring talk? They say that, you know, about *Separate Tables*, about *Baby Doll*, the great *Glengarry Glen Ross* — all that talk. I wanted talk, they say, I'd tune in Bill Moyers on the public network, I'd go see me a play. Like, where's the action? So I'm with you in this instance. I'm feeling the same way.

"But I'm thinking, you looking at us the way you did when we come in, fixing on us the judgment look, I'm just reminding myself how quickly a party can jump to the, like, erroneous conclusion. I mean, you've seen Cutt, is anyone lower than Cutt? Then *we* walk in. The *criminal* element? So right away there's this sour disposition beclouding the room.

"Mr. Giocametti, I —

"Let me ask you, Ms. Peru, do you know Pat Fish here wrote Martin Luther King's March on Washington speech? Practically wrote it. Well, let's say, helped out. Or was it the other one? The really great one, the *white man black man from the red hills of the one place to the black hills of the other*. That speech. The *I have a dream* one. He has a drink or two he will recite you the whole thing. He will recite you even the passages he and Martin decided to leave out.

"What I'm saying, he's good-looking, no one would say Pat Fish wasn't bright, but you wouldn't know he was the leading speech-writer of his generation, not to look at him, would you?

"So what I'm saying, another thing, is I like to keep that in mind when I'm looking at certain people and making the judgment call.

"But heck-fire, you are a busy woman, I can see those buttons flashing up and down your phone gadget, so Pat Fish can tell you that story in his own time. He has the inclination, which is pretty rare. On a desert island, he might. I mean, you got to hold a branding iron to his chest before he'll agree he even knows Martin Luther King ever existed or that at one time, the two of them in a George Wallace jail, Martin gives Pat Fish his *shoelaces. Shoelaces!* — what do you make of that? Martin's got laces, his pair, but Pat Fish, they've taken away his, the jailer telling him *You're a bad nigger, you open your mouth agin I'm takin' 'way your shoes, takin' 'way everything, leavin' your black ass naked, you hearin' me, boy?* Then Pat Fish and Martin thrown in the same cell, Pat Fish saying *The fuckers took away my shoelaces,* Martin saying, *Here, you take mine! Take'um!* Martin not hip to the fact that the jailer has put Pat Fish in there, in Martin's cage, following a certain arrangement, understanding concocted between the Montgomery Police Chief, the Montgomery mayor, the Alabama National Guard, Governor George Wallace's top lieutenants. Like Pat Fish is to go in there and cold-cock the bastard, beat Martin into a squished tomato so he won't look so good on the Nightly News.

"But forgive me, here I'm telling it anyhow, I can't help myself. Can't, because I see someone looking over Pat Fish, asking themselves Who goes there, making the judgment, but *do they have a clue?* No, they do not have a clue.

"Now you're saying, what, did he come all this way to make a speech?

"No, Ms. Peru. Here's my check, one million, which ought at least to be enough for you to get yourself over to Vietnam, Cambodia, see who you can find.

"Later on, I wrangle out of Pat Fish the rest of the story, him writing Dr. King's speeches. It's Zippo's bag, he says — just something Zippo has talked himself into believing. Zippo likes you, he's got to inflate your virtues. He'll tell you his daughter, Doe, scored the highest marks anyone ever did, on her, what you call it, S.A.T.s, but you ask Doe, she'll say no, let's just say I was in the upper echelon. Or how *Gump, Forrest Gump,* isn't merely a stinking picture but the *worst* stinking picture ever made that won the big prize. You see, how it was, down in Montgomery, the Miss Lucy bus thing, the church rallies, the police put Pat Fish in a cell with Dr. King. It's all arranged that he will break a few of the doctor's bones, pesto his face, the higher-ups figuring another black man is perfect for the job. Like who's going to complain, one black man beating the living shit out of another? They've got Pat Fish on a felony charge, looking at hard time, he beats up on the doctor, they will set his tail free. That being the agreement Pat Fish, the law, have. Like the police has just assumed Pat Fish is so stupid he has never heard of Miss Lucy, the NAACP, Stokely, Rap, the Southern Leadership Council, Dr. King. The Movement.

"*Slam,* he's in the cell. There's Dr. King.

"Dr. King with a writing pad in his lap, scribbling away, working on what became his famous *Letter From A Birmingham Jail.*

"Dr. King says to Pat Fish, 'Which do you like better? Do you like, *They can sic their dogs on us but they will only have to go back and get more dogs because we are still coming!* Or do you like: *They can stick us with their cattle prods but they will only have to bring more cattle prods because we are still coming.* Or do you like this one: *They can haul us off to jail but they will only have to build more jails because I tell you, brothers and sisters, we are still coming! We are still coming!* So which one do you think is better in terms of getting our message across?'"

"Pat Fish's answer is immediate. He says, 'You know what I think, Reverend? I think all three.'

"Ten minutes inside and he's Martin Luther King's *editor*, for christsake."

Pancho didn't know what had got into Chantelle Peru. It was like she had taken a talk pill and had to go on talking until the pill's effect wore off. But here's Ish, Ishmael, the boy Sweet's Big Brother — the Digger — and from how Chantelle's eyes lit up as Ish introduced himself Pancho knew his own time with her, for the minute, was over. The Counselor is in love.

"What do you do?" Chantelle Peru asked the Digger. Asked Ishmael.

"Do? What do you think? I'm one of two hundred on hire with the Special Prosecutor's Office, digging up shit on Lewinski one and two.

"Well, shit. Well, you don't mind my saying so: Ish, that is foul."

"Isn't it?" said Digger. And grinned in the famous D.C. way, that of the two shoes dancing, each unaware of the other. "Four unmarked vans strung around the complex, me out there, supposed to be dealing, dressed in threads I wouldn't wear to a circus. The vans got schoolkids banking on the sides, asking, 'What's Monica saying?' Crazy, huh?"

Chantelle liked the Digger's looks, liked his jaunty moves, what he did with his hands, the shoulder weaves, his hip play — liked how he talked. The whisk of those silk trousers. How he looked at her. Oh God, yes, how he looked at her. Going over to Pancho's Bar, their shoulders now and then grazing, talking about Sweet and what had happened to Sweet, slinging the word on Zippo, Chantelle got secretly excited because suddenly, just like that, it blapped into her mind that in all probability, and very soon, maybe within the next fifteen minutes, maybe even sooner, she was going to go to bed with this man. She could even in her mind see them doing it, a mental leap that truly fascinated Chantelle and made her that much more excited and limp with wonder all in the same moment. Then she thought, what, will this be the fourth or fifth black guy I've made it with? Then mad at herself for trying to isolate the exact number, because so long as she thought, Is it my fourth or fifth? — then she was still seeing these men as blacks before she saw them as people, as lovers, or merely as good-looking sexy guys she imagined it might be good to go to bed with. So that bothered her more than a little, the latent racism such thinking implied.

It didn't help any that Ish seemed hip to what she was thinking, and had revved up the flirtation notes to increase the dynamics.

So to make herself feel better about it, more able to cope with these unaccustomed emotions — both the sex flutters and the latent white middle-class liberal daughter-of-the-republic racism that you could hardly help being born with if you came to birth in this society — Chantelle decided she wouldn't any longer consider that she *might* go to bed with Ish. Just put that part out of her mind and go on to something else.

Like why he was here.

"Did you get Sweet to a hospital?"

"Sweet in good hands."

"I'm glad."

"Yeah, Sweet's a sweet boy. He thinks you're sweet too — asked me to pass that along."

"He say, 'That honky bitch?'"

"Something like that."

"Poor Sweet appears to be developing a racial attitude."

"And at such a tender age. Wonder how come?"

"Something in the Shangri-la air, I guess."

"Everybody susceptible, it seems."

"You think I am?"

"No. I think you just a long time between lays. Your psychokinetic outlook in warfare on account of your bones too long been deprived. Plus, you probably not been eating regular."

When did she last eat? She can't remember.

"What do you intend doing with those people who assaulted Sweet?"

"What I'm going to do? I'm going to assault them. They up on eighteen this minute. I don't see identification being a problem."

"But you are passing the time with me first?"

"You a good-looking woman invited me for a drink. Be insulting, I was to refuse. Also, I never before met a woman bringing a forty-million dollar suit against her government. I want to see what she made of, do she have good shoes for when the coals get hot."

"I'm betting you were over there."

"Un-huh. Made me the man I am today."

"There are two of them, I understand. Tilers."

"Un-huh. I'm real worried."

Chantelle liked Ish's smiling ways. He laid down an easy patter, without thinking he had to enrich it with an overload of horseshit. She was thinking she wouldn't mind if they passed up on the drink, hailed a taxi, and went straight to a hotel.

But there already was Pancho's Bar. They had been loitering. Time had flown. Okay, admit it, along the way there had been some heavy touching.

The bar interior seemed dark after the strong light outside and both were a moment adjusting. They halted in the doorway, making out the silhouette of Pancho behind the bar by the cash register, the cash drawer open, a second man beside him, holding up something dark against Pancho's head. Another man, fattish, wearing a fatigue jacket, a visored cap turned backwards on his head, was seated on a stool — spinning to look them over as they entered and now pointing something at them that looked oddly like a pistol. Chantelle was thinking this, asking herself, Is that a pistol? — just as Ish shouted, "Get down!" The next second she was flying, her shoulder aching where Ish had stiff-armed her shoulder, her head ringing when the table's metal base struck her, that table overturning, her knees and hip sliding. Then Ish's full weight was on top of her, pinning her to the floor and her head was ringing louder. Gunshots sounded, some of these coming from Ish, the table top exploding, the glass behind them showering onto the street. It was all over in a matter of seconds, Ish still on her; she turned her head and saw two men stumbling through the exit, one holding a hand over his bleeding neck, blood oozing out between the spread fingers, the other man moving in a swift crouch. The two stumbled by the blown-out window, no more than four or five feet away, Ish with his gun raised though not firing, both of them watching the men move across the street and climb into a dusty Chevy pick-up.

She couldn't breathe then felt the weight lift from her chest, Ish rising to his elbows, his hips still on her hips, his legs between her legs.

Funny thing was, it occurred to her later, that there for a moment she was someone else; she was still out on the street walking, jabbering away, then turning into Pancho's, coming through the door, and the thing that had happened, happened all over again. Her mind heard Ish saying, "You do know how to pick the *in* spot, Ms. Peru," while another part of her brain knew that neither of them, for what seemed the longest time, said nothing. She heard groaning, but whose groan was it?

Then Ish was off her and she was picking herself up, looking around, smelling the gunfire, feeling for broken limbs.

It was Pancho, on the floor behind the bar, moaning. Then Ish was kneeling over him, and she was herself there kneeling, shaking. Pancho's moaning came up inside her and she couldn't stop shaking, the shaking worsening as she suddenly realized the moaning was no longer there and Ish had a hand on Pancho's neck, feeling for a pulse. Then Ish was looking at her, she at him, and poor Pancho was looking at nothing.

She said a foolish thing. She said to Ish, "You didn't shoot him, did you?"

He was still holding the gun in his other hand.

She knew the split second she said it, something in Ish's eyes, that theirs wasn't a relationship going any where.

"No, Counselor, my shots went pretty close to where I was aiming."

She could not bear to look at the wounds in Pancho's chest so she looked at Ish's gun and said a second foolish thing:

"Is that a Mauser?"

Ish hefted the weapon.

"No, Counselor, this little bitch is a .38 Smith." He looked to her like he wanted to say, "Do you want to hold it?" She wished he would say it, for that would make him as foolish as she was. What he said was, "Take deep breaths. You're shaking."

Then he found a stack of checkered table cloths folded on a shelf in the counter, and placed that over Poncho's upper body. The sight of Pancho's protruding legs made her shake more, and she knew she had to sit down or she would fall.

After a few seconds, she felt better. She felt a mounting anger.

"Did this feel like a robbery to you?"

Ish shook his head. "No. It seemed to me somebody had in mind a spring-cleaning."

"What do you think?"

"I think somebody disapprove of yours and Pancho's social ethics."

"Ethics?"

"Maybe somebody think forty million, that's a bit greedy. Even by D.C. standards."

"Christ. I can't even get a court date."

"Your clients all die, maybe the Senator's saying you won't need one."

"You're saying Cutt's behind this?"

Ish shrugged, looking down at the .38 Smith in his left hand.

"Or Jude. The Friends. You know, Jude."

"Jude is a goddamn fraud! The fucker was at My Lai."

"He *was* My Lai. Forget Lt. Calley."

Chantelle touched his arm and Ish put the gun away. "The police will be coming. You'd better go. I'll look after this."

Ish glanced back to the street. He gave Chantelle a quick hug, a sad smile. "Twenty-three years," he said, "the poor sucker comes back for this?"

"They'll fucking pay. Someone will."

"There's my lady," Ish said. At the door, he turned: "By the way, that pick-up was out there? That was a Friends' Chevy. Seen it at the Watergate."

Then he was out of there.

Only as she sees his flying backside, Chantelle Peru looking at the wilting flowers, at dead Pancho, to think:

Qui est-il?

Well, her French is rusty. *Quién esta ahi?* Who goes there?

CHAPTER TEN

ZIPPO

Glo asleep. Eyeglasses bent on her face, *Emma* open on her chest. Page seven. She's really cooking with that book. One entire month now.

Zippo flicks on the den TV. Grab a second, stroll the stations. There's the Grow-New-Hair guy singing his pitch, in CU as the movie people say. Cut to TCU, the client's new rug. Thirty days and you ugly bald-headed guys won't recognize yourselves. He was always a bit shy on top, the Grow-New-Hair guy, way back in his *I Spy* days when hooked up with the black comedian fellow, what's-his-name?

Never mind, it will come to him.

Well, look at that. There on the oldies channel is Veronica Lake, all five foot one of her, giving Bogey the come hither through that hair.

The refrigerator is a maze. Every shelf loaded, not a jot of space to be found, but is there a single item in there a man can eat? Not unless Zippo dabs a finger in dijon mustard, in the Hellmann's, in tamarind chutney, horseradish, relish, pickle juice, sun-dried tomatoes, chipotle salsa, ancient pastes, preserves, sauces. No-fat yogurt a year past its 'Best Before' date. Not unless he cares to fill up on jalapeno peppers, coconut flakes, rock-hard raisins, almond slithers, bread crumbs, unidentifiable smoky jams, baking soda, shrivelled ginger roots. Volatile fumes exuding from the trays. Withering lemons, limes, onion halves; soupy lettuce in a smelly bag could fire rockets to the moon. Tai juice, tabasco, tomato juice with a three-inch crust of mold.

Countless cottage cheese cartons dating from the previous century.

Arugula, parsley, artichokes, romaine, parsnips, radish, turnips, zucchini, green onion, cilantro — all drowning in six inches of pungent brine.

Black, squishy cantaloupe shrunk to the size of a golf ball.

In the cheese drawer romano, cheddar, jack, roquefort, swiss, stilton, parmigiano reggiano that you can chop at with an axe without making a dint.

Gangster life.

Nothing doing in the pantry, either, short of killing off nine bottles of extra-virgin olive oil. Rusting tins of escargot, clams, bamboo shoots, water chestnuts, hearts of palm.

Spiders, Daddy Longlegs, roosting in every corner.

Mouse manure everywhere.

No more jerky in the hiker's pack. Glo has consumed all the jerky. No more Appalachian Squid Oil.

He spills into his mitt something called Mule Train Trail Pellets. Like Meow Mix.

Your gourmet gangster fare.

Let the free citizen breathe, he's thinking. Your own government shooting you every day in the back, slashing welfare, unemployment benefits, health, gouging John Q. at every turn — what's wrong with a gangster extending the common citizen a little mercy?

Pat Fish is wrong about that coin job, however. He has genuine interest, excitement, in that job. No crane, however. Too bad forklifters won't suffice. Forklifters he can get by the yardful.

How he figures it, according to Cutt's timetable received directly from the mint, he's got the southbound coin train arriving in the Raleigh yard at 2:14. The northbound pulling in three minutes later. His own flat-beds directly between them. Both trains there for exactly twenty-nine minutes. Leaving a five-minute clearance on either side, he's got precisely nineteen minutes to shift two thirty-ton units from the southbound to his flatbed, his dummy units to the coin car.

Can it be done?

Absolutely. But everything depending on the crane and the crane guy.

Be nice, though, to have a dry run.

Six million, the rough estimate.

A sweetheart deal, practically no risk.

He needs it, too. Lately, his trucks seized, slapped with fines, the weight stations declaring overloads, mechanical violations. Half his fleet grounded. Mining quarry rights withdrawn, the politicos applying pressure every minute. Pay-offs these days not being enough; you got to share the political philosophy, toe the party line, or your butt's in the sling.

Ah, well — they pull this job, maybe then they all retire.

What's that? The phone?

Get the phone.

"Zip?"

"Speaking."

"It's me. You don't recognize your own brother's voice?"

Every week or or two the past months Dominic is goading Zippo, faxing yet another photo of his estates, his cars, his grayhounds. His three daughters beating back all comers, acing every endeavor, chips off the old block. So many A-plus brains under one roof you'd think they were going for a spot in Guinness.

Dominic on the phone saying he's down in Colombia, was in Rio yesterday, tomorrow is on his way to Saudi Arabia. Working the deals. "All those New York retirees," he's saying, "with their big cars.

I can pull off the street, what, a Lexus, fifty-sixty K over here but you get the machine to the Arabs, right away it's tripled, quadrupled, off the map. I'm turning bucks would make Henry Ford cry like a baby."

His new thing, cars.

"It's like they opened the mint, told you to dip your hands right in."

Dominic yakking away without end because it's his dime and . . . "

Like, you know, Zip, we ain't conversed heart-to-heart in some time."

Two thousand wheels a month he's now moving out of Charleston harbor — out of Jacksonville, out of the Big Easy, out of Shreveport. "You see a cargo vessel riding low in the water, Zippo, you can bet that vessel is mine. Soon I'm buying my own fleet. I got wheels crated on the docks in sealed containers marked COFFEE BEANS, marked ALFALFA SEED. Marked MISSILES, SALT — whatever comes to mind.

"Like here in OJ land, we're suddenly producing coffee beans — but Hey? is anybody suspicious? Does anybody snap? The beauty is, see, the beauty is, the ship don't have to declare its manifest, its goods, even its destination, until two, three days out on the water. Even they send out Whirlybirds, aren't my vehicles already in another nation's waters? Isn't it? I'm unloading in Egypt, my client sniffing the new car spray before the police over here have so much as responded to the victim's call. Tell you the truth, I think last week I moved more vehicles than the Big Three. For a joke sometimes? Just to show I'm playing fair? I slap stickers over my containers, STOLEN AUTO, the stickers say. THIS RIPPED OFF CARGO BOUND FOR THE ROYAL FAMILY, KUWAIT. Ain't that a honey? But you got to have fun, right? Otherwise, what's money? You hear what I'm saying?

"I figure ten more easy years before the dumbfuck lawmakers take their fingers out."

Dominic down there in Bogota, rattling on.

"But, hey, How ya doing? How's Glo? How's Deborah Greenpeace? Uncle Pat, he okay? Man, I got to tell you, sometimes I ask myself,

'Walking down the street, do they hold hands? Do they stroke each other's rump like the fag couples down here?' Just kidding, Zip."

Zippo lets the phone slide from his ear a minute to cool while he munches on the cat chow.

Dominic says, *"Hey! You there?* What I'm saying is I'm converting same as you. Going legit. Putting my main marbles into AT&T, into Blue Cross. I even got my own bank now, did I tell you?"

"Yeah, yeah, what I'm saying.

"Say, Zip, Zippo baby, you know Papa's worried about you. Tells me your health is in peril. You got Senators disappearing, people running you off the road. You been too long without tithing the Pope, pal. You're walking too many limbs, darling, like with that coin heist. Quarters, *quarters,* Zip? I'm feeling how Betty felt her bottom sag, her bones collapse, when Gerry Ford told her he's got to pardon Tricky Dick. Betty knowing that very minute her clinic is too far even to think about making it on Number One, whereas the Jack Daniels is right there."

What?

"Now another thing."

"Yeah?"

"What's this I hear about you out in Vancouver cutting off a certain guy's hair?"

"Hair?"

"Capone, your godfather, sick as he was with syphilis when he died — Zippo, a barber! — he would turn over in his grave."

"Now this guy Jude . . . "

"Jude?"

"Hey! I'm sitting right here, minute ago, putting my shoes on, and what do I see floating across my screen but this plea for me to send my charitable dollars to the Friends for their bright new Christian Theme Park. I was remarking in my mind, see," Dominic saying, "asking, Is Zippo in on this? Is this his scam? But there's Jude on my TV in his metal suit, his hand out, and I'm saying to myself, 'That's the fucker my brother got to watch out for. He's working down here, too, you know, big with the Dump Castro crew, which is just about everyone. These Friends, Zippo, are so far right wing they think baseball is a Jewish Conspiracy, because it's got all those lefties on the mound. Know what I mean? A lefty or a switch-hitter comes to the plate, the Friends want to shoot him.

"So you're looking for who arranged the Tilley Hat hit, I'd say, stop looking. You listening to me?"

Zippo thinking, Jeez, all these years I been underestimating my kid brother. The guy cares for me.

"You with me, Zippo?"

"Yeah?"

"Cutt? You're shacking up with a guy dresses a child, dear God, as his mother? Cut that rope, sweetheart. But who you got to look out for, big brother — is Bud."

Bud?

"Bud, that's right. You see Bud coming, all you can do is hide. So long, pal. Love to the loved ones."

"Dominic!"

Click, Dominic's gone. Dominic so oozing with brotherly love, so overflowing the pitter-patter, Zippo feels his eyes filling like Hoover dam.

Zippo there, his hand clutching the sweaty phone, reviewing the conversation, when — *damn!* — it rings again.

"Zippo?"

"Yeah?"

"Hold on. Let me put Mama on the line."

Mama and Papa Giocametti, putting in their two cents.

Mama saying, "A whole week you have not phoned. A whole two-hundred hours of eternity I do not hear your voice. And Glo telling me, what's this, you can't afford water? What's this, you can't afford a barber to come in, give you a shave, cut your hair? Did I raise you to have hippie hair, a son too high and mighty now and then to call his mother? A minute ago, Dominic dials me all the way from Botega, yesterday was Rio, tomorrow will be the Saudi Republic. But Mister Zippo, I guess he's too busy. I guess he's too busy getting himself shotgunned, run off the road, to call his only mama."

Papa Giocametti saying, "Zippo Zippo Zippo."

Like it's the end of the world and he, Zippo, is responsible.

"Yes, Papa?"

"I have to give the credit to Dominic. He's got, what, to knock heads with the Cubans, the Haitians, the Colombian cartel, the Panamanians, the Jamaican beadheads, the poppy growers of Asia and Indonesia — but is he being shot at? Is he being run off the road?"

"I'm okay, Papa. Not a scratch."

"So I have to say to Mama, I have to say to her, yes, Mama, it must be that Zippo is on the wrong wave beam. It must be that he is no longer the smart boy we raised from scratch."

"I appreciate your — "

"I have to say to Mama, do not worry, Mama, if Zippo is alive he will call. But did you call? No, the rumors fly, we hear our son has gone over a mountain in a Jaguar, but does he call? We hear a Tilley Hat has pumped a thousand bullets into his guts, but does he call?"

"I didn't want to worry you, Papa."

"It's what I say to Mama, Mama, he has not been the same since seeing that picture show with the head of the horse on the white pillows in . . . was it *The Godfather* one or two?"

"One, Papa."

"Now it is rumors I am hearing of U.S. Senators sealed or soon to be sealed alive in walls, and I have to ask Mama, I have to say, 'Mama, in the raising of this son, where did we go wrong?'"

"I'm not following you, Papa."

"A Senator sealed alive inside walls, that does not disadvantage the nation. A hundred such senators sealed inside walls, what's the harm? But innocent school girls, son? To align yourself with a reptile senator who abuses the trust of innocent school girls, now that, son, is undermining the youthful generation's trust in their nation. That is troublesome, Zippo, to your Papa and Mama. I've got granddaughters, how many, they are school girls. It is like as Mama says, Zippo, 'A man who does not keep his hair trimmed, who makes his wife ride around in a thirty-year-old Cadillac, what can you expect of such a person?' We worry, that's what I'm saying. You are drifting far adrift, Zippo. I am thinking you need help of the kind once peculiar to Vienna. I am seeing my son in a box surrounded by flowers."

Zippo says, "Papa! Papa! I'm hip to the concern. Don't worry, my behalf, Papa."

"I am remembering you say that to me as a boy and the next day you are on the stage of the Canteen Theater, Roosevelt High School, pretending to be a filthy grave-digger digging up skulls and speaking in the unnatural way you claim to me is the iambic pentameter. Mama says to me that terrible day, 'For this did we leave our Old Country?'"

"It was a play, Papa."

"I am looking at you that day and I am thinking, This is a boy who does not know of skulls. This is a boy who does not know of graves. This is a boy who knows only the iambic pentameter. This is a boy with whom my good friend Capone requires the serious talk.'"

"I let you and Mama down, Papa, I am sorry."

"A thief, I am remembering."

"Oh, Papa!"

"A thief who says to me one terrible day, 'But Papa, Papa, in Bangladesh are people starving.' A boy who would steal from his own Papa. I say to Mama that very day, 'Mama, we have lost our boy. A different world this son of ours occupies.' And your mother, she says to me, 'No, our boy's brain does not hum with the precision of the foremost deity on high, so easy with the strap, Papa.' And easy I was. Which now, look at you."

"Five dollars, that's all I took!"

"And what did I say to you that day? I said to you, 'The pot not to pee in is the melting pot, my son.'"

"For the starving people of Bangladesh!"

"So, still. Forty years your Mama and I live in wait of the thief's apology. Now look at him. Sealing U.S. Senators alive inside walls."

"It's a lie, Papa!"

"Yes, as in five dollars is a lie. As in, 'I did not spend the five stolen dollars on an ice cream cone.'"

"I didn't, Papa!"

"When with my own eyes I see you eating the ice cream cone. Double scoop. Your Mama, she says to me, 'Is he eating the ice cream cone for himself or for the starving people of Bangladesh?' You killed us, son. Your cold arrows pierced our hearts."

"I'm sorry, Papa."

"Now he speaks. Now he confesses."

"The ice cream only cost a quarter, Papa. The rest I gave to Bangladesh."

"I say to your Mama that day, I say, 'Never again is he to be trusted. He is not fit to be a decent crook.' But these questions aside. How is Miz Greenpeace? How is coming along the dear wife's search for water? By the way . . . "

"Yes, Papa?"

"On the subject of Miz Greenpeace . . . "

"Yes?"

"The grapevine it tells me not only is Miz Greenpeace, the pacifist environmentalist rabid feminist contemplating holding hands with a man who suddenly has gone bald . . . "

"I had nothing to do with that, Papa."

". . . but also she is contemplating new employment opportunities."

"You talked to Dolores?"

"Me? Who will talk to me? The grapevine tells me my beloved granddaughter Miz Greenpeace is being offered prestigious positions in Europe. In Brussels, no less."

"You're kidding."

"At the Hague, I believe."

"She'd have told us!"

"Chasing criminals!"

"No!?"

"War criminals. A prosecutor."

"Papa, please!"

"Papa has to go. A fourteen-course meal your Mama has prepared — "

"Don't hang up, Papa!"

"With sips of vino for yours truly. Guard your backside. Be wary, son."

"Papa!"

"Look out for Bud."

"Who?"

Bud?

Click.

Zippo mulling over this flood of news — Doe at the Hague? Bud? — wiping his brow, crunching the meow mix — when the window explodes behind him.

All hell breaking loose out there.

Zippo looks in disbelief at blood surfacing on his arms in that scant instant before it comes to him that guns are blazing, glass flying, and if he means to live he'd better scramble his ass for cover, assuming already it isn't too late.

Am I hit? he thinks. *Am I dying?*

Qué va ya. Go away.

CHAPTER ELEVEN

BUD

Idena was wearing a dog suit made of real dog hair, with a real dog head. Idena's own head was in there, the dog head flipped partially back, falling just short of Idena's eyes. So Bud, entering the room, had the dog's eyes to look at, plus Idena's eyes, enriched with heavy mascara. The dog's eyes were not imparting anything special, being glass; Idena's eyes were saying, How do you like it? — in a way that suggested she had doubts.

The dog suit was white: a long-haired dog with floppy ears, a long tail. The tail wasn't swishing. It was a do-nothing tail. The fur looked recently washed and brushed. It looked luxurious, as did the dog's leather collar, decorated with silver pellets.

Idena made a good-looking dog, trim and chic. She was on the bed, on all fours, pointing his way when Bud came in. Bud wondered would she say bow-wow. Bud could see the dog had shed a good bit; dog hair was all over the green carpet, on the green duvet cover.

Idena's own hair was tinted red, the color of hearty wine, a deep merlot. When Bud had last seen her Idena's hair had been black. Or her wig had been. Maybe this new merlot color was a wig also.

Bud crossed from the doorway in a circle around the foot of the bed. He wanted to get a look at Idena in the dog suit from all angles; trouble was, Idena on all fours kept turning, turning just the way a dog might, protecting her rear. Idena's arms and legs were inside the dog suit; otherwise, the suit was open.

Idena was wearing the dog suit and nothing else.

It was open down to her waist, the zipper perhaps broken, though not so open that Bud had a full view of her breasts. Partial contours only, now one nipple, now the other.

"Why you looking at me like that, Bud?"

As Bud said nothing, Idena then said plaintively: "Bud Bud Bud."

Bud still didn't reply, so Idena leaned back on the dog's hind legs, pulling the tail up around her hips.

Bud looked around at the three walls, at the large window forming the fourth wall — he looked at the lamp, the dresser, at the telephone, at Idena's knickknacks and beauty products spread out over the dresser — before settling his look again on Idena the dog.

Idena's new hair color, what could be seen of it, Bud decided was an improvement over the black wig. The black wig had given her flesh a white painted look, like a Kabuki dancer.

Idena had a new lipstick, too, in a shade almost identical to the new hair color.

She had really done a job on those eyes.

Idena flicked a tongue out over those new lips, looking up at him; then she circled about as though she were a dog thinking about the nicest spot for lying down; in the end she didn't lie down, only relaxed a bit more on her haunches, head tilted.

Now she was panting.

The mouth open, the tongue out, the bed a bit bouncy, just as it would be if she were a true dog there, panting.

Idena liked a hot house; maybe that was why she was panting, maybe she could use a bowl of water.

Bud poked out a hand to pat the dog's head, but Idena quickly drew back. Her mouth open, tongue lolling.

Bud was amazed at how much she resembled a genuine dog, even given the movie eyes.

Hanging from the dog's fine collar was the dog's name tag. Bud came close, thinking to take a look at the tag, check out the dog's name and where it resided, who you were to call if you found a lost dog — but Idena quickly was up, pedaling backwards, letting loose a deep growl. Showing some teeth.

So Bud dropped that idea.

Over the next few seconds Idena the dog had a ferocious battle with fleas, scratching deep with her claws — eyes unfocused, teeth snipping — then whipping her head back, crunching the fleas.

"Whew!" she said.

Bud rocked his weight from one leg to another, took a deep breath — started to speak, then decided against it.

He shook his head and left the room.

After a moment Idena called in a petulant voice: "What do you have against dogs, Bud?"

Then: "Are you going to be difficult?"

Then she said,"Oh, Bud Bud Bud." She spoke this sorrowfully, as one might who was caught in the rain, or like a mourner out standing by a graveside.

In the kitchen Bud poured himself something to drink.

For a few seconds he studied the dishes arranged on the drain board. One plate, one saucer, a fork, a glass. The sink sparkled. Idena disliked a dirty sink. If you went into a home where there was a dirty sink, she claimed, then you knew you were in for something horrible.

He took from his jacket pocket the small efficiency travel case containing the miniature razor, toothpaste, fold-up toothbrush. He put these on the table, then removed his jacket, hanging it on the back of one of the two dining chairs.

Bud came back into the room where Idena was, taking first sip at the drink which a lot of people said they liked, a sixteen year-old single-malt Scotch. The Scotch tasted smoky. It tasted like an old keg, or an old shoe. It was old, plenty old, but Bud made a face with the first sip, coughed, and was pretty sure he would not have a second.

He was trying to wean himself off Coke.

"This dog cost me practically nothing," Idena said, meaning the suit. "I got it at a vintage clothier."

Bud nodded. He liked everything about the suit except that it shed. No, he didn't like the limp tail, either.

Idena said, "This suit was exactly my size. It had my name on it."

Then she had to call, "Bud Bud Bud!" — because Bud had turned on his heels and gone back into the kitchen.

She could hear him at the refrigerator, or at the sink — somewhere in there — knocking out ice cubes.

"Well God knows," she called, "no one is making you drink that stuff."

Then she fell silent, listening, although there was nothing even a silent person could hear, because Bud was a person who rarely made any noise. He almost never did. He lifted the occasional eyebrow, like just now when he saw her in the dog suit, but he never lifted his voice. Idena could say truly that he was the first man she'd ever known who made no noise. He never, never lifted his voice, and after a lot of that you would — or she would — often forget he was in the house. She thought this silent practice must be some kind of rule he had established for himself. It was an instruction to his being. Like a light foot, a light tread, were instructions to his legs.

Or maybe it was how he'd endured being inside those walls on the island of Iona.

Idena wasn't sure she totally liked this not lifting the voice routine. It made her own voice sound brassy and hollow, even vulgar. Then he would say, "Why are you whispering?" and she would get all mixed up.

"What are you doing in there?" she now asked.

"Eating," she heard him say. Only that one word, eating, like his words were rationed.

"Eating what?"

Then he was suddenly in the doorway, showing her the wedge of cheese, the scrap of stale French loaf he was eating.

There with his Coke, a thick lemon wedge in the glass the way he always had to have it.

"Oh, Bud," Idena said. "If I'd known for certain you were coming I would have baked you a loaf of Mother's Best Bread."

Bud had food in his mouth. So he didn't have to answer.

Bud almost always ate standing up. He ate on the fly. If you could call his nibbling at this or that eating. Idena liked this about him. She was developing the same habit herself. She'd already lost seven pounds, following Bud's example. It was why she now could fit into the dog suit, which actually was sizes below her usual size. Getting into the suit, she'd ripped one of the sleeves. The suit was awfully tight under the arms. It was also pretty hot in there. She wondered how a dog could stand it.

Bud didn't talk much either. One whole week since she last had seen him, but had he yet even said hello?

Then Bud spoke.

Idena knew this was the work of ESP. The only trouble with ESP, which she'd had a lot of luck with over the years, was that hers didn't work with Bud that often.

"Does the dog want any cheese?" Bud asked.

He held a small wedge just wide of her nose.

Idena nodded, thumping her dog paws. She felt extremely happy. She loved it when Bud directed these intimate, very personal questions her way. She loved to have him put food in her mouth. If he let her have the cheese she would lick his fingers the way a real dog would.

"What are you called?" Bud asked. "Are you called Fido?"

Idena barked. She thumped her paws harder, waggling her head and blinking her eyes and sneezing.

"Let me put the cheese on your nose," Bud said.

"Okay," Idena said. She was smiling. She was really enjoying this. This was an extremely beautiful, intimate moment with Bud. It was about only the fourth or fifth such moment she had had with him. She hoped it would go on and on, like when you punch the CD replay button ten times to get John Lee Hooker doing that boat song. That boat song about the boat that is bringing your beloved back to you, but the boat never comes. What comes is a boat mirage, a ghostly boat, and your beloved isn't on that boat either. Your beloved has gone down in the real boat in a bad storm, but hasn't yet crossed over into the spirit world.

"Then you flip the cheese and catch it in your mouth," Bud said.

Idena was looking long and hard at the cheese in Bud's hand. Now and then at Bud's eyes. It crossed her mind to ask him had he shot anyone on this trip. Had he killed anyone. Bud believed Idena had no idea what he did for a living, but the way Idena figured it at this moment there was almost nothing about him of importance that she didn't know.

He didn't mind what she knew, he said, although she ought to know Bud wasn't his real name and if anyone ever put the two of them together she was to tell him about it, and under no conditions was she to let anyone know where she lived.

"Safety first," he would say. Like he was a crossing guard outside a kid's grade school.

"I can do that," Idena said. Meaning the cheese. "That's easy."

Bud put the cheese on her nose. On her own nose, that is, not on the dog's nose, which was a nose made out of black suede and slick with oil from all the people who had rubbed the dog's nose for good luck.

"Fifty bucks says you can't do it," Bud said.

He had a wad of folded bills in his pants pocket; he peeled off a fifty and let it float down onto the nearest pillow.

Idena flipped the wedge of cheese and caught it and swallowed the cheese whole, just the way a dog that had been trained in a dog act might.

Then she laughed. She rolled over and held her dog paws high in the air, kicking them up, so pleased was she with her performance.

Idena had never had anything going with a man who was as good at inventing games as Bud.

'Who Put These Yellow Bricks On My Road' was maybe her favorite game of all those he had invented.

He was the Tin Man in that game, and she was obliged to sing like that white mouse with the pug nose, Judy Garland.

"Does doggy want more?" Bud asked.

She shook the whole of her body, especially her hind quarters, and they went through the full routine again. Idena now had the dog suit head down over her nose, only her chin and mouth showing. She was sneaking the odd look at herself in the vanity mirror, quite struck by the dog's reddish hue and loving how the ears of the dog dangled down. If she sprayed them with a starch spray she bet she could make those ears stand up.

"Bud Bud Bud," Idena finally said. "Why are you so good to me?"

Bud had let about five hundred dollars flutter down onto the pillow by the time she said this.

She sniffed these bills but without keen interest because it was only money and hardly even had the smell of Bud's hands. The bills had the smell of a thousand other hands and she knew if she looked long and hard at Andrew Jackson's face she would see Andrew Jackson doing the terrible things that Andrew Jackson had done, to the Cherokee Nation, for instance, just to mention that one thing she could already see Andrew Jackson doing.

Bud was sitting on the side of the bed. He didn't have any more bread or cheese and he was sitting there with his knees open, his arms dangling between them, his shoulders slumped.

He was looking forlorn, like he had temporarily forgotten where he was and what a good time he was having.

The single malt glass was over on their rented vanity, leaving its ring.

All the room's furniture was rented by the month, including the carpet, the bed, the night tables, the drapes over the big window, and the CD which played John Lee Hooker's boat song. But the duvet and its green cotton cover and the green pillow cases were Idena's own, although Bud had paid for them.

Idena reached over and grabbed the glass and drank all of the single malt down in one gulp. Then she passed the glass to Bud who put it back right on the same ring. If Idena asked him did he shoot or stab or maim anybody on this trip, she knew what he would say. He would rake her with his eyes and say, "Nobody special."

Bud looked after her. He would never let anything bad happen to her. He would not be around long, just looking at him, looking at him the first time they met, she had known that. But in the meantime he was good as gold.

Idena asked, "Do you want to take off your clothes, Bud? Do you want to sleep or make rapturous love? I would really like to, myself. Whatever you want."

Bud smiled at her. He lifted a hand to pat her dog's head but she quickly frisked herself back, out of his reach. She crouched down on her front paws, waggling the dog's high rear end, and snorting — exactly as though she was a dog ready to play.

Then she laughed and let Bud pat her head and thump her sides a few times.

She said, "Do you want me to tell you what I've been doing all the time you've been away? Bud?"

Bud removed one of his shoes and before she could hop around on the bed and take off his other shoe he had done it himself.

So she nipped at one of Bud's ankles, then grabbed one of the shoes in her teeth, shaking it like a live thing.

Bud was unbuttoning his shirt.

Idena sniffed at his naked chest, then sneezed several times, making her ears flap this way and that.

"Do you, Bud? Want me to tell you?"

Sometimes Bud liked her doing that, telling him what she had been up to in his absence. He could listen to her for hours. His face went solemn when her experiences were solemn and when an exciting or happy event was being reported on he was there smiling right along with her. Sometimes he would say, "I wish I had been with you," or "I wish I had been there," and Idena found these moments thrilling.

She felt so close to him at these times. She felt she wanted to climb right up inside him, because until Bud came along, never in all her incarnations, had she known a man who was willing to demonstrate that empathy was composed of living tissue.

Which was strange, given his low opinion of ESP.

But now Bud had rolled over and stretched out his legs on the bed and pulled the duvet over as much of his body as he could with her on it.

He rested his head on the pillow, not the one where the money was, and closed his eyes.

Poor Bud, Idena thought. He gives his whole being to his projects. They tire him out. The poor man is pooped.

Despite the sympathy Idena acknowledged, she was feeling very hurt, and a small anger was beginning to simmer as well. She hadn't seen Bud for days and days, days in which she had not the smallest idea where he was or what, precisely, he was doing. They were supposed to be having an affair, she was supposed to be his devoted mistress, but here he was falling asleep on her.

Bud Bud Bud, she thought.

His hand closed softly over hers and instantly she felt fine again.

Bud was such a wonderful man. She couldn't get over how much she wanted to soak herself in who he was. Like you'd soak yourself in a long hot perfumy jacuzzi with the jets roaring in your ears.

Idena rooted herself under the duvet and stretched out beside him and closed her own eyes.

Then she hopped up and switched off the light and leapt back in beside him.

Then she hopped up a second time and took the empty glass off its wet ring and hid the glass under the bed, aware of how much she and Bud were alike in liking things tidy.

The split-second thought she had, pressing tight against him, was of a dog, a loyal dog, nestling beside its master, but this was an image so stricken of truthfulness that it sickened her to think that she had even thought it.

Out, brief candle, she thought.

This morning she had received a call from a man who had held her ear to the phone for the longest time before he spoke.

"Is Bud there?" the man finally said.

The voice was an unkind voice and this was not supposed to happen in the first place. No one was supposed to know Bud was a person who existed in her life.

"Bud?" she had said.

The party had postponed speaking for a long time. Rice could have cooked and you could have eaten an entire dinner in the time it took that caller to respond.

"Bud don't live here," she finally said. "It's only me and Udran."

Then the man severed the connection.

Afterwards, Idena had stood a long time patting one foot while saying to herself over and over that there was no way in hell Bud would ever have given anyone this number.

The man who had called had not sounded to her like he was an ESP kind of person.

The room was very dark now. Bud's was a shape just slightly less black than the room's other darkness, and if he rolled his head and looked at her she would look exactly that same way to him. Idena found this thought wonderfully attractive and comforting. She felt wonderfully excited. Like if she put her mind to it and concentrated with every ounce of her being she would never be able to figure out what next in her life was going to happen.

Everything was amazingly silent in the room, so silent she imagined Bud's soft breathing was her own breath. She lay a paw on his chest and her mouth against his shoulder and in a second she was inhaling and exhaling to his very same rhythm.

Except that his inhalations were longer and deeper and this twinning stuff was not as easy as it sounded.

Bud Bud Bud. She said his name over and over in her mind, certain that her voice was penetrating to the very depths of his consciousness.

Then she thought, There ought to be music playing, maybe that "Boat" song. But Bud would rarely allow this, even with the music turned to a whisper, because Bud had to be alert for whoever might be trying to blindside him.

More than one person, if you wanted to know the truth, wanted Bud blindsided. They wanted very much to see Bud dead, as did for instance that man who had called earlier.

She knew that was what that man's call was about because she could hear it in his voice. When the man said "Is Bud there?" he was envisioning a world without Bud in it, even if that man didn't know it his own self. The same as with Andrew Jackson who wanted the entire Cherokee nation to disappear and had little regard, besides the irritation, for how this came to pass.

Bud Bud Bud, Idena said, almost aloud, and with a quiet, quick hand swept the money off the bed.

She could see a box filled with this money, and batted her eyes to keep herself from seeing where that box was. Then she was momentarily grief-stricken because she saw not only where the box was, but that the box had human company. The box was down in the basement, which Bud trusted her never to enter, not even in the spectral way she was entering it now, and the human company was a woman with red hair, laid out on a cot she also saw down there.

Then she felt relief, because the woman was breathing.

Anyway, as for the music, because of his blindside Bud had to forego music, his love of music, and tap his feet only to the music that was in his head.

She ought to tell Bud about that call. She ought to wake him and tell him, if in fact he was asleep.

He wasn't entirely asleep, she knew that; he was on the edge of sleep. From the edge of sleep he could rise in a flash and protect her and himself from anything that threatened.

She had full faith in his powers.

Every time she saw Bud he was driving a different automobile. They were always the latest models, the luxury kind, fitted with the very best radio and CD player and so much secret stuff Idena could barely keep up.

Bud said she could work if she wanted to but she didn't have to work, although he thought it was demeaning to do that lap-dancing business at the tables. She had said that time they had this discussion, What does demeaning mean, Bud? And he had explained it in such a nice easy way that suddenly she understood with utter clarity.

So she would never ever again do that lap-dancing business any more than she would go upstairs with anyone who was not Bud.

Bud Bud Bud, she thought again, feeling sorrowful now and giving in to the faintest nub of self-pity.

But after a while, struck by how much she was being the backwards child, Idena gave up this line of thought. She relaxed and wondered if she and Bud would fall asleep, truly, deeply asleep at the same eternal moment and be possessed by the same happiness.

"Are you happy, Bud?" she asked.

He didn't say he wasn't.

But she waited, aware that omni spirits were present in the room, and in another moment these spirits would compel Bud to squeeze her hand.

Bud squeezed her hand.

Bud could hear a person speaking even in his sleep, even if that person spoke in a whisper so low even the lowest beast could not say for sure a sound had been uttered.

He squeezed her hand three times.

Y

E

S, he was saying.

Idena felt wonderfully relieved. She felt elated. She believed she could say with truth that Bud was the one person, man or woman, she had ever in this life made happy. Oh, for fifteen minutes, yes, she supposed she had made people happy, made them forget themselves or release some of their anxieties — but never this way, never the way it was now with Bud.

Idena said, "On this trip, did you sleep with other women?"

Bud murmured from his edge of sleep, "Not many."

Idena thought that a fabulous answer. She cuddled herself closer to him, wrapping his waist in her long paws and kissing the warm flesh of his neck and shoulders. She heard his breathing stretch out, become like sighs, light and airy. He was falling into cosy slumber and she was too.

"I love you, Bud," she said.

"I know. You've loved me since antiquity."

The biggest fault Idena could find with Bud is that he did not believe in a beforelife any more than he did an after one. She could cite a thousand proofs of both, but Bud would remain unimpressed. She had known for a fact, the minute she slipped into this dog suit, that in a prior incarnation she had been this same white dog with the floppy ears and long tail. What her spirit control, the wonderful and scary Neste, told her about Bud — but which made Bud fume when she told him — was that Bud's decisive incarnation had been on the island of Iona thousands of years ago. It had been so decisive that all his other incarnations, down to the present day, had been born with painted eyes.

At that time on the isle of Iona Bud had been the monk Udran — or Odran, Odan, some called him. Udran had been canonized by the church through several centuries for having had the pluck to volunteer to be buried alive in the foundation of the monastery erected on Iona by St. Columba. But eight centuries after being buried, Neste said, it had been decided that his bones would be dug up. Lo, the surprise of all, when it was discovered that Udran was still alive. Alive, though not the same, having turned bitterly blasphemous. Promptly upon liberation from those walls, Bud or Udran began preaching that there was no heaven and no hell, neither a god nor a satan, no begotten son, and that the whole of the monks' religion was a skimble-skamble of myth and legend, of outright lies and ideas derived from the becrazed cults belonging to previous eons. He was so bitter, Neste said, that blood shot from his eyes and his very intestines and kneecaps and testicles ran crimson. St. Columba's monk devotees, recovering from their shock, drove spears through Udran's heart. He went on ranting. Decapitation followed. Whereupon, sea-hawks flapped from his every orifice. Through several horrendous minutes, the monks stomping and gesticulating, Udran wriggled about in the dust in serpent form. Boiling water was poured over the serpent, which was then cut into a thousand wafers. Only towards midnight did the serpent go back to being Udran's bones. But then, lo: a mighty storm beclouded the isle, waves tossed, the heavens raged, every monastery wall collapsed, towers tumbled; in the conclusion every man present was buried alive in the rubble and the island itself sank into the sea under glow of fiendish moonlight. There the island remained for a thousand years, until a phalanx of fish of the deep and then cranes of the air brought it back.

"I really do, deeply, deeply, and forever love you, Bud," Idena said.

But Bud was asleep and so beautiful and warm within her embrace that Idena was perfectly content to let herself drift right in there where he was.

"Ka, ka, ka," Idena said in her sleep — which was the name given Brahma's twinned soul, and means *"Who, who, who?"*

Ka yha lu: who goes there?

When Idena awakened she felt a moment of tremendous exhilaration, imagining that she had been transported to another civilization — which was something that happened with amazing frequency, especially during love-making. Then she realized it was Bud shaking her, because there was his hand on her shoulder and his face above her. "Stay in here," she heard him say. "Don't make any noise. If you hear shooting, go fast as you can out of the window."

"Okay, Bud."

Then he left, pulling the door shut.

She sat up in bed, glad to see that she was no longer wearing the dog suit. It was ruefully warm in the room. "My goodness," she said to herself in the vanity mirror, "is this the tropics?" She remembered now that sometime in the night Bud had pitched back the duvet, undressed her, and they had made a love so beautiful that she believed she was afloat among the stars. She had climaxed about eleven times, with lots of little halves and almost-coming.

Until Bud's arrival on the scene Idena had not had one orgasm in this life; she had told all her friends that she was frigid, an Ice Maiden.

It occurred to her that it could be that was how the man who telephoned had known to do so, because she had confessed to more than one or two of her truly bosom friends at the club that her Ice Maiden days were over, thanks to the new love in her life, Bud. She hadn't seen the harm in that, despite Bud's warnings, thinking there must be at least a thousand Buds around, so how would anyone know that her Bud was *the* Bud? But word must have got around and now if anyone was to hurt Bud it would be her fault. If someone hurt Bud, her fault or whoever's, she would just have to kill herself and go back to being nothing, which, truly, is what most of the dead were, horrible though it sounds.

She sat a moment in a near trance, to calm down.

She needed to visit the ladies, but Bud had told her to remain in the room and make no noise and when Bud said a thing you knew he meant it. So she only opened the door a fraction, to peek and listen. Then she heard car doors slam outside and flew to the window.

Right out in front was a long white limousine. Two burly men with porcine eyes, needing a shave, in army fatigues so dirty they were almost stiff, had got out and now another person was alighting from the big space in back. The man alighting was having trouble and looked like he needed help, though no one was offering any. All three had a terrible aura, of a muddy gray color, and scummy. Idena knew who the one man was because of the crutches and because of his spastic movements. This was Jude, the invisible soldier who had been returned from foreign wars. His picture was on big billboards all over town, and as she studied him now she could see a white golf ball slicing off into the trees, although not exactly who had hit it.

Now Bud was going to really be mad at her, although, to give him credit, he didn't seem to have been mad a minute ago, only concerned for her welfare. He had been holding a revolver in the hand that had not been shaking her, so he was ready for trouble. Now there was Bud coming in view. He had been waiting outside their front door and now he was crossing down to greet these surly visitors. She heard the crippled man say his name, it coming out "Bud Bud Bud" — which tickled her, since she often said his name that way herself, although this man's tone was not exactly caviar on a cracker. It was not friendly. Bud did not say the man's name back. Bud had his nice regular aura, greenish, but with red or orange swipes mixed in, which was Bud's usual aura in situations fraught with danger. Bud's was the busiest aura of any person Idena had ever seen, all swirly and bubbly, with the smell of red clay.

The Jude one, when he was four or five feet from the car stopped, and said, "Gimme a hug, Bud."

Idena could see that Bud did not want to hug Jude. But Bud did, just for a second, their auras wary and not touching, just the way had happened on TV at the Masters golf tourney when Jude shook hands with Tiger Woods, or Wood, and Tiger's aura took on the shape of a spitting cat.

Then the Jude one said, "Miss Chudd is highly pissed off at you. I think I can say the Friends as a whole are. The cash, that's nothin', but why did you have to burn her house down? She'd just finished renovatin', hadn't been in the house six fuckin' months."

Idena was curious to hear Bud's answer. He did not allow cursing inside the house, and might have wanted to apply the same rules to the yard. But he didn't say anything. He slouched there, looking at his nails. The group was now in the yard proper, slowly drifting towards the front door. They were all keeping a close eye on Bud, and Idena thought, Well, wouldn't you?

"I didn't like how she'd done the house," Bud said. "Too much black marble."

The Jude man's mouth dropped open, and a second went by before Idena heard what she knew, even without her powers, was a kind of put-on laugh.

Jude said, "You burn her house down, her sister goes over a mountain. Car accident. A hard day for the Chudds."

"Too bad," Bud said.

"Then there are all those other matters."

Bud shifted about so that Idena could see his face. It seemed to her that his glance came right at her, before sweeping on to the other two men and settling on Jude. Bud did not look nervous or even remotely bothered. He looked real together, as did his aura. He had both hands under his suit coat, under his arms pits like his hands were cold. Bud did sometimes have cold hands even in the warmest weather, which was why Idena had been grinding up aspirin and sneaking them to him in dishes of ice cream. Aspirin was good for cold hands because it thinned the blood and thin blood could better travel to one's extremities. Even in the Egyptian tomb they had known about aspirin.

Jude said, "One, there's the Senator's girl, that Twinkle Toes. He was highly pissed off at you, I will say that. Although what the Senator thinks, or thought, hardly matters. But you know as I do, Bud, that the girl is sick and ought to be in an institution. It appears you absconded with her. Where'd you put her? We want to return the poor thing to her distraught Mama."

Bud said, "That might prove difficult. Her Mama is dead."

Idena had no idea what the Jude man was talking about. She must have been sleeping, or generally occupying another plane, when all that happened.

Jude and the other two men had moved on up to the door, almost out of Idena's sight. But Bud had stayed out in the yard, and now they were having to come back.

Jude said, "Where'd you hide the intern?"

Idena thought about President Clinton as the crippled man Jude employed that word, and her head spun, because sometimes the President's intern walked right into her mind, wanting to take over.

Bud shrugged.

"Then we come to the hard one. What'd you do with Motel Molly? My people saw you coming out with a body. The deal was you'd leave the witch there to burn."

Bud was smiling. Idena was smiling, too, because she saw the basement woman sitting up on the cot, holding her hands to her head because she had a terrible headache and the taste in her mouth, the fumes in her stomach, were so awful. But she was alive and Bud had done a wondrous thing. He had stepped between the victim and the serpent.

"You gone soft, Bud?"

Idena could see that the two men with Jude were getting itchy with all this talk. They had squared off to either side of Bud, their gun hands out of sight.

"She dead, Bud?"

Bud was smart. He made no comment.

"It don't matter. We'll find her. Find both of them. Maybe we already have."

Idena was feeling uncommonly cold. She stuck her legs into the dog suit and pulled it on.

"Then there's the case of our Neck people. I know you'll be relieved to learn the two officers made it."

"I thought they had a good chance."

One of the other men said something and Jude told him to put a foot in it.

"Although they may be brain dead."

Bud said, "That will be a step up. Now you can run them for public office."

Jude's metal legs and crutches went clankety-clank. Idena saw that he was mad. His aura was leaping like fire from a pit.

"You got a weapon under that coat, Bud?"

Bud said, "I don't think you want to see it."

"You know how many people I've killed?"

"Where? At My Lai?"

Jude's jaw popped open again. Then he laughed. "My Lai. Did I hear you say My Lai?"

"Wasn't that where you first made your name? At My Lai?"

"Goddamn," said Jude. "I had almost forgot about My Lai. Now you say to me, 'My Lai.' Are you real, Bud?" Then Jude turned to his gang and said, "Can you believe this guy?"

The woman in the basement was off the cot and twisting the door knob, which wouldn't turn. She was naked except for the white sheet wrapped around her, which she kept losing. Idena thought she was very beautiful.

Jude had hobbled back to his limousine. He sat on the seat, the door open. He was perspiring, although to Idena's mind the day was not that hot.

"Don't tell me you were the pansy wrote those letters to Congress, let the cat out of the bag."

Bud didn't reply.

Then Jude was again turning to his associates, saying, "347 we got at My Lai, men, women, and children. I reckon about a hundred children. Like it mattered a fuck. 'My Lai,' Bud says to me. Wait till I tell Calley."

The associates laughed.

They had real pig eyes, Idena thought.

"You ought not to burnt down the Senator's birthplace, Bud. That was an insult against the republic."

"I had permission."

Jude got himself properly in and one of his people closed the car door.

"You can shoot the son of a bitch if you have the nerve," Jude told them.

Idena could see the man at the car door and the others were thinking about it. They were itching to do it.

Bud Bud Bud, she thought.

The sheeted woman in the basement had found a hacksaw and was sawing off the doorknob.

Idena pulled open the drapes hiding her. She was careful to make a big noise and direct all her best ESP thoughts out onto the grass. She stood at the window in full view in her dog suit. Jude saw her and then all of those out there turned to see what had made the noise.

"Shit," one of them said. "I can't kill a man in front of his dog."

Idena scratched at the glass with her paws. She whined to get outside where her master was.

The other man had his gun out but Bud already had his beside that one's head, grinding the barrel into the man's ear.

"Maybe you can kill a man in front of his dog," he said.

"No," the man said. "No, I can't."

Bud took the man's pistol and stuck his own inside his belt.

After a minute Jude spoke from the limo's open window: "We can't have Little Miss Muffet and Motel Molly hurting the Friends, Bud."

"They got new friends," Bud said.

"I can't get over the shit you pull," Jude said. "Just like your old man."

The limo pulled away. In the second it did, Idena in her dog suit went flying, because the sheeted woman was out of her locked room and climbing upstairs in a rage.

Idena supposed she would have to proffer some kind of good explanation.

CHAPTER TWELVE

ALONZO

"I need to talk to you," Alonzo said to Pat Fish.

"Okay. Talk."

This was after Zippo had gone in to raid the fridge and before he'd taken a bullet through the window. They were sitting out in the swing, watching white clouds float across the moon.

"Where should I begin?" Alonzo asked.

"I don't know," Pat Fish said. "It's your story."

Following his unconsummated, painful love affair and break up with a girl named Lottie Pons, Alonzo spent the little money he had on a cheap room down by the tracks, payable by the week. He kept back ten dollars to spruce himself up. The sprucing led to any number of menial jobs, those which found his arms up to their elbows in grease in this or that kitchen, sometimes tending counter, doing back work with cartage companies, once working security at a Brinks depot gate. The pay was get-by pay, fall-more-and-more-in-debt pay, but he applied himself. He made a point of cleaning his nails regularly, shampooing his hair, keeping his shoetops shiny, his room tidy. He kept himself more or less fit, working pick-up scrimmages, basketball, with guys at the Y, all so Lottie Pons one day would respect him. He couldn't have her love, he'd at least have that. In his spare time he read up on bailbonding, computer programming, dog breeding, hawking, and any number of other professions at the public library, but found nothing that fit very well with his sparse preparation for entry into the job market. "You'll regret it" were words that had haunted him since his youth, and now were with him more or less constantly, those words issuing from the lips of his otherwise faceless parents, this and that teacher. He could be strolling along the street, to or from work or the library, longing for Lottie Pons, and the Dewars man in tails up on the billboard would suddenly be wagging his cane, saying the same thing. Women on the billboards would glare at him, saying, "Alonzo, you'll never amount to anything." At other times they would employ the past tense, "He never amounted to anything," which made him feel that he'd already passed over to the other side with no one taking the trouble to inform him.

At 7-Eleven, where he was filling in on the night-till-morning shift, two men strung out on dope pointed revolvers at the cash register, then at his face. "Open it, dipshit, or die," one of them said, just as they would on TV. In fact, Alonzo could lift his eyes and see them in the monitor, see himself too, although the angle was screwy, the three of them there like in a circus fun mirror. Both thieves had baseball caps on their heads, the bills slanted, their shirt fronts open, their chests bare. The one speaking wore a belt in his pants that was about a foot too long, hanging almost to his knees. Gaunt face, pallid, oily hair, the pair's eyes so bony it looked like the eyes were trying to escape their sockets and run away.

"Do it, dipshit," the other said.

Alonzo had never been on their side of the counter, not exactly, although his sympathy was with them. Their case was as hopeless as his was, ignoring the immediate circumstances. But they had never had someone like Lottie Pons in their lives to offer the fellow a direction in life and enrich his life with the misery of being smitten by love's lost cause.

Alonzo lifted a thumb to the sign just behind him. The sign clearly spelled out the facts. There was never more than fifty in the till and the night clerk did not possess a key to the safe.

The thieves were in no special hurry. They took the time to peruse the message, reading it, Alonzo thought, about three times. But the message made little imprint on their combined cognitive processes.

"Don't shoot me no bullshit," the one said. "We know better than that crap."

Both had rings in their ears. One had tattoos cut into his brow, talons leading up from the eyebrows — a flapping bird coming Alonzo's way above each of the boy's eyes. Alonzo looked hard at the birds, caught off balance, unable to determine whether the birds tattooed there on the boy's brow were water birds, herons, say, or hawks or eagles or, possibly, even vultures.

Alonzo moved aside as they rounded the counter and hit the No Sale button on the till. The cash drawer sprung open.

All Alonzo had to do was shift his foot an inch or two to press the alarm button in the floor. He lifted one foot and then the other, avoiding the button. The thieves did not look to him as though they would make it through the night, regardless of what he did. They would melt into eternity. A few weeks from now no one would know they had ever existed.

"There are twenties under the change drawer," he told them.

"Who asked you?"

For reasons known only to himself, the speaker, the boy with the tattooed eyes, swung the gun butt, but missed Alonzo altogether. His momentum all but toppled him over.

The other one was sweeping cigarettes into a white pillowcase. These two bad boys every week or two, just as he did, would troop down to the washeteria nearest their place, stuff the machine full, and ram in the quarters. Then they'd sit and smoke and fart and oink trivialities at each other, leaf through ten-year-old mags, and eye the housewives and the spinning detritus of their lives through the machines' soapy portholes.

They scooped up the twenties. They swooped toiletries, pills, other goods, into the pillowcase. They were ready to go, though still in no hurry. They hadn't even glanced up the aisles for other customers or once looked at the door. The one with the eyebrow bird tattoos was stuffing Tylenol caplets into his mouth, just about the whole bottle.

"I think me I'll shoot this motherfucker just so I can sleep tonight," the other one said.

"Yeah," the one with the eyebrows said. "Shoot the grim motherfucker."

The word *grim* shocked Alonzo awake. It was not a word he had been expecting to hear. He found himself cocking his head, wetting his lips, nodding, his own brow somehow going hot and sweaty. It was like the word grim, in the thief's mouth, had the force to whirl him back through time, through all the grimness involving Lottie Pons, even back to his life with his parents, who certainly were grim. But *grim* was not a word that he would have thought applied to himself. As he looked at the wasted thief, the thief with the cadaverous face, with two birds flapping at him from the boy's eyebrows — this boy chewing the Tylenol, yelling *"Shoot him! Shoot him!"* — Alonzo realized, with Lottie Pons never having said so, why Lottie Pons had done her best to avoid him and why finally she'd refused to speak to him or ever see him again. He had seen himself as one not exactly full of life, not bubbly or a laugh a minute, certainly, but certainly not grim. Yet here was this boy with birds of prey across his brow, this boy who possibly would not survive the night, saying, yes, shoot the grim motherfucker.

Likely, one or another of the pair would have done so. But a customer chose that moment to come through the door. The robbers didn't know it — Alonzo didn't either — until the ping. They all whirled simultaneously and in the instant one of the thieves fired. Fired three times. One bullet shattered the plate glass window, another went into the ceiling, the third took out the door. The customer took a step back and crashed on his backside through the glass door. The thieves were screaming at each other. Their legs were moving, it looked like they were running, but in fact all they were doing was jittering in place, going nowhere.

Alonzo grabbed each by the hair and banged their heads together. They crumpled at his feet. He kicked their pistols away and hurried to see about the man who had fallen through the door onto the sidewalk. He was sure the man had been shot. The man was still down on his back, glass beneath and around him, bleeding cuts on his hands and face. Each time he made the smallest movement, he yelped.

"Stay cool," Alonzo said. "Help here in a minute."

That was how Alonzo became a hero. He was written up in the local paper, along with a photograph, Alonzo looking happy — embarrassed, innocent — not grim.

He bought twenty copies, thinking he would mail the story to friends — one to Lottie Pons, certainly — but in the end he didn't. He didn't have twenty friends, or even one, and he decided Lottie Pons would respect him more if he honored her with his silence.

And his fame was fleeting. Inside two weeks the newsprint yellowed. Alonzo threw it all out. Shortly afterwards, 7-Eleven laid him off. The Mom and Pop store in the next block had shellacked them, Slurpies among the pubescent crowd being about all, in this neighborhood, the chain had going. He could have a transfer to another store, but it would mean moving or buses, getting there and getting back, so Alonzo said no. They gave him his last pay in a manila envelope the size of a vest pocket. The manager had misspelled his name. By Alonzo's accounting, his pay packet was six hours short.

When Alonzo pointed this out, the manager, a Mr. Elves, got a certain light in his eye, and said, "So sue me. I hate you fucking happy-go-lucky cowboys."

Alonzo didn't say anything. He'd done okay. He wasn't mad at the manager or at himself. The thirty dollars held back would go into the manager's pocket. Maybe that way a thousand or so would be added to the man's annual income. He would move on to a bigger, better store. Grow old, retire, and die. All would equalize itself in the end.

When the cops carted away the two strung-out thieves their baseball caps were left behind on the floor. Alonzo tried them on for size, first one then the other. The thieves had small heads. The caps wouldn't fit, even with the straps fully expanded. They smelled; the bills were sweaty, oily. Alonzo could sniff the insides and remember the boys and what they said. The press stated one was nineteen, named Owen Butts, the other seventeen, named Oslow Meadows.

In the phone book there were pages and pages of names identical or nearly identical to these. Alonzo would look at the pages and think about the lives those people lived. He speculated on whose life was better and whose worse and how his own stacked up against theirs.

Once, with nothing to do, he called the number listed for a woman named Jewel Meadows. Jewel said, "Hi!" She said, "Hi, from Jewel Meadows. Jewel can't come to the phone this minute, on account of being otherwise engaged. If it's orders you want to place, then please call between the hours eight and eight." It wasn't until the beep that Alonzo realized he had got an answering machine.

She said she would get back to him at the earliest possible moment, but she never did.

Maybe he was out.

Later in the month, looking for rent money, his hot plate burnt out and needing a replacement, Alonzo made instant coffee tepid from the tap, and caught the number 62 bus down to the unemployment office. He said to the woman there that what he wanted was a job at her desk, since they never seemed to do anything except tell the person at the head of the line that there was nothing for them today. He told her they ought to put their spiel over loudspeakers so that all the people waiting in line could get the message at once, and go on home.

"Or do you think your way of doing things helps build character?"

The woman said to him that his problem was one of attitude. "You're a sour-ass," she said.

Tons of jobs were up for grabs, she said. Only look at the board. There were employers just crying for good men and women, but the men and women were unwilling to dirty their hands. They came in here and lied about the jobs they had looked for. A generation of welfare handouts from liberal do-gooders had made the common man and woman so common they held employment involving hard labor of any kind in outright contempt.

Alonzo said, "Where are these crying employers? I want to see them."

The woman said, "Excuse me, did I just see you wink at me?" She was trying to catch the guard's eyes. She was repeatedly pressing a bell on her desk. "Your attitude belongs in the ape age. I think you better move along."

Over on the board were about three dozen yellow cards announcing job openings, but they all seemed to be for the same job. They were for jobs in another end of the state, or in Alaska or on Mars, and it would cost you an arm and a leg to get to them. It was the women in the lines with babies on their hips, tired women standing on spread legs, looking at the floor, that tended to get him down. Across the street from the employment center was a flophouse for the homeless, thirty-two beds, and the city had to lay in first a zebra crosswalk to condition the traffic flow, and then a traffic light, and then to station a traffic cop permanently there because so many drunks were being run down. Alonzo didn't like to say so but he had been forced to give up his single room, sell off the mended hot plate, and, until his luck changed, take up temporary residence in the flophouse.

Alonzo was in the soup line one day, waiting to get his nourishment, when he saw two goon-like creatures casing the joint. He looked at them and they looked at him, then both sidled up to him.

He was asked was he in the market for day work or night work.

Alonzo said he preferred something out in the sun, but him and night work could get along.

"Zippo," one of them said, "is looking for machine men. We hear you are a machine man. For novices he pays twice above minimum, a bonus for those who can keep their traps shut."

Other exchanges led to coffee with the two men at a nearby donut shop.

Alonzo was quick enough to understand that Zippo was in the rackets, since they told him so with the first sip, and in the second sip he was led to understand why and how they could use him. A shoe shipment was in the works, more than the usual gang could manage, so Zippo was recruiting extra staff. You worked under a full moon in a quiet environment, hardly got your hands dirty, plus you had the benefit of comradeship with a close-knit group pulling together in a common cause.

"Plus one thing leads to another," a heavy said. "There is definitely upward movement, the vertical ladder like on Wall Street."

Then they got down to it.

"We hear you can work cranes?"

"Cranes?"

In the heavy equipment course at Paradise Business College Alonzo had sat for five minutes in a crane cab. The instructor had pointed out the functions of the various gears, levers, pedals, buttons. He had told Alonzo it was important to keep the cage clean. To be wary of steep inclines. Oversized boulders could be a menace. Spiked boots were a no-no.

Alonzo had not been permitted to actually touch any of the gears, levers, pedals, buttons. He could hardly get the door open.

"The proficient crane operator is good for sixty to eighty an hour," he said, negotiating.

"It's a matter of responsibility," he said. "The proficient crane operator is sitting in a million dollar piece of equipment. You push the wrong lever and there goes your million dollar investment."

The men signalled for a refill.

"One swoop of the ball and one of those machines can collapse a forty-storey building."

"How are they with trains?" the heavy said.

"No problem," Alonzo said. He hadn't a clue.

"Say whole boxcars filled with U.S. quarters?"

"Easy as pie."

It surprised him when both men stood and shook his hands.

"Follow us," they said.

"Are you finished?" asks Pat Fish.

"Yes."

"Well, that's a most informing tale," Pat Fish says. "But I have to ask why you've kept me awake, not a drink between us, telling me this grim story."

They have risen from the porch swing, are passing down the stairs on their way to the cabin in the woods. Ready at last, daylight almost upon them, to hit the hay.

"I thought you should know something about me, for when the time comes."

"The time comes?"

"Yes."

"For what?"

"I'm all over Lottie Pons. Lottie is ancient history."

"Glad to hear it. Lottie a woman without virtue, far as I can see. But I am still in the dark."

"It's like this. Over at the bighouse, doing Glo's laundry, putting that laundry away, I see Dolores Giocametti's photograph."

"Yeah?"

"I'm looking at it and I fall in love. So I was thinking, because of how close you are to the parents, it's appropriate you know something about me before we marry."

"You're going to wed Doe?"

"Dolores. Yeah. I know it. I can feel it."

A few seconds later, there comes the bullet for Zippo through the window.

CHAPTER THIRTEEN

PERU

Two policemen arrived in a cruiser at Pancho's bar. Chantelle Peru was showing them her ID when one of them said, "Yeah, we know you, doll. Don't touch anything." She was seated at the table by the broken window, drinking Pancho's muddy coffee from the Black & Decker, smoking a rare cigarette, a hefty glass of cognac to the side. "I guess you got good reason to drink," said the cop, moving the VSOP bottle a shade. "Since half your law suit's dead on the floor." He was thick-set, with squat legs, a limestone face and insufficient eyes. The second one was in the cruiser radioing in for a homicide team.

Wally came. He'd seen the cruiser turn the corner, Chantelle guessed, maybe had even heard the shots.

Half-a-dozen gawkers stood across the street. The policemen with the chip told Wally to shut the fuck up, although Wally hadn't said anything.

"No, you stay the fuck out."

So Chantelle took her cognac outside. It was hot, maybe that explained why the cops were so surly. But then, Jude and the Senator had done everything they could to make Jude the genuine article and Wally and Pancho dregs out for a quick buck. Maybe the birdbrain cop watched golfing tournaments.

She wondered if she possessed a mothering instinct after all because the first thing she did was take a comb to Wally's ragged hair. She adjusted the doorman's coat over his shoulders, brushed dust from lapels and sleeves.

"There," she said. "Spic and span." Just the way a mother would.

"Ish do this?"

"Not Ish. Ish was nowhere near here. I think this was a hit, Wally. I'm not sure how safe any of us are."

The cop said, "Dint I tell you two to shut your faces?"

"Why don't you sit on it?" Chantelle told him. "And if you look at me like that again, I'll throw a sexual harassment charge against your redneck ass."

"Look at me shake."

The press beat the detective team there by a good twenty minutes. Chantelle had done pretty well rounding up a press corp: three TV people with their crew, one radio person, the news services, a reporter from the *Post*, a *New York Times* stringer.

"What happened?" they wanted to know.

"Another tavern knocked over," the cop said. "Strictly routine."

Standing on a chair, Chantelle told them that Pancho's killing was not the result of a simple robbery but was in fact an act of political assassination. Pancho's death, she maintained, was not unassociated with the forty million dollar suit being waged against the federal government. She would tomorrow file in district court new documents intended to increase the value damage of said suit to one billion. Yes, one billion. Her clients, she stated, would not be intimidated by the loathsome murder of one of their party, a man whose government had stolen three decades of his life and now taken that life altogether. She had every faith that justice would triumph in the end.

She reminded the press that the U.S. Congress, the Office of the President, Defense, Foreign Affairs, together with other federal offices including the First Lady's soft-soap commission, had dragged butt on this Invisible Soldiers issue from the beginning; moreover, assorted bureaucrats and elected officials had erected roadblocks all along the way. A conspiracy existed. But she and Wally, for the sake of the thousands still over there, would not be deterred. She affirmed that her mission to find and return these soldiers to native soil had received not one cent of public funding but was being funded solely by a private citizen whose name she was as yet not privileged to reveal. Yes, she believed this party would provide sufficient funds to take this case all the way to the Supreme Court if necessary.

In the rump quiz that followed her opening remarks, the *Times* stringer requested clarification as to the identity of this anonymous donor.

Chantelle Peru refused such clarification.

The *Times* man said that he had heard that organized crime was funding her cause.

Chantelle said, "If true, then organized crime has taken over the rightful duties of our Federal government."

The radioman, from a rock station catering to eight-year-olds, liked that part.

"Why is your benefactor providing this assistance?" persisted the *Times* fellow.

"Because our cause is just."

Everybody groaned. Since elimination of the national debt had become the mandate, D.C. had not gone in for that kind of talk.

"To right heinous wrongs insofar as they can be righted," Chantelle said, making matters worse. The press people were putting away their notepads.

"How much has been contributed?"

"One million."

"Should your case succeed, will your donor receive any part of the proceeds?"

"Only the mercies derived from God."

One of the camerawomen panned around to get a shot of a near-by church steeple. Chantelle sensed then that the scum was dead.

"What proof do you have that Pancho's death is, as you claim, 'a political assassination'? Where's the conspiracy?"

"I have no further comment on that at this time."

"So you have no proof."

"I did not say that."

"Earlier you have stated that extremist or fanatical factions in this country have — " The *Times* guy wouldn't give up.

"I have said that Senator Roy Otis Cutt, a defendant in this suit, has enlisted the aid of his umbrella organization, The Friends For A Restored America, in combatting our goals. That, I believe, is a matter of public record."

"Are you aware, Ms. Peru, that unverified reports have been circulating as to the Senator's possible death?"

"No, I am unaware of . . . Wait a minute." Chantelle was flustered, thinking *Where've I been? Did the world move while Ish was fondling my ear lobes?* "I find that more than passing strange," she said, "since not three hours ago a dozen people must have seen the Senator entering the N Street building not one hundred yards from where we stand. I — "

But that was where she totally lost them.

The press scrambled away to the building in question.

In this way did the nation first learn of the Senator's death in the N Street penthouse and the connection between that penthouse and one known Mafia don, Zippo Giocametti. The discovery of the Senator's interment within the penthouse walls, with extensive footage of cameras panning the new tilework, the whirlpool, the hot tub, the Senator's room devoted to bizarre John Edgar Hoover memorabilia, the even stranger room devoted to his dead mother, blew the Pancho story, and Chantelle's accusations, into media oblivion.

Muriel Goering wasn't mentioned. It would be later in the day before the second body was discovered and in the confusion early reports would suggest the corpse was that of a young intern recently seen in the Senator's company. How investigators could confuse a skinny thirteen-year-old's body with the obese frame of seventy-six-year-old Muriel was never adequately explained.

News reports that night stressed the Senator's lifelong support of militarism, tobacco subsidies, the death penalty, space exploration, his vehement opposition to welfare and education expenditures, to Fidel Castro's Cuba, to abortion, equal rights, arms control, civil rights for blacks in his native south, public funding for the arts. His many America First patriotic initiatives "around the globe" were exhumed and trumpeted as being consistent with the great American ideals.

Throughout the press scrum Wally sat on the curb, his limbs no longer twitching and thrashing; he seemed himself to have died. Chantelle decided he had been around death so much that he had become shy in its presence, and reluctant to defend himself against its summons.

"Do you want a drink?" Chantelle Peru said, sitting down beside them. "Cognac? Pancho's best."

"Sure," Wally said. "Pancho's best."

Chantelle, nuzzling his shoulder, said, "Let's cry. Do you want to cry?"

"Sure," Wally said. "Let's cry."

"Pancho was good," Wally said a little later. "That's why he got it."

"Right. That's why he got it."

"Un-huh. Why he got it."

"Right. Do you want a drink?"

"Right. A drink."

They sat on the curb, passing the bottle back and forth, toasting Pancho.

Wally said, "All these centuries, you know, we've had it wrong."

"How's that?"

"The bad don't get it."

"No, the evil never get it."

"They don't get it. The good get it . . . in the belly, the head, the heart, but the bad death never touches."

"Never. Right. Have a drink."

"Thanks. Or it gets them by mistake, I think, and they instantly come reincarnated in different disguises . . . "

"I'm following you. I know where you're coming from."

"They wear different suits, have different hair-cuts, speak with different accents, but they're unrolling the same ball of twine — "

"Yeah?"

"But they're the same people. They didn't get it. The good got it but the bad didn't."

"I get what you're saying. Have a drink."

"Thanks. They are with us forever."

"Maybe so. But we are going to take their bad little asses for one billion bucks."

CHAPTER FOURTEEN

DOE

Dolores, Doe, on Air Canada 246 out of Vancouver, in fresh despondency over deceitful government policy and prick forestry giants who would stripcut, denude, violate each inch of the entire northwestern continent in pursuit of ever-increasing profit . . . Dolores on the jumbo 740, arrival time, Dulles, 2:32, only two hours late thanks to delays on the tarmac, turbulence over Moose Jaw, then slowed by headwinds, lightning bolts over the Corn Belt . . . Doe, Dolores, packed back there in coach with two hundred eighty-six other sardines, thinks, as the movie winds down, as the aisles clog with the head's vanguard, as she hides her eyes from blinding daylight flashing through the shade slit . . . Dolores thinks:

Okay. Calm down.

Oh, my poor Papa. Oh, please, God, do not let my Papa die.

The pinched-faced woman occupying the window seat says to Dolores: "I was complaining to my mother one day about a year ago that I never seemed to make any new friends. My old friends, you see, had sort of disappeared from the picture. And my mother said, 'You need to find a way of breaking the ice. Say you're with a group of people and you want to make an impression. Ask them what is their favorite recipe. Men especially will be charmed by this.' So that's what I've been doing. Do you have a favorite? It's become a hobby of mine, collecting recipes. What's yours?"

The woman says: "One day my husband came home announcing he had a new sure-fire diet plan. We would eat anything we wanted. We could eat as often as we wanted. The secret of his new plan was that you never swallowed any of this food. You chewed, you masticated this food that went into your mouth, but you only swallowed the juices. The juices would supply everything the body needed."

The woman says to Dolores: "I was happily married for thirty years. The secret of our happy marriage was this: once every six months or so my husband and I had a 'Get-Acquainted' night. Our marriage would not have lasted except for that. Are you married? You don't look married."

Doe does not tell the woman that she has no intention ever of getting married. She was going with a guy — ever so briefly going with him — and she is pretty sure now that her father has flown five thousand miles to cut off this boyfriend's hair and destroy this relationship, or the possibilities for there ever being a relationship — not that there ever was that possibility, Otis proving to be so right wing and stupid and such a rat. When she was a kid Zippo smothered her, and still he was doing it. She is going to Brussels soon, launching herself on an exciting new adventure, and putting even more miles between her and her gangster father.

The goofball.

None of this she tells to the woman seated by the window. It is none of the woman's business. She is tempted, however, to tell the woman that her father flew five thousand miles to cut off the so-called boyfriend's hair and to tell her this suitor's name, because this would impress the woman. Not every gangster's daughter goes out with the son of a U.S. Senator. But Doe locks her lips. Why would she want to impress this perfect stranger?

"My dear," says the woman, "why are you crying?"

"It's my father," Doe says. "Apparently someone has shot him."

CHAPTER FIFTEEN

ZIPPO

"Thank goodness," Zippo Giocametti hears his wife saying, *"it was only a head wound."*

Why can't he open his eyes, move his head?

When Zippo Giocametti was rained on that early morning by shattered glass, the bullet missed but a glass sliver thin as a needle was embedded in his scalp. You could see the cut, you could wash away the blood. If you applied your thumbs and opened the wound, dug with a knife, you would see the glass. Otherwise, looking, all you see is the cut. After a time, with tending, the cut stopped bleeding; without the blood, the wound didn't seem very serious. Nothing to get excited about. And it isn't anything, really, to feel dismay over because already Zippo's body is working to reject this foreign element. In a few hours, eight or ten, the glass will work its way to the surface, the incision begin to seal. In the meantime, for all practical purposes, Zippo Giocametti appears, to those assembled by his bedside, unconscious. In the meantime, the hidden glass is there awash in blood invisible to the naked eye, sometimes pressing a nerve. If Zippo were in a position to do so, he would tell you how it feels to him. It feels to him like this foreign object is forming itself into some kind of second and separate brain. It is developing some kind of small, tight universe unto itself, crying out for independence from the rest of his brain. He can feel his blood pulsing, this foreign element shifting, and each time this happens he has to steel his bones, to combat this foreign matter with all the energy he can muster. Otherwise, the invader intends to take over his entire brain — And if that happens . . . well if that happens, how can a person live? So Zippo is putting all his energy into this battle for survival. As a result, he's got the chills one minute, he's burning up the next.

This is good, in one sense, because otherwise those who love him might take him for dead.

A doctor has arrived and departed. He has rolled back Zippo's eyelids, probed with a light his eyes, his mouth and nose, his ears. Perused with strong fingers Zippo's chest, his back, his neck — yanked on Zippo's toes. He's examined the scalp, but what was there to see except a man losing his hair, the same as the doctor has lost his?

"Built like a horse. You never know with these things, but he's breathing calmly, his vital signs are a-okay, pulse normal, temperature iffy. Keep him covered. I'd say you got nothing to worry about."

Zippo wants to say to this quack, "Yeah, but what about my second brain? How about you tell my loved ones what is going on in there?" But of course he can't do this. He can't even twitch. If he relaxes even a second that little brain is going to consume his total being.

"I'm calling Dolores," he hears Glo saying. "I'm going to ask her to come home."

Zippo is finding it hard to focus. He hears a voice and his thoughts spill off into something that happened, or something he heard about, twenty or thirty years ago.

Like that German guy, the actor, who showed up one midnight at Frank Sinatra and Ava Gardner's Van Nuys house. The German guy says to Frank, "Your wife and I have had a torrid affair this entire incredible year! Tonight I am taking her away from you." Frank goes storming to Ava. Ava having to tell Frank, "Frank, I am telling you. Frank, would you listen to me? Frank, rest your tonsils, Frank, it is a joke." The guy in the living room on the down sofa the whole time, having a drink, then saying to Frank, "Frank, what can I tell you? She's a woman, it takes her a while to pack." Frank pitching a blue fit. Then, later on, Frank marries Mia Farrow, and Ava is saying, "I always knew he'd go to bed with a boy. Like those little guys, you know, they got to stick together."

"Why is he smiling?"

Zippo hearing someone say that, but that second brain up there pulsing, so that he can't tell who's talking.

The way Zippo sees them in his mind when in his dreams he sees the people he loves they are all in a beautiful ballroom, arranged on long sofas, chairs, some on each other's laps, quietly conversing one with the other. Crossing a leg, fluttering a bejeweled arm. All waiting for Zippo Giocametti to put in an appearance. Tuxedoed waiters float through, champagne on silver trays, canapés, petite bird-feather morsels on these dainty, ridiculous crackers too small to pick up with human fingers.

Relaxed, all of them, but searching the wings, saying to each other, "Where's Zippo? When is Zippo coming?"

Eventually milling about, offering a cheek, clasping a newcomer's hand, embracing late arrivees, forming small units for conversational purposes, bursting into sudden laughter at this or that witticism, whispering to one another the odd rumor, nugget of information. Explaining how it was, their last trip down the Amazon, how the Ritz isn't what it used to be, what the past Christmas was like down on Mustique.

Obscured by foliage, by the flow of beautiful men, by beautiful women in long gowns with plunging necklines — heels, glitter at the throat — stands a grand piano, lid uplifted, flowers arranged in a gold vase upon the piano's sparkling surface. Indeed, throughout the vast room, everywhere one's eyes turn one is greeted by a lavish abundance of these inspired blossoms — by *ferns, moss, resplendent greenery.*

"— Oh, that's Zippo's work! The man would run a mile to sniff a rose!"

French doors sweep open, seen in a path of radiant sunlight.

A pleasant-looking fellow, handsome as the devil, the very incarnation of your debonair, ludicrously talented being, is seen entering the hall, striding to the piano, bowing. Next, lifting the tuxedo tails, sitting, arranging the black bench to the exact position required — then, as tease only, ripples five elegant fingers along the shining ivory.

— "My God!" people are asking. "Is that Zippo?"

Then Zippo gets down to it: not a polite Brahms, if you please — nothing autumnal, no waltz of empty stars, no leaf at play over moonlit water . . . but lightning arpeggios, fire and ice, water and wind, hell and earth in utter confrontation.

Zippo thinking even with his hands' first romp of the keys that here is a performance that will bring down the house. Immortal gods will awaken and shiver in terror.

But the entire ballroom is now sinking into darkness, Zippo's friends and loved ones all have been forced back into the shadows. There sitting at a long head table are all his enemies.

Zippo continuing his performance.

— "Brilliant!" he hears. "Who would have thought that gangster could play the piano?"

Zippo to humbly rise, take his bows, convey to these many the saintly news: *"Discern, my friends, over the rims of your golden goblets, within the champagne's effervescence, within your very own eyes, the new worlds, the new and different tribes, newly advanced civilizations ever in existence beyond the range of our puny, hopelessly human vision. Discern, my friends — if only you would — those other worlds, these parallel lives, in which magical events — marvels beyond compare — transpire with the ease and regularity of falling rain."*

Then all these enemies in retreat, as if cast away by a spell, his friends and loved ones again apparent in the beautiful ballroom, their eyes shining, the house filling with applause.

Not far from their house here Glo and Zippo have discovered on a hillcrest pasture a weathered bathtub with claw feet, put out in long-ago days as a watering trough for the great animals venturing in from the woods. From the tub one can look out over the whole of the beautiful mountains: rippling hills, misty valleys, meandering streams, great rivers. On the grass beside the tub rests a picnic basket, champagne in a bucket of ice. Glo and Zippo sit very still, in the tub filled with creek water. A deer has walked into the picture and is this minute drinking from the tub.

Dolly in for a tight two-shot, Zippo thinks: the deer and Glo, their heads touching.

"She is on her way."
Who? Who is on her way?

Glo's voice. "Pat Fish, did Zippo ever tell you about his cousin Peppi? Peppi Giocametti?"

"Nope."

"Peppi ran the numbers racket for Papa Giocametti way back when. He was convicted of tax fraud and sent up the river for something like two hundred years."

"No, I don't remember that."

"Peppi is the only inmate of Sing Sing ever allowed a dog."

"A dog? Come on!"

"Peppi made a deal with Mr. Hoover. He'd snitch on Papa if he could have his dog with him in his cell. See, he loved his dog. That dog was a big animal, about up to my waist, which means he would have come to Peppi's chin. So the FBI agents go out to Peppi's place, what do they find but that the dog has expired. From old age or missing Peppi, who knows? The agents are in a fix. Peppi won't snitch on Papa without he has his dog, and Mr. Hoover will boot the agents' butts out to South Dakota if they don't come up with a solution. It is

Peppi's wife, Pieta, who makes the proposal. Her bright idea is to dig up the dog, take it to a taxidermist, and have that pooch stuffed.

"Which they do. Mr. Hoover drives the dog out to Sing Sing, says to Peppi, Here's your dog."

"So what happens? Did Peppi snitch?"

"No, he didn't."

"Why not? He didn't like it his old dog had died?"

"It wasn't so much that. Peppi looks inside the dog's mouth and what he sees in that mouth is another dog, the head of his own dog. His wife has had the one dog stuffed inside Peppi's own dog, which was Pieta's way of telling Peppi that if he snitched on Papa Giocametti Peppi's whole family, including those back in the Old Country, were going to suffer the same fate as those dogs."

Zippo in the bed, in a war with his second brain, knows that he has never heard or told the story that he knows Glorianna Giocametti has just finished telling. Glorianna Giocametti is embellishing family history. She is out there where myth is.

"Later on, Richard M. Nixon got that dog. A gift from Bebe Rebozo, if Tricky Dick will let him hear the missing sixteen minutes in those Watergate tapes. Dick had the dog down in the Florida house, right up next to the grand piano. You remember how Dick liked his dogs?"

CHAPTER SIXTEEN

BUD

First there was the sheeted woman to deal with, and there had been quite the row about that. Bud said he'd saved the sheeted woman's life in the only way he knew how. The sheeted woman said she hadn't wanted to be saved, what with her whole family being turned against her because of the financial issue, and, furthermore, in saving her he'd left her with an excruciating headache from whatever drug it was he'd fed her. Plus he'd driven her across the country locked in the boot of a car, and she didn't know where she could go or what she could do now. Bud said, take that money in the box and run. The sheeted woman said, I don't want anyone's money. If I had wanted money I wouldn't be in this pickle and my own daughter and sister would not have betrayed me and wanted me dead.

Idena told them both to calm down. She told them this was not the end of the world, that being a subject she knew a thing or two about.

Bud shot her a puzzled look. She hadn't told him about any end-of-the-world incarnations.

Then the two women went away and had a quick shower and Idena dressed the woman in some of her pretty clothes.

"You are quite a pair," the woman said.

But did she mean this as a compliment?

That was while Bud was driving the woman to a bank. They were going to get a safety deposit box to hold the money in the other box, less ten thousand cash which the woman would take with her, and from his own account Bud was going to have a cashier's check drawn up in the woman's name, enough to get her through a year in Europe, like maybe on the Greek Isles. After a year the woman could return and reclaim the money in the safety deposit box, do whatever she wanted to do, because in Bud's opinion her family by then would be glad to learn she wasn't dead, and that Friends crowd wanting her land for the Christian Theme Park likely would be looking at daisies.

"In a year," he told her, "your daughter will have discovered new majorette uniforms were not so important after all."

The woman was crying. She was crying at the bank, and on the way to the airport, and in the lounge waiting for her plane to Athens, Greece.

Then she hugged their necks, and went aboard the jumbo, no longer crying, her head erect. She called to Idena that she would mail back the dress. Don't you dare, said Idena. It's a gift.

Bud said to Idena, "Honey, that was a brave thing you did at the window with that dog suit."

Bud had never called her Honey before. He hadn't called her much of anything. Idena felt her eyes moisten.

She was under his arm in the front seat, the duvet and bed linen, her knickknacks and beauty products and a few rags from the closet, her waffle-maker, thrown in a hurry into the back seat.

She was going to miss their cute bungalow. She had been a nice little homemaker in that house, making Bud waffles in the morning when he was there, and cooking up French onion soup and stir fry and her other dynamite specialties in the evenings. She wished they'd had a better vacuum. Bud was a man liked things real clean. If he saw a dirty dish in the sink he'd go bananas.

Idena said with a smile, scrunching up tighter against him, "Where we going now, handsome?"

Bud winked, giving her shoulder a squeeze. "I'm beginning to like your friend Neste," he said.

Idena was thrilled. Hardly anyone except her liked scary, moody Neste, who brought news to Idena from other worlds.

"How is old Neste doing this morning?"

"Fine and dandy, sugar candy. That's Neste!"

Probably pooped, though. It had been some time since Neste had dropped in on Idena out of her rays of dazzling light. Neste was known in her own world as 'the she of the seventh tower.' Neste, long ago, had worked as a whore in the sacred brothel in Rome created by a papal bull of Pope Julius II. Neste had been one of the seven women alongside Mary Magdalene at Jesus's resurrection on Golgotha hill. The apostles hadn't known shit about any of that business until Mary and Neste told them.

Earlier, Neste had seeded the oceans and given ovent to the sky. This was in a place called Hoven, which did not yet exist in another human mind except Neste's own. Later on, in her next incarnation, she had been a mollusc attached to first one rock then another, this at a time before seas possessed names or anyone on two or even four legs was to think about naming them. Neste had been relentlessly pounded by waves over an unfathomable stretch of time called Qfwfg, as indeed she was herself called. Another mollusc had made his existence known, in a manner her mollusc mind at the time could not comprehend. The other mollusc, riding a wave, crawled right up inside her own shell and began such insane vibrations within her salty folds that . . .

Qué va ya.

In one of Idena's own earliest reincarnations she had been Divine Sepulchral Princess, whatever that meant. It hadn't meant much, title-wise, especially that divine part. Idena had the strongest feeling, these days, that it meant she was handmaiden to a prick god — locked away alive inside a tomb when the god died. Oh well, that much was sure fact. This was in the pre-Essene period, long before the many sons of the one God walked the earth. For the one God to have that many sons walking the earth he had to fuck a goddess every night. The goddesses gave birth to one thousand sons who had themselves to fuck a thousand goddesses every night if their ten thousand sons were to walk the earth and carry on the birthright. But they did — the ten thousand — fuck their one hundred thousand goddesses, and over primitive time and through the medieval years up to the present day it all got so diluted, the practice so popular, that the average person now thought he or she had every right to do the same.

In none of these prior manifestations had Idena possessed anything that could truly be viewed as a personal mission; she wondered now, riding across town under Bud's arm and punching the skip button on the car's CD with her naked big toe, what was Bud's or did they have a twin mission. Like (she was thinking), were they *khaibut*, meaning were they shadow one to the other, or did the matter go deeper than that? It could be that she and Bud were creatures of the same *garbha*, or *delphos* — offspring of the one primordial womb.

Idena was wearing cutoffs that dug into her crack and displayed her wholesome cheeks; she had on a Beethoven T-shirt, loose-fitting, though it still revealed her nipples; they were like lovely little tree stumps, proud and beautiful, those nipples, and Bud's pleasure in the sight had not gone unnoticed.

Om mani padme hum, was how Idena thought of it. Oh, how my Bud craves his yoni!

Idena couldn't believe how good she felt today.

She had her nail polish out, doing them in this neat-o fab color that one of her club friends had brought in.

Idena said, "Don't hit any potholes, okay?"

Bud bought the Sunday *New York Times*, which Idena dropped on the floorboards beneath her feet; after a while she began to feel a prickling sensation pass up through the soles of her feet. Opening her knees wide, she looked down and saw on the *Times* front page a photograph of Senator Roy Otis Cutt. The prickling got stronger, like needles stabbing her feet; her body felt hot and the leather seat was hot too, sticking to her body.

"You're quiet," Bud said. "Something bothering you?"

"Nothing I can't handle. Unless you want to talk. You want to talk?"

She peered down between her legs again and saw blood running out of Senator Roy Otis Cutt's mouth.

She blew on her new nails.

She had entered this present life a four-year old in Dayton, Ohio; she hoped she wasn't nearing the end of her term, now that it was just beginning to take off.

Bud asked if she was in that tomb again with the rotting corpse of her master.

"Their embalming was better than ours is today," Idena said. "Salt mixed with pig blood and excrement, that's mostly all it was. He did get this smelly mould, though."

The soles of her feet were burning now; she had to bite her lower lip to keep from screaming out.

At least the blood had stopped.

"Bud, did you ever think about being a really good man? I know a lot of bad things must have happened to you, but did you ever think about it?"

"I was good that year in the caves."

"Bud Bud Bud," she said.

He was looking at her in a really wired way, a way she'd never seen him look before, regardless of who he was looking at. His eyes were lit up, his flesh almost radiant. Idena had a shocking thought: she was a good influence on Bud. She almost fainted with excitement.

Then she said, "The only time I was truly a bad girl was that time I was a slave in the Mississippi cotton fields."

Idena hadn't told him much about that time. No, and wouldn't, either. That time was a time best lost in the mists of history.

She wondered about all of those in her line who had come back as George Washington or Elvis or Napoleon, always as somebody famous. Whereas she came back almost always a nothing, a zero. Frankly, she thought a lot of that hokey business was made up.

The headline said, CUTT DEAD BY MYSTERIOUS HANDS. The G. Gordon Liddy talk show on WJFK had received an anonymous call directing police to a penthouse on N Street. A deviate or sexual pervert or left winger had killed him because of the Senator's patriotic work with the Friends For A Restored America, the caller said.

"It's a hell of an incarnation," Bud said. "To come back as a sex slave to a dead god."

Idena told him to shush. She closed her eyes and moved her naked feet back and forth over the *Times* front page. Her feet stung as if mosquitoes were down on the floorboard going orgiastic on her; sparks flew up her legs, all the way into her tailbone, into her ribs, up her spine. She wasn't any longer aware that she was riding in a car through the city streets of the nation's capital, although Bud remained beside her. For all she knew she and Bud were in a space ship streaming through the Nebula Oblinsky. But a picture was forming in her mind and she pressed one hand hard against her brow, sucking on the other. Her ears were ringing.

But the picture cleared. It was there in a box in her brain, exactly like she was watching it on a TV set. Another party, not Cutt, was upright inside a wall, with something indiscernible smearing the flesh. Idena didn't know what this substance was. She sucked her fingers harder. Then she saw false eyelashes, a pug nose, painted lips, a yellow parasol, and knew her party was female. She pressed her eyelids tight. Policemen with sledgehammers were banging away at a wall of beautiful new tiles, raising clouds of dust; they removed the Senator's body; the female was begging, "Please release me also," but the police were

paying no attention. "Don't leave me hanging here," the woman moaned, but because she was a woman the men were alike in the pretense that a voice was not calling to them. Each belonged to a line so ancient and their rights to oppression of women so deeply entrenched throughout the eons that their ears were sealed.

"What the fuck was that?" one of the policemen said.

But that was limit of their response. Each of the men in the room was the son of one of the ten billion sons of the one million gods who every night had fucked the ten thousand goddesses, back when there had been such things.

Idena unclenched her eyes, pressed her feet hard against the newspaper, and the instant she did so the Nebula Oblinsky vanished and the street she and Bud were travelling down vanished, as Idena's mind searched D.C.'s thousand yellow pages in hunt for G. Gordon Liddy's talk show on WJFK.

Idena became aware that Bud was looking at her in a peculiar way.

"You were moaning. What's the matter?"

"See if you can find a drugstore. The bottoms of my feet are covered in blisters."

Bud braked the car at the curb, to inspect her feet, and wouldn't you know it, there was a telephone booth right there. Fine lacy bubbles covered the whole underside of her feet, the blisters even at that second in slow boil, the surface folding over upon itself while simultaneously being sucked under — like candy cooking on a stove, when it reaches the soft-ball stage.

"The blisters will go away after a while," Idena told Bud. "I'm going to do my civic duty and make a phone call, Bud. Got a quarter?"

In the phone booth, looking out at Bud looking back at her with what might prove to be a fatal concern, she said to the station party answering, "Pass me through the G. Gordon, please."

"Not here," the party said. "Not live at this hour, lady."

Idena politely requested the answering party to please pass on to G. Gordon an important message. Another party, a woman, would also be found sealed in the wall where the Senator's body had been found, and someone should go there to release her at once.

She then hung up. She felt full of grief. This was what bugged her so much about these astral realities. A person could bend spoons, levitate, cross oceans in asp shape, read minds, speak forgotten languages, make watches tick faster or slower, abide in other centuries — employ telepathy, clairvoyance, clairsentence, clairaudience, all of that — but what did it add up to? When had it ever helped so much as a single individual off the breadline or stamped out squalor or stopped a war?

"Calling your mother?" asked Bud.

He knew well and good she'd arrived on this earth four years old without a mother.

There were times when even the best of men irritated.

He didn't appear in the least worried about the Senator's fate, however. That was a relief.

"What's the worst, the absolute worst thing you ever saw, Bud?"

"I don't know. Jumping kangaroos? How penguins walk? I get uneasy, seeing how kangaroos jump."

She could see he was kidding and slapped his hand.

"Fields and fields of cotton, me out there in them, dragging that heavy bag, that's the worst thing I ever saw."

"Who goes there?" asked Bud. The next second he was holding her face in his hands, kissing her mouth.

Idena was rubbing Polysporin on the soles of her feet, up between her poor inflamed toes, rumbling along the streets with her own thoughts, when Bud suddenly pounded the wheel, his face flushing. "Jesus Christ," he said. "If they've killed Tabita Banta, you are going to see one highly pissed off Bud."

"Bud Bud Bud," Idena said. "What's happening, Bud?"

They had come to a place way out of the city where only poor people could live. There were bleating horns, and catcalls, people running one way and another, and a thousand policemen directing all their attention at a low cinder-block house. Men in commando uniforms, in SWAT gear, in a big-wheeled jeep-like thing with a machine gun mounted in the rear, were streaking this way and that.

"*Qué pasa*, Bud?"

She hadn't known where it was they were going; she had no idea whose drab little house this was. Her feet were burning, bringing tears to her eyes, and she wondered whether this time she hadn't really hurt herself. Every other time the skin had cleared up in a matter of minutes; this time the pain was climbing up through her legs, giving her flesh the ugliest rash and turning her heart heavy and the inside of her head hot and cloudy.

Light seemed strange.

Bud was mad. Bud's face had wrinkles around the eyes she'd not noticed before. And those eyes furious. It was the first time she had ever seen him angry. He was thumping the steering wheel, cursing under his breath. Bud who never cursed and would tell her she needed to wash out her mouth with soap when she used that word.

He was saying that word over and over.

An ambulance had backed up near the cinder-block's front door. Now a gizmo was being pushed across the bumpy yard; someone's body inside a black bag.

"Do we know that party, Bud?" Idena innocently asked.

But before he could answer, here came another gurney. This one had a wobbly wheel, like happened with every supermarket cart Idena had ever tried pushing. The gurney attendant was losing his patience with that wheel, having to lift it over spotty clumps of grass. A tall ceramic jug by the front door, holding a cute bush with red balls, tinsel, had been knocked over. The front door hung by one hinge. Windows had been smashed, and although police, and soldiers, too, were running in and out of the door, you could still see smoke sifting from the windows and smell the nasty chemical odor riding the air.

Bud was out of the car. He was over mingling with the onlookers, engaging one and then another in brief conversation. Almost all the people out there, the sightseers, were black people, all sizes and shapes, wearing loose shoes, housecoats, and other such stuff that clearly they had pulled on in a rush. Children were squealing, rushing about. Dogs slunk about. A black cat sat in a window of the adjacent house, undisturbed by the melee. Beside that house, midst a raft of Harleys, weaved a score of bikers in T-shirts, leather jackets, having what looked like a party. A bullhorn squawked: *Please disperse. This is a police matter. Please return to your dwellings.* This announcement was met with a chorus of boos and cat-calling. Someone threw a shoe. Then other items rained down upon the cops and soldiers. Near Idena stood a man in a business suit, wearing a straw hat, drinking a Coca-Cola. Beside him another man, with plaited hair, holding a rum bottle. Here came a woman in a wheel chair waving a broom. There, another woman fresh from the shower, wiping her hair with a white towel as she ran. A woman swinging a tire iron. "Hey, Officer. How many of us you killed yet?" the woman called. That won a cheer. A lot of shoving and yakking, name-calling, ensued. An old man with ribbons in his hair, walking by, playing a Smokey Robinson tune on his Amigo boom box, smiled at her.

"Bud says, 'Hold on,'" the old man said — then sashayed away.

Bud had gone. She didn't know where it was Bud had gone.

She closed her eyes, thinking, *I can't bear to see these people hurt.* Then immediately reopened them. Across the street someone was building a boat in the front yard. Old, the paint flaky, as though the boat-building had been going on for decades. The boat was mounted on crossed poles of descending height so that the prow of the boat had the look of a vessel zipping though water. On the deck, beneath a flag depicting a red lightning bolt, sat a large family in straight back chairs, observing the proceedings. A vacant lot beside the boat place was heaped with rusting refrigerators, washing machines, bedsprings, abandoned sofas, all ringing an ancient automobile turned to its side, walking stones leading to a viny wooden arch over the car-house door, where a hand-painted sign said CHRISTIANS WELCOME. WIPE YOUR FEET.

"Come on, fool," Idena heard someone shout. Turning her head, she saw a young black girl with spritzy hair tugging a white man's arm. "You're in enough trouble, now come on."

"Excuse me, Miss," Idena said to the girl. "Can you tell me what is going on?"

The young girl leaned her head in the car window.

"Honey, do I have the time?"

"I hope so."

"Well, see that house? The asshole military has stormed that house and killed Ginger McCombs. The other dead we don't know yet."

Now the girl's white partner was sticking his head in. He pointed a long arm at the biker house. "See that house? See all them roach machines? Them SWAT fuckers was supposed to be raiding the biker pad. But it seem them SWAT fuckers had the wrong address, so it's Ginger's house they stormed. Kicking in Ginger's door, shooting tear gas through the windows. Blamming away at anyone they see moving in there."

"My Lord!"

"Mine, too. It seem every time them SWAT fuckers come out here to raid them motherfucker bikers they git the wrong house."

"Why the military?"

"Here, honey," the girl said. "You look like you could use a toke."

Idena clenched shut her eyes. Her fingers smelt of violets, formaldehyde. She concentrated hard, pressing fingers against her eyes, but couldn't see whose bodies were inside the body bags. All the pressing, the concentration, did was give her a headache. She didn't know why she was crying. It wasn't because of her hurting feet or because she had the faintest idea why she was here, or had even the smallest personal reason to be concerned about whose bodies were in those bags. She was crying, she sensed, for the full unfathomable mystery of the human enterprise and for all this death that surrounded her wherever on earth or among the stars she found herself.

She could remember vividly being locked in that ancient Egyptian tomb with the corpse of the spent god. Had he been a good god? Had he been bad? It was frustrating that she couldn't remember. She had come to believe that, really, her whole existence as a member of the spent god's harem was confined solely to the spent god's post-death experience. If she had served him in life, been one of his girls, surely she ought to remember. Recall at least some little detail, like what his bed was made of or what he liked to eat, or did he like a whole bunch of his wives at once, or prefer the more private, genuflective pastime. Was he occasionally kind or was he habitually mean? Humble or arrogant? Did he drink? Did he have a thousand children?

No, all Idena could remember — here now pressing her eyes — of that time of her life as the god's Divine Sepulchral Princess was that part of it endured in the fucker's tomb. Surrounded by all that blinding gold. His coffin — sarcophagus, she guessed it was called — was gold. The floor, the ceilings, the walls — nearly all you saw anywhere was gold. A thousand cups, goblets, vases, chests, tapestries — art work galore — all gold. Cats, dogs, cows, hawks, jackalmites — gold. Multitudes of foods — meats and fruits — these aplenty and plenty good to look at but smelling to heaven of stinking embalming juices. Herself and all the other sepulchral maidens hungry, always hungry, but knowing that with every forkful stuffed into their mouths they were embalming themselves.

But her predominant sense of things was of all that gold. Gold heaped up everywhere. Like in that *Lost Ark* movie, though without the pit of snakes. Thank goodness, in the spent god's tomb there hadn't been any nasty snakes slithering about. Snakes she could do without. Snakes on hand, she would have slit her throat with one of the thousand golden knives. Or hanged herself, as some of the other girls did, on one of the many golden ropes.

Gold, yes, but what a messy, unlivable place that tomb had been, even so.

No bathroom, for one thing.

Not much air, either.

Plenty of light during the day, but the nights awfully cold.

The coffin — the sarcophagus, she meant — right there in the room's middle, taking up the most valuable space, so that you couldn't move without having to shift around it. Stubbing a toe, hitting your knee, next day you were a walking bruise. You came to hate the spent god — or she did — because he was always there, always in the way.

"We can close the lid, girls," she had said. "Can't we at least close his fucking lid?"

Though not speaking quite like that, of course. No way. They were all spitting it out in some kind of Egyptian pharaoh's tongue, of course — but getting pretty raw in the lingo sometimes, you bet. Spats. Endless spats which any little nothing thing could ignite. Clawing at each other's eyes, pulling hair, kicking — yelling insults as they wrestled over the golden floor. Jealous bickering day and night.

"Close the fucking lid! Okay, he was our god and we worshiped the son of a bitch, but now he's *spent* does that mean we have to spend every minute in this *mammisi* looking at his dead stupid face?"

Not that you could actually see his face. That face, the whole body, was wrapped inside strips of golden cloth, giving him the look of a giant cocoon. His mummy wrappings sewn with stones of chalcedony, some milky white, others carnelian. Rubies, too. Him smoked and pickled, salted and oiled beneath those wrappings — that much clear from the exposed big toe — that toe filled with bitumen and spices.

She had been one of fifty-six such Divine Sepulchral Virgins imprisoned alive there, one for each year of the spent god's life. All young, twelve and under, plus a cry-baby eunuch or two. A drag those eunuchs were, so vain about their appearance they'd drive you bonkers in a minute. Some of those girls had been dearly besotted with the spent god, maybe were his own daughters, and prostrated themselves around the body, hurled themselves hourly upon the corpse, wailing lamentation, chanting their dreadful heartbreak. Sucking on that exposed toe because then the penis of the spent god would move in death and the lucky girl conceive the spent god's reincarnation.

Fut. That was his name. The great god Fut. Fut the Father and Fut the Son and Fut the Holy Ghost would be reborn and the lucky mother herself removed from the tomb, be enthroned, live in Fut's palace where she could spend all that gold, command a tide of servants acceding to her every whim — if only Fut's dead penis could be made to levitate. If only it could be inspired to get on with its business.

The girls bellyaching, forming ranks, each believing, she guessed now, that they were the chosen one. That toe oily and bitter, no way was she going to put it in her mouth.

Some of the girls claiming the sacred semen from the dead penis would fly out of the spent god's tool by invisible magical tube extending into their vulva — *"It does!" "It does not!"* — ; others asserting the fluid was to be taken orally, toe to mouth. — *"Does!" "Does not!"* Yet another faction saying the seed would be transported under realm of darkness in the beak of a Holy Dove, entering by way of ear or nostril. It would be delivered by lightning bolt, by Incubus, by magic.

All of the girls united in the belief that by stealth of night the eunuchs, themselves to conceive the new Fut, were sucking the spent god's toe into oblivion.

That toe, for sure, wearing down day by day.

How long Idena remained entombed she could not say, but long enough that she saw dust thicken on every surface and flesh erode from the bones of all present. Strange insect creatures, alike unto those of the ant world, traipsed hither and yon, across the floor and up the walls, sullenly conveying bits of flesh in their black jaws. At last her own spirit to flutter out . . . her last glimpse that of these same insects scuttling into darkening crevices with morsels that at one time had been herself.

Policemen were telling the onlookers to move on now, that there was nothing more to see. But the people by the cinder-block house were having none of this. Many, mostly housewives with big bottoms inside loud stretch pants, hair in rollers, clutching babies to their bosoms, keeping rein on infants with scurrying feet, clearly were angry. People were shouting, shaking fists in policemen's faces; the officers were swinging nightsticks, soldiers thrusting bayonets; people were being pushed one way and another. But more and more were arriving, swooping in from the other cinder-block houses, screaming profanities at the pigs. Lights were flashing, sirens going.

She saw Bud in the crowd, throwing frantic signals her way. What? What was he saying? Oh, she said to herself, embarrassed, at last catching on. And me psychic, she thought. He was telling her to move the car, take it around to the little alley running behind the cinder blocks. She wanted to yell out, "Bud, you know I can't drive! You know in none of my many lives I never learnt how!" But she was already sliding under the wheel. She was already slipping into gear, jouncing away — now passing the cop cars, the armored vehicle, passing a man in a blue suit with a phone up to his mouth. Turning the corner. Up ahead she saw Bud running. Signalling wildly. Yes, honey, she thought. I know. Down this little alley.

Then Bud was jumping into the passenger side, keeping low, saying, "Get me to the rear of the biker house?"

"Okay, Bud. How am I doing?"

"Magnificently."

"What's happening, Bud?"

"They missed our girl. She's hiding out with the bikers. I'm going in. When we leave, we leave in a hurry. Be ready."

"What girl, Bud? Not another one?"

But Bud was gone. In an instant he was across the biker yard, leaping rubble, wheels, handlebars, going through the bikers' back door. A host of men could talk a good game but her man Bud was a man of action.

In another instant a bunch of them — burly, leather-clad dudes — were crowding that same door, swilling beer, looking her over.

It didn't take Bud long. He came out, leading the girl by the hand, trailed by a big biker with a bloody nose. A bunch of other bikers were rah-rahing, shooting high signs. Bud wasn't even breathing hard.

The alley was a dead end; they were going to have to return the way they had come.

"We need a diversion, guys," Bud said to the bikers.

"You got it, Bud!" they said.

He has such a way with people, Idena thought. *How does he do it?*

In a second the bikers were revving their machines. One by one they roared out of the yard.

"Bud?"

At Ginger's cinder block the police, the soldiers, and the blacks were mixing it up. A fire truck had arrived; the hoses were out, spraying the protesters, knocking them over. By the doorway of the wrecked house a woman in a housecoat was crawling on the ground. She had one hand up, trying to protect her baby from a cop who was beating her across the backside with a nightstick.

Idena said, "Honey, stop that man."

Bud has his pistol out. The barrel was curved, he once had told her, and could shoot around corners. This time, though, he drew a direct bead.

He drilled the son of a bitch beating the woman squarely between the eyes.

"Mind the curb."

In her excitement Idena had bounced the car up over the curb, mowing down a row of stunted bushes, almost doing the same to a weaving biker. The biker waved a high sign. Then they got out of there. After a few blocks their motorcycle escort peeled away. No one was coming after them.

Tabita Banta — Little Butter — sat in the back, her head whipping.

"I'm never coming to this fuckin' city again," she said.

"Dint I tell you?" Bud said. "Don't use that word."

"Don't say *dint*, Bud."

"Okay.

"Who's *she?*"

"My girlfriend, Idena. She's psychic."

"I'm psychic, too, Bud. In my mama's womb I could see her looking at me. I could see her ring. I could see that hand rubbing her belly. She's going, Hello, my little darling Butter, how are yous liking it in there? And I goes right back, Hello my darling mother, I have not the smallest complaint. Yous think she heard me, Bud?"

"Don't say yous."

"Okay, Bud. It's only I'm rattled. I sure did like those bikers, though. They were some nice to me. Where we going now, Bud? What's going down next? I don't know what it is with me back here. It's likes yous — *you!* — two are my only surviving family. It's like you are my new mother and father."

CHAPTER SEVENTEEN

WHO GOES THERE

In the spring previous to the time of this story's events a farmer by the name of Clovis Hemp, living a few miles up from the Giocametti place, had been plowing his land when a strange adventure befell him.

Clovis Hemp has a favorite mule named Willy. Clovis, that past spring, hitched Willy to the plow. They were breaking up a certain field when Willy began behaving peculiarly. There was an area of that field which Willy would not enter. Clovis Hemp scolded, he switched Willy with the reins, he led Willy by the bridle — begged him — but over this certain area Willy would not transgress.

Clovis Hemp said, "By golly, Willy, do you see a snake?"

So Clovis trampled over the ground, looking for a snake. He did not find a snake. What he found was yet another pothole. Clovis Hemp knew potholes. His ninety cleared acres were riddled with potholes, these mostly of long-standing origin, though frequently in recent years new ones had appeared.

The oddity about this one was that Clovis Hemp, on his knees peering into the hole, could not see bottom. He arose, kicking his boots against the earth. The cakes of earth Clovis dislodged tumbled down into a silent darkness. He probed with a long stick, and touched nothing. Finally, he rolled up a large stone, and poked and pried this stone into the hole.

After what seemed to Clovis a very long time he heard a splash, following by an echoing rumble that vibrated the earth.

It came to Clovis Hemp that the ground on which he stood could any minute give way beneath him. So Clovis hastily retreated. He stood beside Willy at the edge of the field, holding his breath, as that entire area the mule would not transgress upon slid away. A greenish vapor, chilling in its coldness, floated up from the vast hole, which Willy was grieved to see now covered fully half an acre.

The earth shook. Clovis Hemp could feel in his boots the force of a great river, water without parallel, thundering beneath him.

Clovis, not a superstitious fellow, even so, crossed himself. He said to the mule, "God help us, Willy, but there's a potent brew building down there."

A week ago, a hottish day in the Blue Ridge, Clovis was out again behind the old mule, this time clearing new ground. Over the winter Clovis has taken down any number of trees, digging holes and planting dynamite within the holes to dislodge the remaining trunks. Old-timers have warned Clovis that he should take a cautious path with all these explosives, but Willy wants new acreage for his soybeans and has gone right ahead. The land is now cleared of all but the most stubborn tree trunks, together with boulders too large to shift, and Willy is pretty pleased. When the crop comes in his wife will have a new dress, his children new shoes for school, and he will be able to pay off the embarrassing debt accumulated at one and another store down in Shenandoah.

So a week ago he said, "Giddyup" to the fine old mule.

But again there was a patch of earth old Willy would not transgress. Clovis said aloud, "Here we go again," and the mule turned its head to look at him. Even as that head was turning Clovis Hemp felt the earth collapsing under his heels, wrinkling in quickly expanding waves and casting up strange clouds. Clovis cried, "Godamighty, Willy," feeling for the plow handles and aware of one rein tightening around a hand.

It is this that saved him: that one rein wrapped around the single hand. Willy was at full trot, then at gallop, then running as Clovis had never known the old mule could run, dragging Clovis behind him.

Willy does not stop running until he reaches his own stall, and over subsequent days Clovis Hemp has come to understand he has lost a willing partner to work those fields. Clovis Hemp's newly cleared acreage has disappeared altogether, fumes rising where that land once was, unseen water coursing beneath those fumes, with nothing more than Clovis Hemp's word, his oaths, to claim land ever was there.

A white limo barrels down highway 69, bound for the mountains. In the rear sits Chantelle Peru, between Wally the doorman and the man whose limo it is.

Peru is on the car phone to Hillary, Chair of the all-but-defunct White House Committee on Soldiers Abandoned in Vietnam. The First Lady is getting an earful.

"The sons of bitches!" Peru is saying.

Who?

"The Friends. The sons of bitches kill Pancho, I speak to the Arlington people, arranging a formal marine guard, the two-gun salute by his grave side in the National Cemetery, what do I find?"

What?

"I find the sons of bitches have had their oars in at the highest levels of Defense, at Congress, at Justice, at the VA, could be even the White House, and guess what every son of a bitch I now talk to is telling me."

I don't want to guess.

"They are telling me poor Pancho, a second lieutenant in the U.S. marines and a forgotten prisoner of war for twenty-three years, never served! The sons of bitches have stricken his name from the military rolls."

You're kidding.

"Ditto, Wally's. They've put their names in the shredder. The sons of bitches are refusing to bury Pancho at Arlington, never mind the goddamn honor guard. But let me tell you this, Hillary. I got photographs, service records, letters, dog tags, even a commendation from a major for heroism on the fields of valor. I can bring a hundred, a thousand, people to court who will testify that he served over there, and these goddamn Friends, and every bastard bureaucrat administering to these lunatics' summons are going to be uncloaked, and *pay the fucking price.*"

The foul language isn't necessary, Peru.

"Let me tell you what's necessary. What's necessary is I'm upping the ante, this class-action suit, to one hundred billion. That's *billion*, Hillary! One hundred billion. Tell Bill. If I have to bring the whole goddamn government down in total disarray, utter collapse, crash the dollar's value below the ruble, I will do it. You think those sons of bitches are going to get away with this? I am going to put all their asses *under* the jail!"

Who is backing you, Chantelle?

"Never mind that. If the sons of bitches think this suit is going to dry up and go away, they've been chewing on the wrong end."

Not that gangster? I hear you have a gangster footing the bills.

"Says who?"

That's what I hear.

"So what. Yeah, a gangster, Hill, that's right. We need another million from him, we'll get another million. Zippo is in this for the full haul. We are going to crucify your asses."

I'm on your side, Chantelle.

"Fuck you are. Anyway, you tell them. *One hundred billion!* Say, Hillary, did I tell you? Who I've got here in the limo beside me? Holding my hand? Patting his foot?"

Who?

"Streicher, honey. Chief Justice, the U.S. Supreme Court."

Holy Mother of God.

"Yeah. Big slam-bang, eat-the-shits-alive Streicher. I figured you'd be impressed."

Streicher's OUR appointment. We trampled all over the nitwits — we BEGGED — to get his nomination confirmed.

"Yeah. But you didn't buy his soul. Streicher tells me . . . unofficially, off the record, we never saw each other, you know?"

Yes?

"— we have a case."

Streicher?

"That if the entire U.S. government is conspiring to defeat our cause, conspiracy afoot from top to bottom, then could be one hundred billion . . . well, like that's just for the duress and strife."

Come by. I'll get Bill, the Joint Chief —

"The Floor leaders?"

— The Attorney General. We can talk.

"Way late, Hillary. The sons of bitches are out to kill us."

Phooey. That's phooey, Chantelle.

"You think so? Check out Pancho — check out Cutt — in the morgue."

Why would his own people kill Cutt?

"I guess he wasn't mean and stupid enough, Hill. Although that's hard to believe. Maybe he was too old. Maybe he didn't fuck enough interns, excuse me."

Low, Peru.

"I apologize. Truly. That slipped out. But you might consider, maybe they want yours and Billy's job."

There is no conspiracy on this, Chantelle. You're wrong there.

"There is *always* a conspiracy, Hillary. You said so yourself on — what was it, *Good Morning America*? — back in January when Billy's kiss-kissy stuff with Monica hit the fan."

Well, fuck you, too, Chantelle.

"Hickory, dickory, dock, Hill. It's way late. Time you got cracking."

Chantelle? Listen . . .

Peru calmly replaces the phone.

"I guess I told her," she says.

Wally pats her hand.

Poor Wally, he's been out of it since Pancho's death

Streicher isn't saying much. Weeks since he's been out of the city, he wants to enjoy the ride. He's pleased, though, with Chantelle Peru. Prime goods. Got the killer zeal. A firecracker is Peru. He spotted it years ago when he took her on, fresh out of law school, the flaming rebel, at his old firm. The Vigilante Kid, he'd dubbed her then.

"I hope Zippo's place has water," Chantelle says. "We may be there awhile."

"How far, Counselor?"

"Another hour. Follow the loon's shriek."

A fellow by the name of Rufus Putz is this minute maneuvring his 10-wheeler around the narrow curving road above Shenandoah, bound from Roanoke. A six-thousand-gallon tank of fresh water rides his trailer wheels. A woman on the phone, giving her name as Glorianna something or other, has said, I must have water! Water! My daughter is coming home!

"All I know is," Rufus says aloud to no one, "they said down in Shenandoah the place was around here somewhere."

The switchback curves are getting to him. It's been a long day. The signs, WATCH FOR FALLING ROCKS, are familiar to him. Even so, he's rarely seen a road littered with so many. Fumy, flaring gasses appear to be erupting out of seams in the rock walls the highway builders cut, and in the dips he's had to splash through rushing water a foot above the road. Last night it rained, he thinks, but this makes no sense.

At the Giocametti house not all time has been consumed in mourning Zippo's worrisome state. Pat Fish has come through. The gang has been rounded up. Glo has revised the master's plans for the coin heist.

Glo said: "Zippo's snatch at the Raleigh depot is all wrong. We went for the coins there, we'd get swept off to jail. Now it may surprise you to learn that when I was a little girl my entire family was in the way of being train freaks. We had a rail system that ran through every room and floor of the house. We had trains moving twenty-four hours a day. Our set-up duplicated to the nth degree the whole continental rail system as found throughout the United States, Canada and Mexico. Some company built a spur line, we build ours. A depot moved, we moved ours. You are following what I am saying?

"Which is why Zippo's plans are inadequate. He doesn't know the tracks. The system.

"It was Cutt, you'll remember, who suggested Raleigh. I say forget Raleigh. Because I think Cutt's friends have penetrated the deal. I see it as a set-up. *They* will be at Raleigh.

"So here's the alteration.

"To reach Raleigh the mint train has to pass through a teensy burg called Fuquay-Varina. That's in North Carolina. Population twenty-seven. But Fuquay-Varina has a regular depot, has triple tracks, even a waiting room, from the days it was on the main North-South run, New York to New Orleans. The old Southern Railroads Zephyr line. Have I lost you?"

"Go on."

"Nearest policeman, thirty miles up the road in Warrenton; nearest county sheriff's office twenty-six miles east, in Warren Plains; nearest highway patrol forty miles southwest, off I-85, above Oxford.

"We hit the coin train in Fuquay-Varina. We shoot the coin cars off onto a side-track, send the regular train on its way, hook up our own engine to the coin cars. Then away we go. No crane required.

With luck, and if our switchman is on his toes, they won't even know we've struck. Do you know? Just three minutes out of Fuquay-Varina there's a line, erroneously believed inoperable, that ends in what is now an abandoned barn. That's our transferring point. Here, I'll sketch it for you.

"Twenty minutes, start to finish. Simple."

Pat Fish said: "You sing a convincing tune, Glo."

Glo said: "I want it understood, however, that after expenses — after a generous cut for the troops and a small contribution for Zippo's old age — every penny from this heist is to go into Zippo's law suit."

"You're the boss."

At this very minute the gang's operations crew is steaming towards Fuquay-Varina.

Ten minutes behind Chief Justice Streicher's limo purrs another. Black, windows tinted, heavy with the receiving apparatus, bearing the license plate GO ORTH. Inside rear, Jude, the Governor, Miss Chudd. Jude has a customized chair: it swivels, rises, descends with the press of a button.

Up front, a no-name driver, beside him the Friends' roving ambassador, Special Agent Lootz. The driver is picking his teeth. Lootz is wiping down a .38 Special.

"You did a good job on that Wisconsin woman, Linquist, Lootz," Jude says. "I ever tell you?"

Lootz beams.

Miss Chudd, wiping her glasses, sees three Lous, all of them stupid. How many times had he failed her civics course? She's mad. It's near here that her sister and the movement's best shooter crashed to their deaths. She can take that. In war, there are casualties. What she can't yet take is that man Bud burning down her house, taking her money.

Her baby, the Internship Program, is in shambles.

"Break ground on the Christian Theme Park tomorrow," Orth says. "Be finished in time for Christmas."

Miss Chudd feels better. Money pours in every day. She can build herself another house, this one in the Park. A lifelong dream, that Park.

Behind the stretch, another vehicle, a white van, Giocametti's name stencilled on the sides. Inside the van, four Friends, two of them excellent tilers, all heavily armed, at the moment downing Carstairs rye and dining from a communal bucket of KFC.

O.O. Orth, looking through the rear window, says to Jude: "The driver back there is weaving all over the road. I hope your guys aren't drunk."

Jude has his leg harness removed. He's sniffing the leather, the metal. The recent rain has brought on rust, mildew. He needs oiling. He isn't getting the attention lately that was his not long ago when he strode the Master's course with George Bush.

"Drink has got us where we are," Jude says.

Everybody laughs.

Lootz is moved to speech by the merriment. "While I was out there I had me some of that famous Wisconsin cheese. Let me tell you, to my mind it was just cheese. Maybe you'd like to hear how I done the babe," he says. "That note, *I have betrayed my country*, was my whole idea."

Jude, a wink at the governor, says, "How'd you do it, Lou?"

"She's sitting by the curb, morning, watching her kid prance into school. I slide in. I say, 'Been tied to any doorknobs lately, Miss Linquist?' Lord, yous ought to seen her shake."

Jude and the governor wink. "No shit, Lou."

"I was wearing a hat, but she recognized me right away."

Jude says, "You see a hat these days, it's on a fruit. Are you a fruit, Lou?"

Lootz' jaw tightens. He shuts up.

"Thank God he's shut up," Miss Chudd says. "I never could stand that boy's mouth."

While Lootz had been talking Miss Chudd had been reviving her own adventure with Bud. He'd sat at her vanity table watching her as she played possum on him. She had a long knife in her hand under the covers but he'd never come near enough for her to use it. She had that knife now, folded inside her purse. She hoped the day would not end without her having used it on someone.

The Governor has a thought. He says to Jude, "I'm worried about Beef."

Jude says, "Worry makes the dick soft. Why worry?"

"I wish he would call."

"He'll call."

They watch an insect of some kind buzzing around Lootz' head.

"Yeah, but what does that fucker, Beef, know about bombs?"

Miss Chudd smirks. "Ask those abortion doctors," she says. "Ask at those baby-killing clinics. Tell the governor about Beef's good work with those nigger churches, Jude."

"Forget Beef," says Jude.

Miss Chudd is ever touching Jude: stroking his hair, his hand. Miss Chudd is in love. In her family it was always her twin sister who had the fast reputation; Miss Chudd was the one who fell in love.

Miss Chudd remembers with a pang her sister's Tilley hat. Her son Otis had sent that hat to Sister, all the way from Vancouver, Canada. That was nice of Otis. The Senator in recent years had gone off the boy. The Senator had no provision for Otis in his will. This was reason enough, to Miss Chudd's mind, he had to die.

She has seen the fly, if that's what it is, rise and flit against the closed window by Lootz' head; now it is in flight again, swooping into the rear. She swats a hand at it, but misses. Then it is up crawling on Lootz' neck. It likes Lootz. It doesn't look like a fly. She watches it sneak out of sight inside Lootz' slicked hair.

Senator Cutt was not highly esteemed in Washington. A more loathed man, in fact, would have been hard to find. This within a geographical boundary wherein the vile and the despised run one hundred to the acre. It was conceded that Cutt's power in many areas, especially with regard to certain nations, exceeded that of the President. Merely by a curl of his lips he could dictate the nation's policy on, for instance, Cuba. As chair of the Senate Appropriations committee, the Foreign Relations Committee, the Banking Committee, etc., his influence stretched far and wide. In private, his cohorts and defenders took considerable joy in being able to say that in Washington Cutt was the single patriotic statesman left who "still could call a nigger a nigger and a cunt a cunt." Nor did he overlook the smaller fish. Singlehandedly, he had seen to it that the Philippines' poor Imelda Marcos was placed in a position whereby she could buy herself new shoes and have a good lick at restoring to her rightful purse the three hundred million her husband had salted away in Swiss Banks. When the Canadian tycoon spearheading the drive to restore holocaust survivors funds lodged through fifty years in these same Swiss banks showed up on Cutt's doorstep, Cutt said, "What holocaust? My contact up there in Toronto — Zundel? — he assures me he's got evidence that business is all malarkey."

It was said of Cutt along congressional row that his goal in life was to fuck up everything in life that worked and to work the life out of everything that fucked.

On Capitol Hill the Senator's office was known as Cutt's Collection Agency. Lobbyists claimed he left the bottom desk drawer open so callers could drop in the cash.

As *The New York Times* said in a succinct editorial noting his passage, "Cutt was for nothing and against everything, except Cutt." Adding in a hopeful note: "It is possible the senior Senator never knew how far from civilized shores the tide had swept him."

Miss Chudd sighs at the passing scenery. Jude's hand rests in her lap. Then she lifts that hand and goes back to trimming his nails.

"There's the road to Luray's Famous Caverns," she says. "It is one of the world's great cave and underwater systems. Did any of you ever visit? I bring my dear students up here every year."

Up front, Lootz squirms.

"You got problems, Lou?"

"Something biting me."

They watch him reach a hand into his collar and scratch.

"What is it?"

"Feels like a flea. Where would I catch fleas? Fucker is eating me alive."

The Governor says, "I still don't see why I have to be here."

Jude says, "What I'd do over there, I'd round up the villagers, I'd say, 'Run, you sons of bitches.' Them that didn't I'd drop on the spot. I get those running it was like popcorn hopping out of a pot."

"That's what we need to do more of over here," Miss Chudd says. "Clear the deck."

Lootz is still scratching. "I think it's in my eye," he says.

Jude says, "You finished cleaning that .38, Lou? Let me see."

Lootz passes the weapon over the seat to Jude who hefts and sniffs, says, "A good job there, Lou." To the Governor, he says, You ever fire a piece?" The Governor shakes his head and Jude passes the .38 along to him.

Jude says, "Anyone notice how stuffy it is in here? Let's lower our windows, why not."

Miss Chudd says, "It's all this smoke."

Jude says, "You like the gun, Governor?"

"Good grip. Bastard is heavier than I would have thought."

Jude says, "Are all our windows down?"

The Governor says, "They're down, Jude."

"Then shoot the gun."

"Shoot the gun? What you want me to shoot at?"

"Not the driver. How about you shoot Lou?"

The Governor takes aim.

"Hey, hold on!" says Lootz.

The Governor fires. There is a clapping sound, smoke, the smell of cordite, and the limousine rocks. Lootz has a look of utter astonishment.

"Jesus," says the Governor. "I don't know what got into me."

Jude says, "I think you missed."

On the road past Luray, Virginia, Wally the doorman turns to Chantelle Peru and out of the blue, remarks: "One day over there the women took me out of my cage and spent a whole day scrubbing me down. They had a young girl in another pot, doing the same to her."

"Why were they doing that, Wally?"

"There were only women left in that village. All the men were gone or dead, and most of the women were shot up or burnt. Maimed, most of them dying. The old ones thought the whole race was about to become extinct. So they scrubbed us up, me and the girl, and put us together in a bamboo hut. We stuck out our heads they whapped us."

"What happened?" Streicher asks.

"The old women told us we were married. I might have a child over there."

"*Quién esta,*" whispers Streicher.

The phone rings in the Governor's limo. Jude snatches it up.

Beef says, "That fucker Zippo's in bed with my bullet, still alive. But I got the bombs planted. All yous gotta do is push the plunger."

"Good."

Zippo dreams.

Zippo's father says to him one day, in a boasting manner, "Capone is requiring a long talk with you."

Alfonso "Scarface" Capone, the shooter.

So many years since Zippo Giocametti was in New York City, but here he is in his dream, a school boy dressed in knickers, knee stockings, soft cap, his ears sticking out.

"What's this your Papa is telling me?" says Capone. "You a thespian? You trod the boards do you, kid? This I got to see."

In the dream Zippo is on stage, just as he was in real life — his old grade school, opening night performance, *Scenes From Shakespeare*. Outfitted in what's said to be Elizabethan gravedigger's garb, holding up a skull on loan from Mr. Yakitis's science lab.

Zippo wants no part of this dream. The *Hamlet*, Alas Poor Yorick fiasco, was not the family's finest hour. Papa and Mama Giocametti, Dominic in diapers, all out in the auditorium. Capone and his moll beside them. Zippo with the jitters, the director in the wings whispering, "When you say your lines, dumbo, hold up the blasted skull!"

Just as the brooding Dane is putting the question to him, how long ere a body rot, a commotion occurs. He hears his father shouting to Capone, *"Who sez I can't take off my shoes? Who sez? I pay good coin to sit down hear my son speak the iambic pentameter, I can't take off my shoes? Who sez, Big Shot, Who sez?"*

"I sez," hollers Capone.

A wild scramble, these two big guys bellowing and shoving each other, the women going after each other's hair and getting in their own *Who sez?*

Zippo on stage in these prissy tights, Alas Poor Yorick's skull elevated, about to unload his *"if he be not rot already* comeback . . . when suddenly the audience is scrambling, screaming, Papa and Capone brandishing their pieces, Papa with his *Who sez?*, Capone with his *I sez* — the next minute emptying their gats. End of *Scenes From Shakespeare*. End of Zippo Giocametti's thespian career.

When Governor Orth squeezed the trigger he felt the surge down to his testicles. The soles of his feet tingled and up through his spine came the shudder of the limo chassis, the vibration of rolling wheels. The explosion shook the car, jingled the Governor's ears, roared inside his head. He unclenched his eyes and looked at his companions, their hands over their ears.

"Where'd the bullet go?"

Although a side of his face is blistered, Lootz is grinning. "Out the window, see the nick? But, hey, did I flinch?"

The Governor says, "It's a heavy mother. Pinched the bejesus out of my finger. Wait, now."

He takes aim again.

"Squeeze. Don't jerk," Jude says.

Lootz screams, "Cut the fuck this out!"

The Governor fires again, this time gripping the .38 in both hands.

The .38 takes out a portion of Lootz' head. Blood and gobs of tissue streak the limo interior, drip from the windows, the roof, the doors.

A black brick has settled behind Lootz' eyes. He hears someone saying, "Why'd you want the man shot, Jude?"

"He had no character. He wasn't a guy going anywhere."

Lootz hears plops, spurts, eruptions; something fizzing, like steam escaping through a valve.

"He wasn't never nothing but a fat pile of shit."

Lootz hears these voices although they exist without meaning to him. Who is Lootz? He feels a strange levitation of his body, oomph sounds, quaking noises along the backbone, like high-stacked dishes falling over. Running feet. He hears the swoosh of closing doors, the click of latches in their slots. It is darkening, air has turned cold. One eye dangles free of its socket. Lootz looks at this hanging eye, fascinated; he is looking at the eye as the eye looks at him. There should be pain, but Lootz feels none. No pain and no concern, either. He thinks it is fine, a good thing, this dangling eye; it is rather beautiful, extraordinary, hanging like that. A black light is slowly creeping up his body, turning all in its path black. This is insulting, Lootz feels; tension, indignation, shakes his body. Then there is release, a sudden shifting of perspective. Now he sees only through the dangling eye. The eye studies with curiosity the remarkable substances streaking the glass, the dash, the door. For these, the eye acknowledges inexplicable kinship, affection. The eye has an odd yearning to join them or have them join him. Black pus seeps into the eye; the eye blinks, swivels about, detecting movement from within its own roots; something is there, making sucking, spitting noises. Gradually, the intruder ascends, scratching the eye's surface. All the eye sees are bent black sticks, these murky, setting themselves down one by one on the eye's surface. The eyes sees a diversity of eyes looking back at him. An insect. A bug? The insect pauses, sneezes, licks, flicks antennae, probes the eye's terrain for malignancy, for food, sanctuary. It flaps a wet wing, licks, flaps the other. Now it begins again its crawl, under, now onto, the eye's lid. The eye sees the insect's quivering behind, the color greenish, metallic, gleaming. It hikes up its rear, evacuates its bowels. The eye is open, cloudy; it sees nothing falling. It sees nothing at all.

"Throw him the fuck out."

The insect waits. It has lost its host, its home. The new environment composes itself around him, shifts, makes room for his arrival. It is a universe rife with danger, menace at every turn, but he perceives the arrangement is not altogether alien. He examines himself. He is intact. Nothing has altered. He grooms himself, scents the air; a certain whine in the distance is familiar, exciting. Female. She can be his. He will fly her down, mount her, ride her on water. His antennae probe: that way is water. He is all powerful, unique, beautiful. He has lived forever. He scuttles forward. Digs. He will bury all his secrets in this place.

He flicks out a tongue. Eats.

Dung.

It is good.

Quién anda.

The story is told of an insect queen named Qfgr, so magnificent in spirit that when any insect in the kingdom was taken by malady of any kind, Qfgr the queen would go and lie down beside it. In this manner did Qfgr take unto herself all sicknesses existent in the insect world. The sick bug walked and the lame were healed.

Over the centuries, old and riddled by disease after all this while, Queen Qfgr continued in the ancient practice. If asked, she would say it was her duty, not merely by whim of her being Queen but because such was the commandment from on high. All should care for everyone. If not, what kind of insect were you and how could compassion reign?

When she herself lay dying in a rocky field, all who were in good health because of the deeds she had performed turned a blind eye. They looked askance at her aged body wrapped in misery, then went on about their business. They had come to believe their recovery was their own brave doing.

Her princely children arrived and stripped her head of its crown, her limbs of their jewels, with never so much as a favorable nod at her entreating words.

This marked the one bitter moment of Queen Qfgr's entire sojourn on earth. With her last breath she prophesied that ever hereafter it would be the fate of the insect world that they should eternally sting and eat each other, eat dung, and therefore never rise in grandeur.

After her death — some say even before — marauding locusts swallowed up her legs and drank the juices from her throat. And thus were disease and death again rampant in the kingdom and her pall embraced the world. Now hers is a hollow husk whisked near and yonder by wind and in its gusting you can hear her mournful cry.

The phone rings in Justice William Streicher's limo.

Chantelle?

"How are you, Mr. President?"

I've had a long talk with Hillary.

"Good for you, sir."

The Ship of State is at work, Chantelle.

"Delighted to hear it, Mr. President."

We are reaming butt. Your friend Pancho will receive his honors.

"That's wonderful news, sir."

Hillary and I will attend.

"Thank you, Mr. President."

Do you remember the case of a social services worker named Euphenia Linquist of Racine, Wisconsin? Sexually assaulted at the Watergate, later found dead?

"I recall, sir."

New evidence has come forward, linking her death to the Friends For A Restored America. Fingerprint on the note.

"Congratulations, Mr. President."

We may win yet, Chantelle.

"Yes sir."

And Chantelle . . .

"Yes sir?"

Refresh my memory. I never saw you alone in the Oval Office, did I?

"No sir."

I have, I believe, conducted myself properly with you at all times, as I would with any beautiful woman. Isn't that true?

"Indeed it is, Mr. President."

"Your tally is a bit steep, Chantelle."

"I can be reasonable, sir."

"I could have certain other reasonable people nudge Congress."

"I believe that would be entirely appropriate, Mr. President."

My best to Chief Justice Streicher and Wally. When you see Mr. Giocametti please tender my admiration.

"That will mean a lot to him, sir."

Stay loose, kid.

"You, too, Billy."

Zippo, squirming up from the pillows, blinks at bright sunlight streaming through the windows, and asks himself: Where is everyone? What gives?

Jesus, I feel great. What a sleep!

He sees, out against the mountainside, a beautiful woman standing beside a huge red tank, under a shower washing her hair. Where did the tank come from? Who is the woman?

Another woman runs into view, this one perhaps younger, naked also. The two women dance under the spray, washing each other's hair. They look familiar.

Glo and Dolores.

He hears noises from the pool area. He pads down the long hall, sneaks a look: there in Zippo's own bathing trunks, bent to dive, is the Supreme Court's William Streicher. There's Wally in knee shorts, Chantelle Peru emerging from the kitchen, carrying a tray on which rides a baked ham. There's the stringbean, Alonzo, arranging flowers. That boy, he thinks, will make some woman a good husband.

He's on his death bed, they've been having a party?

The pool has water?

He feels a sting in his scalp, lifts a hand — there's the glass: his see-through second brain, glistening like a diamond.

Clovis Hemp, as is his custom, arose early this morning. He called his dog, Helen, and he and Helen strode across to his field that had turned into a lake of water. Yesterday on his property, off in low-lying woods where his every tree and bush compete with rock cast up during the glacial age, he had noticed new cracks in the rockfloor. Bubbling water fizzed up through some of these cracks, trickling away, although in a half-dozen places smallish pools had formed, the water not bubbling here, but pure and warm to the tongue. In more than one place he saw what he would call geysers, these pencil-thin, scarcely more than a foot high. He had put a finger in the hole, and there that dwarf geyser came in another place.

Clovis's idea this morning has been to determine whether there exists any pattern in this business of the splitting boulders and the bubbling water. He wants to ascertain whether this new trick of the mountains leads towards or away from his own farmhouse, and per-haps call on a neighbor or two to inquire what they might have observed about this funny business. He has figured Helen as a vital partner in these explorations, as has proved to be the case. Clovis has held an ear to the rock veins, the open seams, listening for coursing water. Sometimes he has heard water and at other times only imag-ined he did; Helen's ears are the more reliable. She needs only to sniff these seams to know. If she sniffs and does nothing, Clovis precedes along. If Helen's ears shoot up, if she hikes a front leg, moans a low moan, barks — then Clovis knows he is on the right trail.

Which is why he has come to stand this morning on an outcrop of rock near a mossy, claw-footed bathtub in cleared pastureland, looking down at the land that the new fellow and his wife have bought. He has yet to meet the new fellow or see him, but he has seen the wife in the village, and passed her old Cadillac on the road. Once these newcomers settle in, in another year or two, he and his wife, under normal circumstances, would have paid a visit. They would have brought the newcomers a Mason jar or two of Mrs. Hemp's jams. But circumstances are not today normal, and any minute now Clovis Hemp means to stride down there and introduce himself.

He's hesitating, though. It had not crossed his mind that the new folks would have visitors. Still, it is necessary. Because if his theories are right, pretty soon now — today, tomorrow, or in a hundred years — the rockface up here is going to split wide open. Water is going to volley forth, and that new place, not much to Clovis's liking, is sitting directly in the path that water will take.

The people at Luray have noticed a dramatic rise in the water table in many of their caverns. They have had experts huddling daily. An aquifer, these experts tell them, is a layer of extremely porous rock or sediment, most frequently sandstone. Water in the form of rain, snow, and frost enters the exposed edge of the aquifer at a high elevation; it seeps downward. The weight of the water above puts enormous pressure on that water trapped below. Thus, for instance, you might have geysers.

"Well, what's the cause of our troubles?" ask the Luray people. "Heavy rains? El Nino?"

"Not rain," say the experts. "The best explanation is that there must have been some unusual disturbance in the aquifer."

The experts are unaware of Clovis Hemp's stump-clearing adventures.

Clovis Hemp's TNT has ripped through the overburden, fractured the bedrock, and penetrated the aquifer. Luray's great underground river is seeking new outlets.

In the limo on the road west of Luray, Miss Chudd is first to see the geysers.

"My goodness!" she says.

Miss Chudd, when heretofore she has envisioned heaven, has not seen geysers within the golden streets and byways of the King's lordly mansions.

But if God is merciful then His heaven must certainly have these geysers.

They are *so* beautiful.

The limo purrs around the switchback curves. They are descending the last high mountain and in a moment will be turning up Zippo Giocametti's road.

"What was it Beef said? All we have to do is push the plunger."

"I want to push it," says Miss Chudd. "Let me."

"Let's flip," says Jude.

CHAPTER EIGHTEEN

CAVES

Idena, woman who predicts the future, reads the past, reads minds, once set up housekeeping in an Egyptian tomb . . . sees in her own mind all this bad shit coming down on Zippo Giocametti.

"I'm seeing it again, Bud. All that water."

"Harp, harp," Bud says.

"You too stop squabbling," pipes up Tabita Banta from the rear.

They are barrelling across the country in their new car, a black convertible Saab, on their way to the Pueblo caves of Bud's youth.

"Zippo is just like my old boss Jack Ruby," Idena says. "He couldn't bear to watch a woman strip. Hide his head in his paws. 'Why you have to wear those spiked heels?' he'd say. 'Who said you got to use a pole? Stick that finger in your mouth?'"

"You stripped?" says Tabita Banta. "Cool."

Idena was looking at the Timex on her wrist a moment ago, a vision smoked in from nowhere, knocked her breathless. That watch the identical melted timepiece Dali sent around the globe. So hot it burned the skin. It isn't the scalded wrist that bothers her. Time and time again, crossing these flat plains, she's seen water. Oceans of water.

"I've got to go wee-wee, Bud."

"Here okay?"

"Okay, Bud."

They are miles from nothing. In the desert, the air rippling with heat. Bud pulls over.

There they are, two winsome ladies, squatting by cactus in the great plains.

Idena thinking, *Like I did way back yonder in my cotton-picking days.* Raise the rags, squat. Nothing to it.

Afterwards, she stoops to read a message in the foamy urine. Nothing doing. She can't read foam. Hers in the shape of a monster with nine bodies, but what does that mean?

She's not exactly jacked up with confidence. Once in a while she's had visions that were strictly out to lunch. For instance, those cotton-picking days. Back there in the way yonder, hundred fifty years ago, half Little Banta's age, dragging the sack, hot sun beaming down, she had experienced Utter Failure psychic booms. Every day, breaking her back, breathing cotton dust, dragging the bitch bag, she saw it: Massa's mansion rooftop collapsing under weight of Yankee cannon balls. Good fucking riddance, too. Pray Massa, Mistress Massa, all their sons and daughters, go with it. Pray them cannon balls turn them into pork chops.

Through four years of war she carried that vision. Yet the mansion, Massa, Mistress Massa, the little mistress Massas and the Massas extra, none were ever touched. Them Massas spying on you every minute, kicking you right and left . . . Massas senior and junior fucking her every evening the moon came round.

On the road again, Tabita Banta between them, taking language instructions from Bud under the wheel.

"D-I-D-N Apostrophe T. Didn't. Contraction of 'did not'."

"Gotcha."

"Say it. 'Didn't'."

"Dint."

"Great. You're improving."

"Bud?"

Bud Bud Bud. That's all he's heard for 1500 miles.

"Yes."

"I think maybe I become a biker after living with you and Idena in the caves."

"That is so sweet," Idena says. In not one of her incarnations has she been a mother. The experience is blowing her mind.

Tabita Banta pinching the inside of a thigh, saying, "I got too much flab."

At a crossroad outside Albuquerque Idena shouts, "Stop the car, Bud!"

She goes running.

CROOKS TAKE $17 MILLION IN DARING COIN HEIST declares a headline.

Night on the desert, tent flapping in the wind, the three around a fire. A coyote howls. Who goes there?

"Don't worry," Bud says. "It won't happen the way you think it will. I sat out on that land a week ago, under a tree, my rifle scope pinned to your friend Zippo's head. I didn't like it so I didn't fire, but I know the land. The rock will split, water will thunder down, but Zippo's house, that whole section, will not be in its path. It'll be hell, though, for anyone along the road. Now let me tell you about these caves. First, the light, it's spectacular, like nothing you've seen. The silence, that, too, will boggle your brains. At night, on until dawn, spirits gather. They hover in crevices, swing on invisible cords over the canyon, swoop and perch on every ledge, conversing one and all, the long night through, in secret code."

"Why do they do that, Bud? What are they saying?"

"They are exchanging, each with the other, the full gruesome details, the outlandish marvels, the very-most intricate wonders of you and me and a million others. They are telling the ancient story."

Who goes there.